ORA AND THE OLD GOD

SARAH DAY

Ora and the Old God

Cover Design by Sara Oliver

Wholesale orders can be placed through Ingram (or any of their distribution partners).

Library of Congress Control Number: 2020914659

Paperback ISBN: 978-1-7355334-0-7

Mobi ISBN: 978-1-7355334-2-1

ePub ISBN: 978-1-7355334-1-4

First Edition 2020

For the witchy women in my life.
You are powerful and beautiful.

ONE

FROM a young age, Ora Widogast dreamed of a land that stretched to a star-bright horizon. Her body knew the dry air, wind, and moonlight. These elements came to her as she slept. And the crevices in the land, the hidden spaces, those came to her as well. It was a slumbering microcosm all her own. When she awoke, the dream lingered, but she never mentioned the desert to anyone. It was too quiet and strange to dwell on for long.

Ora grew up in Fel, a small trade village in the country of Nor. There, rain came across the ocean in shining, silver clouds. From atop the basalt cliffs, she felt as though she could reach up and brush her fingers through the bellies of storms. She liked the sensation of being small under those heavy skies, but she loved the forests more, even if her mother told her to stay away from the dark old growth.

ORA AND THE OLD GOD

The Hy Borea Forest was not a place for girls, her mother would tell her. The meandering trails were for men like her brother Hademar, who hunted for fine furs to trade in Port Besil. Fur from the Hy Borea was famous for being thicker and softer, whether it be fox, beaver, or rabbit. In the evenings, the men of Fel would gather in Mathilde's inn to brag about their hunts. The colorful stories enthralled Ora, who wanted nothing more in all the world than to have exciting tales of her own.

If only her mother would leave her be. Ora tired of chores in seconds. Dusting seemed pointless if dust would settle again within the hour. Why sweep if Hademar would arrive with mud on his boots later that afternoon? And cooking. She hated cooking. No matter how often her mother showed her how to make burberry pie or rabbit stew, she would add too much salt or leave the pot over the fire for far too long.

As often as she could, Ora would sneak away from chores to meet Hademar behind the shrine house. They would leave an offering of salt, bread, or fresh flowers for Farig, their silent god, and she would follow her brother into the woods. She adored him for these small acts of disobedience. Still, he never took her hunting. He only showed her beauty—the tumbling creeks, the boulder fields, the waterfalls, the curtains of moss glistening with dew.

Then, they would return. Her mother would give them a stern look, but Hademar was not a child anymore. He would laugh and say they had not gone far, though they had. That they had not strayed from trails, though they always did. If her mother began to argue, he would give her a giant hug and tell her not to worry. She always worried.

They lived in a cabin beneath a hemlock pine. Like all the other buildings in Fel, their home was made from weathered, gray cedar. Moss grew on the roof, and pine boughs scraped the windows when the wind picked up. The wind blew more often than not. On stormy winter days, Ora would run down the street to pester her Uncle Lupin for stories.

When he wasn't drinking at Mathilde's inn, he liked to watch the rain blow by as he smoked a pipe on his porch. Ora often showed up soaked and grinning with her frizzy black curls matted to her head. Half the time, she left her shoes at home and had smudges of mud on her face.

The day before she turned seventeen, she had something other than stories to ask for. "Uncle Lupin!" she said as she leapt past the stairs and onto the porch. She had been running. Red blossomed on her cheeks, and her chest rose and fell with heavy breaths. "Can I ask a favor?"

"It's freezing cold. What are you doing in the rain?" he grumbled, ignoring her question. "Inside with you."

She did not wait for him to stand up but burst through his front door to sit on the hearth. As he came inside after her, she placed another log onto the dwindling fire. Lupin was a giant of a man, and the floorboards creaked under his heavy footsteps.

"Tomorrow is the Tabas hunt *and* my birthday," she said.

"I know it."

"Well?" She had been impatient for her seventeenth birthday. Among the Nors, turning seventeen meant she would no longer be viewed as a child. At last, she would have the freedom to do as she pleased.

Lupin sat down at his big wooden table to tap out his pipe. The knock of it against the wood was a familiar, cozy sound to Ora. Her uncle's cabin housed a permanent, herbal cloud. "I spoke to your ma if that's what you've come to ask for."

"It is." She sat shivering beside the fire. Flames glittered in her black eyes, and she looked devilish as ever. "What did she say?"

"She said it's up to your brother."

This made her smile. She had spoken to Hademar the night before.

"She also said you'd be the death of her if you carry on like this. Gives her such a fright, you going into the woods." Lupin pressed more mageweed into his pipe as he spoke, then nursed a flame with a lighting taper.

Ora took up the fire iron and dug at the white coals beneath the burning logs. "*Everything* I do frightens her," she said. Then, with a sly glance at her uncle, she added, "Hademar said I could go with him."

"Hm." Lupin puffed at his pipe. Smoke soon filled the one-room cabin along with the sharp, crisp smell of mageweed. "Ora, get that box. Bring it here." He pointed with the stem of his pipe at a wooden box on the mantle.

She pulled it down straight away. It was about as long as her arm and had a satisfying weight. Though tempted to open the box herself, she placed it in front of her uncle. Setting aside the pipe, he lifted the copper latch and then the lid to reveal a polished silver short sword nestled against dark blue velvet. The hilt was made of ruddy leather, and silver wolves danced on the guard. Her eyes lit up as Lupin took it from the box. The sword appeared small in his giant hand.

"An early gift for your birthday." He turned it so the blade rested in his palms and held it out to her. "It's silver."

Speechless but beaming, she took the hilt in her hand. She raised the blade so the firelight would reflect in the polished silver. "Thank you, Uncle Lupin. It's beautiful."

"I had a sheath and belt made for it too. It will be finished today."

She placed the sword back in the box and flung her arms around him. He patted her back.

"Don't tell your ma," he said as she pulled away.

"Never." She winked. For years, she had practiced the sword with her uncle. Lupin would meet her in a hidden cove when the tide was out. There, they would spar on the hard sand with dulled blades. It was one of her dearest secrets and painstakingly orchestrated so that neither Hademar nor her mother knew.

"If you are to go with your brother tomorrow, I want you to take it along. Should you run into any fae, the silver will—"

"I know, I know."

"Didn't your ma teach you not to interrupt?"

"She tried," she said with a laugh, then added an apology.

Before he could give her a playful clout over the head, she ducked away and sat down across from him. She knew he didn't mind. Most of the folks in Fel thought Lupin a touch mad for his stories about the fae, but Ora loved to listen to his tales. For that reason, he let her get away with almost anything.

Lupin coaxed the pipe back to life with a few long drags of air. He spoke around curls of smoke. "Listen, child, even a small cut from silver is poison to the fae. If it does not kill them, it will fester and drain their magic. Do not forget this."

"Do you think we'll cross paths with the fae?" she asked, almost hopeful. The idea of magic had long fascinated her.

"You shouldn't wish for it. Haven't you listened to your old uncle all these years?" His brow wrinkled. "The fae are cruel beings. Best keep your wits about you. And, above all else, do not speak your true name."

"Yes, Uncle Lupin." But her voice sounded distant. She sat staring out the window as if being inside felt the same as being in a cage. "I don't think it will be raining tomorrow."

"And what makes you say that?"

Ora's dark eyes returned to him, and she wore a crooked smile. "It's my birthday. Why should it be raining?"

He laughed. "You little imp. Why shouldn't it?"

"It's never rained on my birthday."

He stroked his scraggly beard, thinking back. "That may be so."

There came a knock at the door, and Lupin snapped the box shut. Ora sighed. "That would be Hademar," she said.

Her brother swung the door open without waiting for an answer. "I thought you'd be here," he said as he stepped into the warmth. He was seven years older and carried himself with a quiet confidence. Ever since he grew a beard, Ora thought he looked like their uncle, though leaner and without the gray peppering Lupin's dark hair.

"I'm glad you came. Your sister here was starting to be a pest," said Lupin.

Ora pinched his arm as she passed by. "*He* was the one being a pest."

"I happen to know you're both rotten," said Hademar with a laugh. "Come on, Ora. Supper has been ready for a while." He tossed a coat to her. She had left it hanging by the door at home. It was lined with soft brown rabbit fur and staved off even the coldest of winds.

They said their goodbyes to Lupin and hurried through the rain together. On the porch, they took off their soaked shoes. As Ora unfastened her laces, Hademar spoke in a low voice. "Ma doesn't want you to come along."

"Of course she doesn't."

"Hear her out."

"I thought this was settled."

"She's more upset than usual."

"Fine. I'll hear her out, but it doesn't change anything," she said. When he did not meet her firm gaze, she nudged his arm. "Hademar?"

Rather than answer, he jerked his head toward the door. "Let's get inside where it's warm."

They carried their shoes to the hearth to dry. The savory scent of bone broth filled their noses. Their mother sat at the table, stirring her soup with a soggy chunk of bread. After they hung up their coats, they joined her. Ora could see the worry working at her mother's features.

"Your uncle spoke to me this morning," said Nel without looking up from her soup. Lamplight flickered against her pale face and deepened the shadows beneath her eyes. She looked more tired than usual, small and worn. Over the past year, her hair had become more gray than black, and new wrinkles creased her brow.

The two siblings stole a quick glance between each other. "He told me he did," said Ora.

Her mother let the bread sink into the broth and placed her shaking hands against the table. The dread in her eyes made Ora feel a pang of guilt, but she would not yield to her mother's fears. When the silence became too heavy, she reached across the table and touched her hand. "Ma, there's nothing to be afraid of."

Nel took a deep breath. "If I asked you to stay home tomorrow, would you?"

She opened her mouth, ready to lie, but she shook her head instead. All her life, she had watched as Hademar returned home in the company of proud and boisterous men. She admired—even envied—their success. Their hunts were the lifeblood of Fel, the reason their small village thrived. Ora felt certain that she was meant for something greater than domesticity, and she daydreamed of being the first huntress to conquer the beasts of the Hy Borea.

"I'm going with Hademar on the Tabas hunt. I've always wanted to go, and he said he would take me," she said, firm and final in her words. Her ma's eyes fluttered closed for a heartbeat. Ora's headstrong manner was nothing new in their household and often the source of conflict between the two Widogast women.

"I know I can't make you do anything, Ora. I never have been able to. But if you could, just this once …" Nel took hold of her hand with a tight grip, her voice rising with a strained pitch. "If I must beg it of you, I will."

Ora turned to her brother, not knowing what to say. Their mother had always been nervous about her venturing into the forest, but this was different. She was almost hysterical.

"Perhaps you could come along next year," Hademar said.

"What?" She pulled her hand away from her mother's and glowered. "You told me you'd take me along *this* year. You promised."

"*Ora*." He gave her a meaningful look, but she would not have it.

"This is ridiculous. I will be seventeen tomorrow." She got to her feet. "Why should I have to wait another year?"

Whatever the reason, her mother seemed incapable of saying more. She pressed her lips together, and tears filled her eyes. When she opened her mouth to speak, she only succeeded in producing a miserable moan before sinking her head into her hands.

"*Hademar*," Ora said, hoping he would speak reason, but he only shook his head. Seething, she glared down at her mother and said between clenched teeth, "I am not a child. I will do as I please."

Though Ora immediately regretted her harsh words, she could not bring herself to apologize. Instead, she stormed out of the house barefooted. By the time Hademar reached the door, she was halfway to Lupin's front porch.

*****

That night, Ora slept on a bed of furs before her uncle's fire. Hademar did not bother trying to coax her into coming home. After all, she was only a few doors down. As for Lupin, he returned with the sheath for her sword to find her feeding his fire and scowling. When she told him what happened, he pulled a quilt from a cedar chest and tossed it to her.

"Why is she afraid of everything?" Ora said as she unfurled the quilt. "Hademar has been on many hunts. He's returned safe every time."

"Don't be hard on your ma. She does not have the same wildness of being that you possess. I'm afraid you got that from my side of the family." The fondness in Lupin's voice quelled her anger, and she settled into the quilt.

Still, her mother's trepidation over the hunt left her perplexed. She lay awake, staring into the flames for a long time and trying to discern what made her mother worry. Lupin, sensing that she could not sleep, cleared his throat. He had yet to go to bed himself and sat smoking his pipe at the table as he read a battered old book on nautical astronomy. He had never been a sailor himself. The guide had come into his possession in Port Besil, after winning a game of traveler on the docks. Ora had been with him and suggested the book when his opponent turned out to be broke.

"You won't be sneaking off tomorrow, will you?" Lupin asked.

She could not stop herself from smiling, so she remained facing the flames when she answered. "It wouldn't be sneaking off if I told you, would it?"

"I suppose not. Your ma ever tell you why she's afraid of the Hy Borea?"

This piqued her curiosity enough to get her to roll over and face him. She had few meaningful conversations with her mother. They quarreled too much, and Ora weaseled her way out of the house as often as possible. "She's never said a word."

"Hm. No surprise there."

"Then you should tell me."

"Seeing as you come of age tomorrow, I think I might, but promise me you won't breathe a word of it to your ma."

By then, she was sitting up. The quilt fell from her shoulders. "I promise I won't."

"Very well." He set his book aside and blew out a small cloud of smoke that swirled above his head. "It happened on a moonlit night before you were born. Your father had been ill with fever for days, and your mother refused to leave his side. Imagine my surprise when I woke up to a knock and discovered him on my porch. He was bent over—" Lupin hunched his back and held the bowl of his smoldering pipe like the knob of a walking stick. "Couldn't hold himself up. I helped him inside and asked what in Farig's name had brought him to my door. You know what he said?"

"What?" Ora asked, her brow knitted with worry.

"He said your ma was missing. She got up and walked out the door, left it open. No explanation. No warning. She just … vanished." He spread his hands wide. The pipe wobbled in the crook between his thumb and forefinger. "Now, you know as well as I that your ma isn't one for midnight walks. Remember that hound I had for most of your childhood?"

Ora nodded. "Thrush?"

"That's the one. Well, I took her with me to search. We went up and down every street in Fel. No trace of your Ma. Thrush couldn't pick up her scent either. I roused every able-bodied man next. We spread out. Sent some down to the beach. The rest of us, we searched the forest.

"For three days, we looked. Your brother cared for your pa with Mathilde's help. Losing your ma only made him sicker. Mathilde said he wouldn't stop calling for her. He wouldn't eat or drink. We all began to fear that he would pass before we could find her or that she would never be found at all. Every night I prayed to Farig to protect her, to save Hagen.

"That third day, I must have walked from dawn 'til dusk through the woods. I could hardly lift my feet anymore. We were losing hope. I remember Mathilde brought me dinner that night, and while I was eating on the porch, I saw something move at the edge of the woods."

"Ma?" said Ora, her voice soft.

Lupin grimaced as if the memory pained him. "Yes, child. Your ma. She stood there in the ferns, naked as the day she was born. Once we got her cleaned up and warm, we tried to ask what happened. But she couldn't bring herself to say. To this day, she hasn't spoken a word of it."

Ora shivered. "What do you think happened?"

"Hard to say. But I'll tell you one thing; I feared the fae had something to do with your birth at first. She learned she was with child not long after that. But the second I saw you, I knew you were Nel and Hagen's daughter. You look just like them."

Doubt struck her. "What if I'm a changeling?"

"No! Changelings are ghastly things," he said, but he raised a brow at the possibility. "Then again, you are an ugly little sprite, aren't you?"

She stuck out her tongue. "Not as ugly as you are."

"Must run in the family." He chuckled and stamped out his pipe. "Alright, alright. Your old uncle is tired at last, and you best get some sleep yourself."

As Ora lay back down, she wondered what had drawn her mother into the woods. She could not imagine her mother rising from bed only to roam naked through the Hy Borea for days on end. The impossibility of it distracted her from other thoughts, and she soon fell asleep with the warmth of the fire against her cheeks.

That night, she wandered the dark land of her dreams, feeling the flat earth firm beneath her feet. But a voice broke through the quietude she had grown accustomed to, calling out a name she did not recognize. The voice made Ora tremble because it felt foreign, like someone had crept into her sleeping world. When she turned, she expected to see nothing but empty land. Instead, she saw the stark silhouette of a cliff elk on the horizon. It stood unmoving, a sentinel against the stars.

TWO

THE cliff elk's shadow remained on Ora's mind as she opened her eyes the next morning. She had never seen another living being in her dreams, and she thought the vision must hold meaning.

A soft knock interrupted her thoughts. She crept to the door, careful not to wake her uncle, who still lay snoring in his bed. When she cracked open the door and saw Hademar, she frowned. He held her coat and shoes in his hands.

"What does ma want this early?" she asked, slipping onto the porch. The morning light had begun to spread across the sky, and the breeze sweeping in from the sea smelled crisp and cool.

"Ora—" he began.

"I'm going whether or not you take me," she said, crossing her arms.

"I know. That's why I came to get you."

Her face lit up. "You changed ma's mind?"

"Not quite. She just knows you won't change yours." He offered no more explanation. "Hurry up and get ready."

She gave him a quick hug and hurried back inside to shake Lupin awake. When she told him the news, he lifted himself from bed and gave her the sword in its leather sheath along with the belt. "Stay out of trouble," he called after her as she rushed out the door.

On the porch, she set down the sword to pull on her coat and shoes. Hademar eyed it. "Where did that come from?"

"Uncle Lupin gave it to me," she said as she tightened her shoelaces. "It's silver!"

"Did he?" He looked up with narrowed eyes as their uncle opened the front door with his pipe in one hand.

"What?" Lupin asked.

"A sword? Why a sword?"

"She's old enough for one."

"You never gave me a sword when I came of age."

Lupin sat down in his chair and shrugged. "I suppose I didn't."

Ora jumped to her feet and tugged at Hademar's arm. "I'm ready. Let's go!"

They said goodbye to Lupin one last time and walked along the muddy street. Once they were out of earshot, Hademar looked down at her and said, "Uncle spoils you too much. You don't know how to use a sword."

"Can't be that hard. The edge is sharp, and I am quick," she said and fastened the belt around her waist.

"We're hunting for Tabas, not battling little hares in the woods. Are you going to duel with a turkey? Lead an affront against the raccoons for stealing offerings from the shrine house?"

She laughed. "They have been getting away with it for too long, haven't they?"

When they passed by their own cabin, their mother stepped outside. "Go on," Hademar muttered, giving Ora a gentle push. She sighed but left his side to trudge up to the steps.

"At least take some breakfast." Nel held out a bun wrapped in a plain, yellow handkerchief. "I know your uncle didn't make any."

"Thank you, ma." Ora's heart softened. She almost apologized for the night before, but as she took the small bundle into her hands, her mother's eyes slid down to the sword.

With a worried look, Nel drew her into a tight hug and whispered against her ear, "I hope your uncle taught you well."

Ora winced. "You know about that?"

"I know more than you realize." She held her daughter out at arm's length. "May Farig protect you on this hunt and see to it that you return to me."

"Ma," Ora said, confused by her mother's words. "I'll be with Hademar. Please, don't spend all Tabas worrying."

"I can't promise that." Her mother's expression became somber. "But I want you to promise me something, Ora."

"What is it?"

"Guard your name. At all costs."

Though Lupin often gave such warnings, her mother avoided talk of the fae. Still, Ora made the promise. "I won't even whisper it," she said.

Nel nodded as her daughter spoke and closed her eyes for a moment, holding back tears. "Very well." She kissed Ora's cheek. "Happy birthday, my dear girl. Stay close to your brother."

"I will." Ora backed away from her mother and tried to reassure her with a smile. "I love you, ma. We'll bring back a whole cliff elk for Tabas. You'll see!"

Before her mother could say anything more, she hurried back to Hademar and pushed him along. By the time they reached the main stretch of road, both were laughing. Bells and blessings reached their ears. Women, men, and children stood on their porches, leaned out of windows, and swirled on the sides of the road.

"May Farig protect you on your hunt!" they called out. "Tabas blessings upon you!"

The Widogast siblings were not the only ones to go out hunting for the Tabas feast. Other huntsmen marched ahead of them, waving at their neighbors and friends. Ora heard someone shout happy birthday to her, but when she turned, she could not decide who it came from. Hademar caught her searching the crowd and jabbed her with his elbow.

"Nearly forgot to wish you a happy birthday myself," he said.

She rolled her eyes. "Some brother you are."

Hademar laughed. They had reached the edge of town. "Stay close. I don't care what age you are. Ma'll never forgive me if something happens to you."

"We sneak off all the time," she reminded him. "Today is no different."

In the woods, the other Tabas hunters spread out, each taking their own favored paths. Ora drew in a breath of crisp air. The rain held off, but thick fog rolled in from the coast. It drifted between the dark evergreens and swallowed sound. Hademar led them along a familiar trail at first. She unwrapped the bun her mother sent, ate it in a few bites, and stuffed the handkerchief in her pocket.

As they left the trail and descended a hillside, her excitement grew. "Hademar," she said. "I dreamed of a cliff elk last night. Do you think it means anything?"

Much smaller than normal elk, the cliff elk of the Hy Borea were lean and as fluid as any fox. Bringing one down took an incredible amount of skill. He considered her dream and said, "It would be quite the offering for Tabas, but we're more likely to catch a brush pig."

They spent the day inching through the ferns and waiting. Hademar spoke little, content in his silence as they made their way deeper into the forest. Ora knew better than to strike up conversation, but she had hoped for a more thrilling adventure. The quiet day left her in a stupor.

They sat on the giant root of an old cedar for lunch and ate salted pork and hardtack. As Hademar finished his last bite, he nudged her with his elbow.

"You're of age now. Is there anyone who has caught your eye?" he asked.

The question took her off guard. Ora did not often think of romance or marriage, and her brother had yet to find love himself, though she knew he once kissed Mathilde's daughter. She felt her cheeks grow hot. "No," she said. "I don't think—well, I'm not very ladylike. I think the boys see me more like a sister."

"It *is* difficult to imagine you settling down," he admitted.

"I don't think I want to."

"No?"

Ora swung her legs and stared at the mossy earth below. "It sounds boring, Hademar. And if I—if I did marry, I'd make a terrible wife. I can barely cook, no matter how hard ma tries to teach me."

Her brother laughed and ruffled her already messy hair. "You are terrible at housework. I'll give you that."

She feigned insult but could not help but laugh along with him in the end. At the piping call of an eagle, Ora tilted her head back and caught a glimpse of the raptor soaring above the treetops. It was the first creature they had seen all day.

"Does hunting always take so long?" she asked.

Hademar smirked. "Have you grown bored?"

"No. I couldn't ever be bored out here."

"Ah, then you're just impatient." He lowered himself from the rock and held out his hand. She took hold of it and jumped down. "We may return empty-handed. Not all hunts are successful."

"But it's Tabas," she insisted. "And I dreamed of a cliff elk."

"Not all dreams are truthful."

The afternoon stretched on much as the morning had. They crouched unmoving among ferns and watched a spring for a long time. Ora felt her eyes growing heavy as the trickling water lulled her.

Successful hunts called for festivities. Or at least drinking. Perhaps for that reason, she did not expect hunting to require so much patience. She imagined dramatic chases through the woods, meeting strange beings, and near-death experiences. As she thought about the many hunting stories she heard in her lifetime, she began to wonder if men enjoyed embellishment.

While her mind wandered, Hademar nocked an arrow with an elegant, practiced motion and pulled back the bowstring. Her eyes followed his, and she grinned. Beyond the spring, atop the crest of a hill, stood a cliff elk.

Unconsciously, she moved forward to see better.

Wood snapped.

Ora's stomach twisted. Her brother lowered his bow, but his arms remained tense as the bull leapt away. The crash of brush lasted only a moment, and the elk vanished almost as soon as it moved.

She lifted her foot from the cursed branch she had trodden on. Hademar's breath clouded the cold air. "A day wasted," he said.

The sky was beginning to turn a brilliant red. The day was over. She knew the walk back to Fel would be a long, quiet one. Hademar would show up empty-handed and feeling foolish thanks to her.

"I don't know how we would've carried it back anyway," she said.

He did not answer. Instead, he stared at the hillside the bull ran up. The evergreens and shadows swallowed any trace of the creature.

She rubbed at her cold nose with the edge of her sleeve and waited. He had an unreadable expression, and the sudden and urgent sound of his voice made her jump. "Go back to Fel. I might stand a chance without you tagging along."

This stung. She wasn't about to go back alone. "Hademar, I—it was only one twig. One twig! All day! I've hardly breathed or farted since we left this morning."

The corners of his lips flickered at her outburst. Instead of letting a laugh sneak out, he made a threat. "One more twig and I'll leave you out here tonight."

"You wouldn't. Ma would never forgive you," she said. Though lighthearted enough, the threat made a fearful energy creep up her back. She shivered. Satisfied at the instilled fear, he waved for her to follow. He had not given up on the bull yet.

As they crept up the hillside, she tried not to fear what could be in the shadows or crouched behind a boulder. Such thoughts could cause her to misstep. She reminded herself that every movement must be measured.

Just as time began to stretch again, Hademar paused. Little daylight remained. She grew still and searched the trees. At first, she did not see the bull. Its body, striped by branches, looked like a part of the thicket. As soon as its form came together in her mind, the slicing of air filled her ears.

Thud.

The arrow sank into the spot above the bull's shoulder. She expected its heart to burst, for it to collapse into death. It turned instead. Its cold, glassy eyes fixed on her brother. "*You fool!*"

They froze. The voice came from the bull but not from the bull. It filled her ears, feminine and secretive. The sensation of an old force crackled in the air, and the hairs on the back of Ora's neck rose. She reached one shaking hand down to her sword.

Hademar had another arrow ready as the bull stepped out of the thicket. "Get back," he said. His eyes did not move from the elk.

Ora did as she was told and stepped behind a tree. Her blood felt like cold water. Her heart raced. Every sensation was amplified. She wanted to run. She wanted to return home.

"Don't be a coward, Ora," she whispered and forced herself to look around the tree.

Despite his steady voice, Hademar's hands shook. "What are you?"

The bull's hide shifted. Thin, white hands parted its chest. Then, the head tilted back and melted into a silky, chestnut fabric. The cloak draped over a fierce, human-like frame. The antlers vanished as the hood fell and revealed a head of thick, black hair. A narrow-faced woman with eyes bluer than summer skies peered at Hademar. She reached one hand up and touched the arrow protruding from her shoulder.

"A dren," Ora breathed, recognizing the elk shapeshifter from her uncle's stories about the fae.

All grew still. Even the wind settled.

Ora had imagined dren as monstrous, fearsome creatures, but the woman possessed an eerie beauty. The delicate curves of her face were not quite human. Nor were her pointed ears. Black tattoos swirled on her ash white skin, and her hair curled in a way that Ora could not help but envy over her own frizzled, dark locks.

The wonderment broke when Ora became aware of several sets of eyes gleaming in the brush. Before Hademar spoke, she knew what he would say. She began to shake her head.

"Ora, you must run."

The thought of him putting her life before his own made her feel sick with guilt. She could not will her feet to move from the spot. She stared hard at her brother. She feared she would never see him again.

"No," she said, her hand still wrapped around the hilt of her sword. "I can't."

"Run!" He let loose the second arrow. It lodged into the dren's chest, and she bared her teeth as she fell to her knees. The air felt like a lightning bolt had struck. The branches and ferns began to shift. A voice rose up from the thick brush, and the bow flew from her brother's hand.

He drew his hunting knife. "Ora! Go!"

But she couldn't. She watched as three more cliff elk shed their skins and stepped out into the open. Hademar charged at the nearest, a female dren almost identical to the first but with tightly braided hair. She sneered and caught hold of his wrist before the knife could pierce her. A fluid stream of words fell from her lips. The knife lit up with a fiery glow, and he cried out, dropping it to the forest floor. The skin on his palm and fingers was scorched red.

One of the others rushed at Ora. Her hand fumbled for her sword. As the dren rounded the thick, old spruce, she drew it from the sheath. He was much taller than her and had the broad, muscular build of a warrior. His square jaw was clean-shaven, and his dark hair, though cropped short, sat in thick curls. He stepped toward her with a self-assured smirk.

Ora held the blade before her and tried not to shake. "It's silver," she threatened.

The dren laughed, golden eyes flashing as he drew his own sword. He took a mighty swipe and knocked Ora's blade from her hands. With a cry, she bolted into the ferns.

Branches and briars clawed at her clothes. She did not stop to look back. She did not stop to think. As she splashed across a creek, a loud buzz filled her ears, and then, a searing force struck her square in the back. She jolted and tumbled hard against the rocks. Pain shot through her head, down her spine. Cold water sank into her clothes. A wild chill coursed through her, and darkness sprang across her vision.

Ora could hear herself panting like a dog, and her pulse thrummed in her ears. She tasted the bitter, metallic zing of blood in her mouth. As she regained focus, she saw the dren crouching over her.

He said something in his own language, and the pain subsided. With a gasp of relief, she sat up. As she did, he grabbed hold of her chin, forcing her to meet his gaze. "Aren't you resilient? That spell should've knocked you out cold." To her surprise, he spoke the common tongue, but the words were mangled by an unrecognizable accent that bit at his words.

She glared. Already, she could feel her strength returning and a burning anger rising within her. "What do you want?" she asked.

A short laugh flew from his lips, and he let his hand drop away. "Your fate will be less terrible than your friend's."

Hademar. What had they done to him? She scrambled backward, unable to gain her footing in the mud. A stone slid beneath her hand, and she curled her fingers around it. It was no silver sword, but a rock would do. With a furious cry, she flung it at the dren.

As the stone cracked against his forehead, she twisted around. Half crawling and half stumbling, she at last made it to her feet and rushed back through the woods, back to Hademar. She would not abandon her brother.

But she was too late.

He lay motionless on the forest floor. The other dren were nowhere in sight. She dropped to her knees beside him. There was no blood that she could see. She pressed her ear closer to his lips. To her relief, breath tickled her ear. It was not until she straightened that she noticed the wiry hairs growing from his skin. In disbelief, she gingerly touched the new hair on his arm.

Then, Ora felt him shift. She teetered backward, her breath coming in short, frightened bursts as her brother began to change.

His limbs twitched, and his back twisted up into a grotesque arch. As his bones rearranged themselves with sickening pops, his body jerked at odd angles. His limbs became shorter, his face longer, his nose broad and flat, his ears bigger and bushier. His fingers fused together; his boots fell from his feet—now hooves. More dark hairs grew from his thickening skin. His body swelled into a new shape, and his clothes became shreds.

Though she had heard of the fae changing people into animals, her mind could not accept what she witnessed. She reached out a shaking hand and laid it upon Hademar's back. The coarse fur tickled her palm. His spotted hide rose and fell with a gentle, slumbering breath beneath her hand. It couldn't be real. She had to be imagining it. It had to be some kind of trick, some kind of illusion.

Numbed by the impossibility, she did not hear the footsteps behind her. Her body felt cold with the shock of what had become of Hademar. The words drifted out of reach at first.

He was … *a brush pig*.

"We do love irony, we dren. The hunter becomes the hunted and all that." Before she could turn her head, she felt fingers dig into her hair, scrape her scalp, and wrench her back. It was the golden-eyed dren. Blood and dirt streaked his face. "How fitting it will be for your own people to hunt him down like the stupid beast that he is."

She tore at the dren's hand as she tried to escape his grip, but he only wound her hair tighter into his fist.

"My brother's not a stupid beast! Change him back!" she shouted with indignation, twisting and clawing as she tried to pry away his fingers. "Let go of me!"

"Don't be foolish, *Ora*. That's what he called you, isn't it?" He crouched down behind her and sang in his own language.

His words filled Ora's mind, warm and sweet. Though she could not understand them, her thoughts filled with the sound of the dren's voice. Her heart danced as if she was gazing on something beautiful for the first time.

A frost-covered field in the morning light.

Fog rising in the mountains.

Clear, turquoise water.

A laugh trickled from her smiling lips, and she mumbled something about how nice he sounded. Then, her body grew heavy and a peaceful sleep stole her away.

THREE

STATELY and swift, Tyg Marigen stalked through the queen's conservatory. The large glass room contained a myriad of exotic plants and butterflies, brought back from the human realm at the queen's request. Human servants tended to the collection, ensuring every bloom and leaf thrived. It was, in her view, the pinnacle of their monarch's mindless superfluity. Out of spite, Tyg did not bother stepping around the yellow, swallow-tailed butterfly that landed in her path. The poor creature crunched beneath her boot.

As the Magus over the Yewolyns' division of mages, Tyg commanded a great deal of fear. Only her husband, the Valor, ranked higher. Though the Yewolyns were known for being Mysanhal's fiercest warriors, she had a reputation for being cruel and cunning even among her own ranks. So, it was with good reason that the head of the palace staff, a thachwing named Wynn, let out a high-pitched cry of surprise as she rounded the corner and came face-to-face with Tyg.

A flurry of colorful wings swirled around them. The butterflies gravitated toward Wynn, settling on her silky, melon-green dress. Despite being a wisp of a fae woman, she always managed to stand out with her extravagant gowns and red hair.

"Sorry, sorry, Magus Marigen. I didn't see you coming," said the thachwing, eyeing the broken swallowtail just behind Tyg's boot. Wynn's long wings flicked behind her, a mosaic of paper-thin, iridescent cells. Like most thachwings, she had an affinity for living beings, no matter how small. She clasped her hands together, resisting the urge to tend to the butterfly in the dren's presence.

Tyg looked down on her with a chilling blue gaze. "Perhaps if you were more aware of your surroundings, such missteps could be avoided."

"Yes, Magus. Right as always. Well, you must have come—"

"To speak with the queen, yes. Step aside."

As Wynn obeyed the shrewd order and pressed herself into the curled fronds of a fern, she called after Tyg. "She's meeting with High Priestess Aygriel. Perhaps you could wait in one of the parlors? The Scarlet Room was just dusted."

The dren halted and turned, her elk cloak whirling around her sinewy figure. "It would be wise of you to remember your place, Wynn."

She bowed her head. "My apologies. It was only a suggestion, Magus."

Without a word more, Tyg left the flustered thachwing and made her way to the center of the conservatory. There, she found the queen engaged in a hushed conversation with the high priestess. The ghostly white dren used more than a pinch of glamour to appear young. To the war-battered Magus, it was a frivolous form of magic.

Though Tyg was a devout worshiper of Cree, their god, she had been at odds with the high priestess for decades. Ever since the elf king, Odharan, crossed over to the spirit realm, Aygriel had gained too much influence over his widowed queen. Her sway too often resulted in the Yewolyns being sent on ridiculous errands and diplomatic affairs, a poor use of their strength. Worse, Tyg was beginning to suspect that Innes was grooming Aygriel to take the throne once she crossed to the spirit realm.

They both fell silent at the Yewolyn's approach. Tyg gave a low bow.

"Your Majesty, I apologize for the intrusion, but I have brought news," she said.

"I am most pleased to see you have returned from Nor safely, Magus Marigen." Queen Innes swept her hand toward one of the empty chairs, the long sleeve of her silken, violet dress whispering across the ground. The queen was a regal thachwing with long white hair and pale features softened by time. Unlike the priestess, she did not bother hiding her age but donned her wrinkles with a marked elegance. "High Priestess Aygriel and I were just discussing matters that you may find of interest."

"Certainly." Tyg had to stop herself from sighing as she took a seat. She found it difficult to predict the whims of Innes, that damned thachwing woman. Innes peered into the dream world too often and consulted with the high priestess for even the smallest matters. "Your Majesty, if I may begin—"

Innes cut her off. "No need, Magus. I know of the girl your husband brought back to Tirnan last night. I heard whispers in my sleep."

As a flicker of irritation passed through Tyg's expression, a taunting smile grew on Aygriel's face.

"Unusual, isn't it?" said Aygriel.

Tyg ignored the priestess. "May I ask what your dream was about, Your Majesty?"

Innes's pale, gray eyes seemed to look through Tyg as she spoke. "I heard whispers in the dark. They said her name will be cherished by the shadow."

"What do you mean?" asked Tyg, forcing herself to remain resolute.

Innes laughed, and her eyes grew watery. "She is more than she seems, my dear. Valor Marigen has invited a new creature among the fae."

"A new creature, Your Majesty?" Tyg nearly laughed herself. The human girl was ordinary, though a tad small for a Nor. When her husband, Callum, had carried the girl to the servants' quarters, her fur coat and wild hair made her look like a small animal in his arms. "We were not far from the human village of Fel. The girl probably came from a family of trappers. It's nothing to be excited about."

Aygriel folded her delicate hands beneath her chin. "Are you doubting the queen's vision, Magus?"

"Of course not," snapped Tyg, avoiding the high priestess's trap. "But I wonder if there's any real cause for concern. Whoever she is, *what*ever she may be, her name is now bound to your will, My Queen. Surely this is all for the best?"

"You may be right, Magus Marigen," said Innes.

Triumphant, Tyg glanced at Aygriel, who had lost their minor political duel. Innes had at last listened to good reason. Intending to shift the conversation to more pressing topics, Tyg opened her mouth to speak, but the queen went on.

"Perhaps you could keep an eye on her until I have learned more."

This was not what Tyg had in mind. "My Queen, I am the Yewolyn Magus. Not a nursemaid."

"You're right," said Aygriel, her voice sweet. "You are not a nursemaid. You are a guardian of our royal city, of our country. I can think of no one more fit to watch over a *new creature*. Your strength and wisdom are called for when it comes to such an … uncertain matter."

Innes clasped a hand against her chest as if the priestess had just delivered an impressive sermon. "Well spoken, Aygriel. Do you agree, Magus?"

Anger simmered beneath Tyg's stoic façade. It was clear that Innes's decision had been made before the Magus had stepped into the room. She bowed her head. "Very well. I will watch over the girl."

"Good. Bring her to court this evening, but do not speak of my vision. I do not want to alarm anyone."

"Understood, Your Highness. But, I did not come here solely to discuss the girl. I brought news of the Cedar Clan."

"Ah yes, the Cedar Clan," Innes said as she smoothed out her skirts. "I suspect they did not give you any trouble. How did they respond to my offer?"

"They will return to our realm and set aside past conflict if they are allowed to stay hidden. They do not want to be troubled with our affairs."

The queen's placid expression revealed little. She poured herself a cup of tea, stirred in cream and sugar, and took several sips before answering. "They are unlikely to cause any trouble. There are only—eight left, correct?"

"There are seven, Your Majesty."

"I will give this some thought."

"I understand. The Yewolyns are at your service. We will await your instruction." Tyg rose and bowed to the queen once more before leaving the pair to bask in the sun and their own foolishness.

As soon as she closed the door, anger burned away her cool demeanor. The queen had become more and more nonsensical in the past few years. In King Odharan's time, harming a Yewolyn would have been reason enough to sentence the girl to death. Instead, she would have to look after the little Nor. And the girl was nothing more than a peasant from the Hy Borea!

She stormed through several of the palace's grand corridors and down a flight of marble stairs. Ladies and lords alike parted as the

Magus of the Yewolyns passed. Servants hurried to hide in nearby rooms. Even the little black cat who wandered the palace leapt into an open window and disappeared.

Once she reached the servants' quarters, Tyg threw open the wooden door to a small room. Like all the other servants' rooms, it had modest furnishings and a single window alight with morning sun. However, this room's occupant was filthy and covered in thin, bloody scratches. Seething, Tyg glared down at the sleeping Norrish girl. *You are the Magus,* she thought. *You are better than this.* Slowly, her composure returned. Once she calmed, she bent down and whispered a spell to rouse the girl.

The Nor opened her dark eyes and, upon seeing Tyg, sat up with a start. Her face paled as she realized she had been captured. "What do you want?" she asked.

"You are a girl?" Tyg asked. "A human girl?"

Taken aback by the question, she only nodded, eyes still wide and wild.

"You were born to human parents?"

Confusion filled the girl's eyes. Impatient, Tyg grabbed her arm and commanded her to answer.

"Of course!" she shouted. "I hadn't even seen a dren before …" Her voice wavered. She pulled her knees to her chest as her brow wrinkled. "Before then."

Tyg huffed and stepped out of the room, slamming the door behind her. Within seconds, she heard the girl tugging and twisting at the brass doorknob. Despite the mystery that now surrounded the Nor, she felt a small, satisfied thrill at the girl's panic.

"Only a spell can open this door," Tyg crooned.

The girl pounded on the door, demanding that she be let out at once. As she listened to her cries, Tyg caught sight of Pons, a human servant, peering out of his own room.

"Come here," she said, voice knife-sharp and cold.

The boy did as told and stood before the fuming dren with his eyes downcast, waiting for orders.

"Draw a bath for this girl. She reeks. And tell Wynn to find her something suitable to wear for court this evening."

"Her name," he said. "Wynn will want to know it."

"Tell her it's Ora. Now, hurry up."

Pons all but ran toward the opposite end of the passage. As he disappeared through a door, she turned to go find Callum. Her mind still reeled with the queen's words. How could the girl be anything but human? She certainly smelled and looked like one. But, if the girl was something else, she might be more trouble than she was worth. The sooner Innes crossed, the better. Then, the human girl could be dealt with, regardless of who she was.

Tyg found her golden-eyed husband lounging on one of the benches in the Great Hall. He seemed relaxed but was no doubt contemplating what fate awaited the girl he had brought back to Tirnan, the royal city of Mysanhal. He thought it funny that a human girl had bested him with a river rock. As the healers took care of the nasty gash on his forehead, he related the story as if it was a joke. Vexed by his behavior, Tyg had watched from the doorway with her arms crossed.

At her brisk approach, Callum sat up and rolled his stiff shoulders. "I might be getting on in age at last," he said.

"Don't be ridiculous," snapped Tyg. "You may have outlived most Yewolyns, but you're still young for a dren."

"You flatter me, Magus."

"I'm only pointing out what is true," Tyg said, annoyed that he would use her title to flirt. She had *earned* her place among the Yewolyns and held onto her position with fierce pride. Her husband had risen in the ranks through tenure and became the Yewolyns' leader only a few years ago. It took countless battles and decades of practicing combat magic to achieve her post as the most adept war mage among an already select group. Though she never dared to voice it, she harbored a quiet resentment for Callum.

"Is the girl awake?" he asked.

"Yes, and Queen Innes will be seeing her this evening, which means you ought to make yourself more presentable. I've told Pons to draw a bath for her. She smells like dirt. And pig." She smirked at those last words, quite proud of herself for pulling off a successful transformation. They did not always change so smoothly. For that reason, there were a few strange, half-human beasts living deep within the Hy Borea.

"And how is Pyri?" asked Callum.

She grimaced at the question. The arrows had missed her heart, but that did not make the healing process pleasant. Tyg's cousin had been at the hands of the healers all night as they rewove her flesh. The pain would last for weeks, but it was nothing compared to what they had endured during training. Pyri would return to the Yewolyns once the healers released her from the infirmary.

"She's asleep," said Tyg, brushing the matter aside. In a lower voice, she said, "I'll walk with you to the bathhouse."

He raised a brow. "What for, my wife?"

She crossed her arms as he languidly got to his feet and looked her up and down. "Not for what you'd like. I have matters to discuss with you."

"Always business with you, but, very well, let's go." He stepped aside so that she might lead the way.

When they walked outside, Tyg tilted her head up to smile at the warmth. It was always summer in Rioc, the fae realm. It was a gift from Cree along with magic and long life, provided one did not meet a violent end. The fae who lived in Tirnan had comfortable, rich lives, eating fine food and hosting lavish parties. Though glad to be home, Tyg had never seen much sense or honor in hedonistic pursuits.

"What was it you wanted to discuss?" asked Callum as they made their way down the steep staircase that led to a large, open plaza with an impressive overlook of the Sylamor Mountains. The jagged white peaks were bright and faint in the morning sun.

It was too early for the plaza to be crowded, but she still glanced over her shoulder to be sure no one walked too close. Then, hardly loud enough to hear, Tyg murmured, "The queen is having visions in her sleep. I do not think she will be fit to rule much longer."

"What do you mean?" Callum asked.

His apprehension did not surprise her. Innes had been revered by many as a wise leader ever since King Odharan crossed over to the spirit realm. After over a century of the elf king's relentless tyranny, Rioc had never known such a long period of peace. Still, historians were divided. Some considered it a golden age for Mysanhal. Others warned that Innes ruled too carelessly, and Tyg agreed.

"I mean, she's spewing nonsense. She's looking upon distant places, and she has devoted herself to Cree too unflinchingly. It may be …" She stole another glance over her shoulder. "It may soon be time for her to cross."

Callum let out a heavy sigh. "There will be bickering among the clans no matter who the oracle names as our new monarch. We have not had a divining ceremony in—"

"Nearly two centuries," finished Tyg. Innes no longer had a direct heir. Her sons and daughters had died in King Odharan's wars, just as Tyg's father had. As a young dren, her fierce father, then the Valor, had seemed invincible. His death still sent a pang of longing and hurt through her heart. Becoming even quieter, she added, "Callum, I think you should make an offering to Cree. To show your devotion. It may put you in his favor."

"That's more than a little presumptive."

"You've more than earned it," she said. "*We've* more than earned it." Of course, Tyg had more than her husband in mind. She had been making secret offerings to Cree for many years, anticipating the ancient queen's eventual crossing. Aygriel be damned.

She made no further mention of the queen's vision to Callum as they walked to the bathhouse. By the time they reached the marble steps, her head had begun to ache terribly. Ignoring the crease between her eyes, Callum kissed her cheek, a rare show of tenderness between them, and went inside to purchase a bath token.

In no mood to join him, Tyg turned to leave but was met with laughter. One of her least favorite dren had been watching from a nearby fountain, and now, she was halfway across the cobbled street.

"Alish," said Tyg as the dren woman reached her. "Well met."

"You and the Valor have a fight?" Alish peered around Tyg's shoulder after Callum. She had grown up with Tyg but did not become a Yewolyn. Instead, she took to the royal city's gossip and parties. A delicate and unusually pale beauty by dren standards, Alish had slept with many more than her fair share of eligible bachelors, even a few ineligible ones. Incomprehensibly, they all adored her despite the fact.

"Our marriage is none of your concern." Tyg began walking back toward the palace, but she soon found Alish next to her.

"I heard he bound the name of a human girl."

Tyg could not smother a thin smile. "It's true," she said, pride swelling in her voice. Even though she felt the girl deserved worse, it was rare for a human to be brought back to their realm. Names were sacred, after all, and name binding was reserved for punishment more often than not.

Alish appeared small next to Tyg and had to walk quickly to keep up with the Magus's long strides. No one doubted the strength of a fully inducted Yewolyn, and the elk cloak and tattoos were visible reminders of that. But Alish did not fear the quick temper of a Yewolyn. After all, she had made many of them turn to liquid beneath her ardent touch. Even Callum—before he married. This only added to Tyg's resentment.

"Queen Innes must be pleased," she went on. "It's been at least a decade since anyone bound a human name. Will she be in court tonight?"

Tyg did not answer at first, hoping that Alish would leave her be. But, of course, the annoying wench kept up, waiting for an answer. "Yes, she will."

Alish beamed. "I would very much like a human girl of my own, you know. I hardly have time to do the dusting or take my dresses to be laundered. It's all very tiresome. I could hire a maid, sure, but you can't really trust them the same way you can a bound human. Surely you understand, Tyg. You don't have one either, do you?"

"I do not, and I do not intend to." Tyg meant it. There was still time to sway Innes. The girl's name was bound. It did not matter who she was placed with.

"You've always been so—"

"Do not finish that thought, Alish."

"What does Callum think?"

"*Valor* Marigen's thoughts are hardly anything for you to concern yourself with." Tyg halted. "Are you finished being a nuisance?"

Without the slightest hint of offense, Alish beamed up at her. "Oh, I had only hoped to catch up with an old friend."

To her relief, Tyg caught sight of Wynn rushing toward them. "Please excuse me, Alish," Tyg said curtly. When the dren did not immediately leave, she lost all patience and shouted, "Off with you, Alish!"

The dren woman flinched and gave a hurt look before leaving Tyg in peace. She watched Alish go, her head throbbing and thoughts churning darkly.

Wynn pressed her hand against her chest. She was out of breath and rosy-cheeked.

"Magus." Her delicate, iridescent wings twitched behind her as she spoke. "I had hoped to find Valor Marigen."

"He's busy," said Tyg. "What is it?"

The thachwing hesitated but then said, "You see, Magus, the girl refuses to bathe. Surely it's nothing, but when I tried using her name, it didn't do any good. Perhaps I said it wrong?"

"Perhaps," Tyg growled through clenched teeth. She stepped past Wynn. "I will deal with the girl."

FOUR

"I'M not wearing the dress," said Ora when the boy, Pons, tried to reason with her. Almost as soon as Wynn left the washroom, she had flown to the door and discovered the thachwing locked it. Now, she stood twisting at the doorknob with both hands.

"At least bathe," Pons said. "You do sort of … smell."

With a growl, she let go of the handle and spun to face him. She didn't like the boy. He seemed incapable of looking her in the eyes, and he did whatever was asked of him. Or rather, whatever the fae asked of him. She could not sway him. "Why should I do anything they tell me to? They've—well, they've stolen me away! Same as you. You're a human like me, aren't you?"

His cheeks turned bright red. "I don't have a choice. They have my name. Don't they have yours?" It was then that he glanced up. The anger in Ora's dark, glittering eyes made him inch backward.

She thought of her uncle's many warnings, and the difference between her and the boy became clear. Rather than let on, she nodded in response to his question. "They do," she said.

Whether or not Pons believed her, he fell silent. In the stillness, she studied him. He looked to be about her age but a head taller. He had auburn hair, freckled skin, and hazel eyes that glistened green and gold. He reminded her of a trader that came to Fel once, eager to procure fine furs for the royalty in Merin. It had been unusual. Merinians rarely ventured past Port Besil, but he had wanted to see the Hy Borea for himself.

"Are you Merinian?" Ora asked.

"I was," he said, voice sullen.

"I'm from Fel," she said. "In Nor."

He did not answer at first but appeared stricken by her want for conversation. At least he spoke common, and she did not have to struggle with her limited knowledge of the Merinian language. When he did not respond right away, she turned to the windows.

"I could guess that you're Norrish. You have an accent," he said, watching her push against the panes with all her might. "Those won't open, you know. They don't even have latches."

A furious cry burst from Ora's lips, and she slammed her fist against the glass. The pane rattled. She pressed her forehead against it, gazing upon an interior courtyard. A single tree with pale, white bark grew in the middle. Wooden benches circled its trunk. Curled in a patch of sunlight beneath the tree was a black cat, the tip of its tail tapping the earth.

"It's not worth all the trouble," Pons said. "They can do much worse than bind your name."

"Oh, I've *seen* what they can do." Ora refused to look at him as she spoke. She focused on the cat instead, her heart wrenching with each word. "They changed my brother. He's all alone in the Hy Borea, and I'm the only one who knows what's become of him. I have to find a way back to help him. Don't you understand?" The cat lifted its head. She thought for a moment that it noticed her standing in the window.

"Ora, I do understand. I—"

Surprised to hear her name fall from the boy's lips, she turned around, but before he could finish speaking, the door to the washroom thudded against the wall. They both jumped as the dren who woke her stormed inside.

"Get out," Tyg said as she brushed past Pons. He fled without a word, pulling the door shut behind him. She towered over Ora. "Why haven't you done as you're told?"

Ora did not shrink away. Instead, she crossed her arms and lifted her chin defiantly. "Dresses are useless."

Tyg looked at the gown Wynn had draped across a wooden chair. It had three layers of fabric: crisp white, sage green, and apple red. Beside the chair was a pair of soft leather slippers. Under different circumstances, Tyg might have agreed with Ora's assessment of the garment. However, with the mandated court appearance rapidly approaching, the fine clothing would be a vast improvement on the girl's current attire.

"*Ora*," she said, her voice dripping with a powerful energy. "You will bathe and dress for court this evening."

But the girl stood firm, tight-lipped, and angry as ever. It was enough to push Tyg over the edge. Her hand shot out in a swift movement and wrapped around Ora's throat. She pushed the girl against the wall. "You will not make a fool of me."

Ora tried to dig her fingers beneath Tyg's grip, but the dren was much stronger. She gasped silently for air. When her face started to darken, Tyg released her, and she dropped to the dusty, wood floor, coughing and grasping at her throat. Despite this, Ora glowed with pride when she looked up.

"Your name, girl, what is your true name?"

"It's Ora," she croaked. "It's always been Ora."

Tyg crouched before the girl. She snatched up one of Ora's hands, drew her knife, and pressed the blade against one of her fingers. A drop of blood welled up against the cold metal. "If you wish to keep your true name from me, know this: I will slice off one of your fingers for every time you disobey."

Ora swallowed hard. She did not doubt for an instant that Tyg meant what she said. She stared at the blade, at her own blood, and then gave one quick nod. "I'll bathe. And wear the dress."

Tyg pressed the knife harder into the girl's finger, and a small, frightened cry escaped her lips. "And if you let anyone know that your name is not bound, I will see to it that you return to your family a gutted pig like your friend. Do you understand?"

The dren's threat made her blood turn to fire as her brother's gruesome transformation flashed in her mind. "It was you? You changed my brother into a pig?"

Rather than answer, Tyg only said, "Clean up. *Now.*"

Ora jerked her hand away as soon as Tyg loosened her grip. To her great relief, the dren left her alone in the washroom. For some time, she stood shaking beside the tub, trying to decide what to do. She wanted to keep all her fingers, and she certainly did not want to be turned into a pig. But she had to escape. She had to find Hademar and help him before he was hunted down himself.

At last, she shed her thick winter coat and her clothes—hand-me-downs from her brother. Though they were worn, she folded them and placed them gently on the chair. As she did, she saw the bright yellow smudge of the handkerchief poking out from her pocket. Aching for home, she pulled it free. The soft fabric still smelled like the warm, sweet bun her mother sent.

She eyed the extravagant dress, wondering where she could hide the handkerchief. "No pockets. *This* is why dresses are useless," she grumbled to herself as she searched the layers of skirts. Finally, she resolved to knot the handkerchief to the innermost layer and prayed that it would not come loose.

Knowing she would have a piece of home close by made Ora feel lighter. She dipped one leg into the tub. The bathwater was tepid but tolerable. It had been mixed with scented oils that were far too floral for her taste. She rubbed the dirt off her arms and face, enjoying the feeling of being clean despite herself. If she had returned home, she would have bathed with nothing more than a washbasin and rough cloth.

As she cleaned off, her elbow bumped against a knob. There came a high pitched whine, and her heart flickered. But the whine gave way to a steaming stream of water. Fascinated, she ran her hand beneath the faucet. The water was hot enough to sting her hand. Torn between delight and irritation, she turned the water off and forced a frown. She did not want to be in awe of the fae.

Ora stood to crawl out of the tub, but the fae from earlier, Wynn, stepped inside the washroom. "Tyg says she has you behaving," said the thachwing as she came to the side of the tub. "I hope you don't consider that clean. You still have pine needles in your hair. Sit back down, *Ora*." She said her name in a slow, deliberate way.

Embarrassed to be standing naked before a stranger, Ora crossed her arms over her chest. Reluctant as she was, she sank back down into the tub, thinking of Tyg's sharp blade the whole time.

"There," said Wynn, sounding pleased with herself. "I must have been saying it wrong after all."

She began scrubbing at Ora's thick hair with a sweet-smelling soap. It took several rounds of dunking and scrubbing for Wynn to be satisfied. After that, Ora had to grit her teeth as the fae pulled tangle after tangle out of her curls with a brush. By the time she finished, the water was freezing cold.

Wynn handed her a towel to dry off as she stood shivering beside the tub. Then, she helped pull the dress over Ora's head and fastened a braided leather belt around her waist. Despite the layered fabric, the skirt felt light and comfortable.

The thachwing picked up a strand of her wet hair. "Now, what to do with this? Some ribbons perhaps?"

"I'm not some sort of doll," Ora said bitterly.

"Of course not, dear. But ribbons *are* fashionable, Ora," Wynn said, dismissing the outburst without so much as a raised brow. "Come with me. I have just the thing."

Ora followed behind Wynn's shimmering wings. They walked too fast for her to get a good look into any of the open rooms they passed, though her quick glimpses didn't reveal anything unusual. Most of the rooms appeared to be like hers, holding nothing more than a bed with a colorful quilt and a wooden chair with a tidy pile of folded clothes.

"Aren't human girls like you supposed to love ribbons and dresses?" asked Wynn as they began to ascend a narrow staircase tucked behind a wooden door.

Ora, despite her best efforts, could not help but like this fae woman. She was not vicious like Tyg and even seemed a bit simple-minded, humming and swaying as she walked. "I don't wear dresses or *ribbons*," she said.

"Hm. How very odd."

They reached the top of the stairs and stood on a small landing. The door before them was painted bright green and had a swirling, blue glass window with sunlight swimming through it. Wynn pulled out an ornate barrel key and unlocked the door. *How come her dress has pockets?* Ora thought ruefully.

"Alright, dear, in you go." This time, she didn't use Ora's name but guided her with a gentle hand on the small of her back. "Have a seat over there," she said, gesturing to a wooden stool by the window.

They entered a large bedroom with a canopy bed and floor-to-ceiling shelves stocked with countless rolls of fabric. A big wooden table on one end had scissors, pincushions, and needles strewn across it. Ora passed all this with an inquisitive eye, even daring to run her hand across a piece of deep, violet silk that cascaded over the side of a shelf.

"Fae silk," Wynn said as she dug through a drawer. "You can only find it in Mysanhal, of course."

"Mysanhal?" asked Ora.

"Yes, dear. More specifically, you are in Tirnan, the royal city of Mysanhal." She tapped her chin. "Let's go with this red to match your dress." She pulled the ribbon from the drawer and turned to Ora, who stood by the window, peeking down at another courtyard.

In the center was a huge stone circle. Beyond that grew stunning gardens with bright flowers, winding paths, and ornate fountains. A waterfall flowed down from the mountainside, fed the reflecting pools, and continued beneath intricate walkways. Ora spotted a group of well-dressed ladies strolling the grounds. They each had wings that glistened in the sunlight.

"Sit, sit, sit." Wynn waved the girl away from the window and onto the stool. Then, with a flurry of words, she mustered up a gust of air and wove it through Ora's wet hair.

It felt like nothing more than a tickle and took mere seconds. In wonder, Ora ran a hand through her hair, now dry and soft, and tilted her head back to look at the smiling thachwing. "How'd you do that?"

"Fae magic. Not so bad, is it?"

Ora did not mention Hademar, even as flashes of his transformation came to mind. She turned pale and looked down at her hands.

"You will become more accustomed to our ways as time passes." Wynn's voice was sweet as honey as she lifted the girl's chin with the tips of her fingers. "You are blessed to walk the fae realm."

"Blessed?" she scoffed, jerking her chin back. "I was stolen from my home."

With a sad smile, Wynn squeezed Ora's shoulder and stepped around her to begin braiding ribbons into her hair. "You were spared a worse fate."

"My brother was not." When the thachwing said nothing, Ora twisted around to face her. "It was an accident. We were hunting a cliff elk."

"You crossed paths with Yewolyns. Count yourself lucky to be alive," Wynn whispered.

"Yewolyns?" she asked.

"They are our queen's finest warriors. They could have just killed you both, but Valor Marigen caught your name. It is the only thing that saved you, do you understand?"

Ora thought of the golden-eyed dren, and her heart filled with resentment. At least he did not know the truth. She fell silent as the thachwing began to pin her braids into place.

"I must apologize for earlier," Wynn said as she finished Ora's hair. "I had intended to fetch Valor Marigen, not his wife."

"What do you mean?" Ora asked and stepped down from the stool.

"The dren who got you to, erm … bathe. That would be Magus Tyg Marigen, the head war mage of the Yewolyns. I wouldn't wish her on anyone, but when you wouldn't do as told, I had to—"

Ora cut her off. "*She* is his *wife*?"

"Yes." Wynn paused. "She did not harm you, did she?"

Though the small cut on Ora's finger could hardly be seen, she tucked her hand behind her skirts and shook her head. "No," she said, remembering the dren's threat. "No harm done."

FIVE

AGONIZING hours passed as Ora waited for court. She could wander the servants' wing but was allowed nowhere else. That did not stop her from trying, of course, but she soon discovered locked doors on both ends. Anytime she happened to pass Pons in her endless, restless pacing, she shot him a dirty glare. He would hurry off, looking ashamed and defeated each time. He did not seem to have any trouble slipping in and out of the long, dim corridor.

Aside from Pons, the occasional human would scurry by, careful to keep their distance in the wide corridor. They all wore simple blue uniforms and only spoke to each other in hushed voices about chores that needed to be done. When Ora tried to gain their attention, they pretended not to see her and shuffled away without a word.

Her heart ached for home and for her mother, whose worst fears had come true. It was not just Ora who did not return home; it was Hademar as well. She prayed to Farig that Lupin would know what to do. No one else in Fel would suspect the fae.

At last, the door on the south end of the wing opened. Ora had expected Wynn to fetch her, but to her great disappointment, it was Tyg. She looked no different than before, still dressed in a soft brown elk cloak and plain breeches.

Ora hated the dren and wished she still had a sword at her side. It did not matter if the Yewolyn was stronger and more powerful. All it would take was a single cut from the silver blade to drain the magic from Tyg's blood.

"Come," Tyg snapped as if scolding a dog.

Though she did as told, Ora did not bother hiding her anger. This turned out to be a mistake.

"Insolence does not become you, you little brat." The Magus tapped the handle of her knife. "Lighten up, girl. Queen Innes will not accept disrespect, and she's the one who will be deciding your fate."

It took some effort to relax, but by the time they reached the Great Hall, Ora managed to soften her features enough for Tyg to be satisfied. Even if she had clung to her resentment, the grandeur of the large chamber would have stolen her breath away all the same.

Rows of benches stretched between ornate, marble columns. Chiseled into each column were four fae women, each holding up a brass lantern with cool, bluish lights glistening behind glass panes. Sculpted garments draped over their figures with impossible fluidity and spilled over their bare feet. How anyone could carve something so realistic and beautiful baffled Ora. When she felt certain that Tyg would not notice, she dared to brush her fingers over one of the skirts to see if it was really made of stone.

The throne drew her eyes next. It was made of polished alabaster that caught the glimmer of the mysterious blue flames. Finely carved flowers and birds swooped through the back and along the arms. A plush, royal blue cushion nestled in the seat, each corner pulled down under the weight of an impressive sapphire and tassel.

The opulence was foreign to Ora's Norrish sensibilities. They did not value affluence or luxury in Nor. Even their king and queen sat on modest wood thrones, symbols of humility, hard work, and devotion to their people.

As the initial shock faded, she began to look more closely at the fae who crowded the hall. She could name many of them from her uncle's stories—stalwart elves, rosy-cheeked thachwings, druids with pale green skin, and more dren. There were also many fae she did not recognize. A woman with a flat nose and long, black hair. A knobby, old man who appeared to be made of branches and bark rather than limbs and skin. A girl hunched on the end of a bench with a seal pelt tugged over her shoulders.

Tyg turned down a row of benches, and Ora caught sight of her captor. A sickening knot formed in her stomach as Tyg shoved her down next to him.

"Well, well, look at you," he said. When she ignored him, he caught hold of her chin and forced their gazes to meet. A twinkle of laughter shone in his eyes. "You're quite pretty without all that mud, aren't you?"

"Callum," Tyg hissed, and, to Ora's surprise, he let go.

Suddenly, a hush settled over the hall. With a rustle of fine fabric and wings, every fae rose to their feet. Tyg shot Ora a look, and she jumped up at once. They all turned toward the grand, arched entrance as the queen stepped into the hall. Two thachwing women in ivory silk dresses attended her.

Queen Innes's hair tumbled freely down her back, as wild and beautiful as sea foam, shifting from moon white to silver like the storms that often swept across the ocean toward Fel. Diamonds and rubies glistened in her golden crown, which looked abnormally large perched above her soft, round features. Her wings, pale silver, were so long they spilled across the ground and joined the train of her violet dress. Though stunning, Ora thought the queen had a strange, distant expression in her even paler eyes as she made her way slowly down the aisle of benches.

Once the queen reached her throne, she turned to address the court. Her voice was pure music, sweet even to Ora, who could not understand her words. The fae took their seats once again.

Ora's eyes shifted about the room, and she quickly sat down a moment behind the crowd. Her anxiety grew as the fae conversed in their own language, sometimes laughing, sometimes debating heatedly for long stretches of time. Various officials rose to their feet and orated at length. Others stood supplicating before the queen. When Innes spoke, she did not raise her voice, and everyone grew dead silent to hear her words. Ora began to wonder if they would forget about her. But then, a different sort of hush came over the crowded hall. Heads began to turn toward them.

"Up," said Tyg, grabbing hold of Ora's elbow. All three of them rose to their feet and approached the throne.

As Callum spoke in the fae tongue, the queen studied Ora wordlessly. She tried to avoid meeting Innes's gaze, but she felt drawn to it, like a moth to lamplight. When she at last looked up, the queen's eyes held her in place. Then, she heard a voice whisper in her mind. Instinctively, she knew it belonged to Innes.

You are quite unusual. Ora is not your true name, is it?

She could not stop herself from thinking of the truth. It rose unbidden, much to her horror. *It's short for Eudora.*

A pretty name, said the queen.

Her secret revealed, Ora felt like crying. She would never escape. She would never save Hademar. She would be trapped in the fae realm forever. Hopelessness blossomed within her, and it took all her willpower to maintain her composure with Tyg and Callum standing on either side of her.

But the voice went on. *Let's keep that secret between us, Eudora. You have a different fate than any of us suspect.*

Questions welled up in Ora's mind, but the queen's gaze left hers at last. The hall came back into focus, and she drew in a deep breath of air.

Tyg bowed to the queen and spoke in the common tongue. "Apologies, Your Majesty. I haven't had time to teach her proper etiquette."

The fae queen lit up with a smile. "No need to apologize, Magus Marigen. It takes time for humans to learn our ways." She looked between the two Yewolyns thoughtfully. "Seeing as you brought her to our realm, Valor Marigen, I am placing her in your home."

These words made Ora's knees weaken. Out of the corner of her eye, she saw Callum bow his head. As he began to speak, she dug her nails into her palms. "Your Majesty, while we greatly appreciate your generosity, we—"

"We would be honored," said Tyg quickly, cutting her husband short. His brow rose in surprise.

Dread spilled into Ora's blood. She opened her mouth to protest but remembered the knife of the iron-willed dren who stood next to her.

"Good. You have more than earned this blessing," Innes said before settling her gaze on Ora once more. "Ora, your name is bound to Mysanhal, and so you are bound to her ruler's will. You will serve the Marigens as long as you walk our realm."

"I—" Ora began but snapped her mouth shut as Tyg's hand clamped down on her shoulder.

"We thank you, Your Majesty, for your generosity," Tyg replied.

Innes nodded before dismissing them with the wave of her hand. The Marigens bowed low to the queen, and Ora sensibly did the same. However miserable she felt, she would not let them see. She followed the two dren back to their place in the hall and sat in perfect silence for the remainder of the evening.

When the queen dismissed the court and left the hall, Ora let out a long, slow breath. This only made Tyg glare. Despite the hard pit in her stomach, she remained resolute beneath the Magus's gaze.

"Ah, aren't you fearless?" Callum said in Ora's own tongue. "How very lucky I was to catch your name. I think any other human would crumble in our household."

"Should I be afraid?" Ora said, even as her pulse quickened. She saw Tyg tense, like a cord ready to snap, but Callum only laughed.

"Shall I see to it that the girl gets settled in?" Tyg asked, her tone sweetening.

Callum raised a brow and said something in fae. When Tyg responded, he shrugged and looked down at the girl. "Go with Tyg, Ora. She will make sure you're comfortable for the evening. Tomorrow, we'll put you to work."

Callum excused himself. Once he was out of earshot, Tyg whispered to Ora, "Do not forget that I keep my blade sharp."

"How could I?" she said.

The Magus lifted her hand as if she might strike the girl, but as Ora recoiled, she composed herself. "Watch your tongue. I will not warn you again," she said. "Now, come with me."

As they exited the palace, Ora blinked at the bright sunlight that greeted them. The warm summer air surprised her, and she wondered just how far away from the Hy Borea she had been taken. The hazy, evening sky softened the tall mountain peaks that rose over the royal city. As she descended into the crowded streets with Tyg, the swell of activity made Ora's heart drum. Compared to the small, cozy village of Fel, Tirnan was an overwhelming, noisy sprawl of foreign life.

Fae of all types walked the narrow paths between stone buildings. Their language grated unpleasantly in her ears. Most were hauntingly beautiful, made strange only by their sharp features, wings, or the crackle of magic that surrounded some of them.

Despite a gnawing sense of unease, Ora could not deny the splendor of the city. The architecture itself was unlike anything she had ever seen. The white stone walls shone like jewels in the dying light, a far cry from the drab cedar cabins in Fel. Archways and doorways and window frames all had delicate, impossibly detailed carvings.

Like in Queen Innes's court, enchanted brass lamps hung outside storefronts and from posts on street corners. Ora caught sight of a small fae girl, no bigger than her hand, crouched atop one of the lamps. When she noticed Ora staring, her lips curled into a vicious snarl that revealed pointed, cat-like teeth.

"A sprite," Tyg said. "Do not stare."

They crossed bridges over crashing waterfalls and jostled their way through crowded plazas. Water flowed from fountains, which came in countless shapes and sizes. The fae stopped to drink from smaller metal spouts that drained into grates nestled in the cobblestone.

They eventually came to a west-facing townhouse near one of the open plazas. Ora hesitated as the door swung open but stepped inside before Tyg lost her patience.

Golden sunlight filled the parlor. A chaise sat near the fireplace, and there were several shelves full of scrolls and books. The home appeared dusty and unkempt. A heavy wooden table in one corner had maps and papers strewn over it. Dishes sat atop the mantle and in other odd places. A brown apple core perched on the arm of a plush, red chair.

Tyg shut the door behind her and stepped toward Ora. "Come with me," she said and led her down a dark hallway. At the end of the passage, she opened a door to a small spare room. Like the rest of the house, a layer of dust coated the furnishings, which amounted to nothing more than a bed, washstand, and wardrobe. "You will sleep here."

Again, Ora hesitated to cross the threshold. Would the door close forever behind her once she did? She would not be much use locked in a spare room.

As if reading her mind, Tyg said, "You may walk freely in our home. Any door that shouldn't be opened will be properly enchanted. I can assure you of that."

Though still a cage, it was better than being trapped in a single room. She nodded in answer, still uncertain of Tyg's intentions.

"Eat what you'd like from the larder," said Tyg. Then, without a word more, she turned and set about enchanting the doors and windows.

Tired and hungry, Ora sat on the bed and listened to Tyg walk about the house. At some point, she heard the front door open and then click shut. She tried not to rush as she stepped into the hallway and made her way to the parlor.

"Hello?" she called. "Tyg? Valor Marigen?"

The house responded with silence. She was alone. Despite knowing the door to be enchanted, she tried the handle anyway. Heat bit at her hand, and she leapt back with a cry of pain. She looked down at her scorched palm. Her skin felt tight as she flexed her fingers, but it did not blister.

"I'll find a way out," she said to the door, but doubt crept into her thoughts. Humans could not use magic. How would she be able to get past the enchantments without a spell?

Ora began to tug ribbons out of her hair. She moved cautiously toward the table covered in maps, notes, and what appeared to be letters. Her hands shook a little as she began to look at the maps. Reading did not come easily in her own language, and the fae script eluded her entirely. Still, she studied the mountain ranges, lakes, and geography that lay before her. Nothing looked familiar.

She turned away from the letters and began to scan the spines of books. She reached out to touch one and gasped. A little spark had pricked her finger. Were the books enchanted as well? She touched another. The same tickle of energy spread through her hand, but it did not hurt or burn the way the door handle had.

Cautious but intrigued, she slid the book from the shelf and opened it. She could not explain it, but she felt there must be power in the fae writing. She could feel it when she touched the pages and ran her fingers over the words. It made her heart patter and the hair on her arms rise. She smoothed her hand across page after page and wondered if she might find something useful, something to help her understand the magic that kept her trapped within those walls.

Though she knew the house to be empty, she glanced around before closing the book and carrying it with her to the spare room. There, she tucked it beneath the mattress. Defying Tyg gave her a small thrill. She stepped back from the bed with a smile. Whatever it took, she would escape.

SIX

FYNTOLOMAH'S Alehouse sat deep beneath the market district, and though it had a bright yellow door, it was not easy to find. Anyone who visited it for the first time had been led there, or they chanced upon it after following a maze of narrow streets. Windowless and damp, the space was lit only by the bluish glow of enchanted lamps. The effect made its patrons look surreal, like underwater spirits.

Old Fyn, an ancient elf, sat in the corner each night, keeping an eye on the crowd of transient merchants. Trouble rarely broke out, in large part due to the fact that he prohibited magic. Spells did not mix well with drunkenness. Despite this rule, he still made a small fortune off the cheap ale. At least, that was what he claimed kept him in business. Callum had watched the old elf make quiet deals with merchants for many years. In exchange for not ousting Fyn's questionable operation, the Valor enjoyed as much free ale as he desired.

"Look at that," Callum said, tipping his mug toward Fyn's corner. "Does that look like Elder Kavyn to you?"

Beside him sat Cyn, the Yewolyn who had carried Pyri to the healing wards after the attack in the Hy Borea. One of the youngest Yewolyns, Cyn had few marks to boast, but his extraordinary swordsmanship had helped him earn his elk cloak two years prior. Charming and cavalier, he loved entertaining dren women with grandiose stories.

"That's a couple of old elves, but that's no Elder Kavyn," Cyn said, having leaned across the table for a better view.

"No?" Frothing ale sloshed over the rim of Callum's mug as he spoke. "The resemblance is there—the beard! Look at it. Hanging like a snake."

"Plenty of elves braid their beard like that."

They stared hard at the elf who sat across from Fyn. His back was turned to them, and all they could make out was a braided cord of hair tossed over his shoulder. Fyn slid the mysterious elf a package beneath the table.

"Can't be him," Cyn concluded. "You think Elder Kavyn would come to a place like this?"

"No! You're right. The smell alone would scare him off, and if that didn't do the trick, Fyn's manners would."

The two Yewolyns roared with laughter. As they settled back into their drunken ramblings, Cyn looked up to see Alish drifting toward them. "Here she comes," he said, not bothering to hide his words from her. "Alish, lover of all!"

"All but you." Quick to defend his friend and brother-in-arms, Callum got to his feet. "Off with you, Alish! We'll have none of you and you none of us!"

She sat down across from the two all the same. "I'm not here for you," she said even as she gave Cyn a sly wink. "I've only come to hear what happened in the Hy Borea."

Tempted by an audience, Cyn snapped his mug back onto the table. "Ah, you've heard rumors, have you?"

"I've heard Pyri is in grave shape," she said, lowering her voice. "And I heard Tyg turned a human boy into a—what was it?"

"A brush pig! It was incredible, really. It was the most graceful transformation I have ever witnessed, more so than …" Cyn's words trailed off. Tyg stood at the end of the table with her arms crossed and head cocked to one side, daring him to go on.

"Right," Callum said and sat himself back down. "Have a drink, my love."

"You must be pleased," said Alish with narrowed eyes. "A bound human will be so nice to have around the house."

Frowning, Tyg sat down next to Callum and took hold of his mug. Then, unceremoniously, she downed the whole thing. Cyn watched with wide eyes as the Magus wiped her mouth on her sleeve.

"Leave, Alish. I'm in no mood for your gossip," Tyg said.

For once, the dren woman had the good sense not to argue. "Another time, boys," she said, biting her bottom lip as she eyed Cyn.

Once she had swaggered off, Callum turned to his wife. "She's right, you know. I don't think either of us care for housework. Might be nice to have the dust—dusted?"

"You're drunk," she said. "And Alish is an idiot."

"This may be so, but you're the one who stopped me from declining our queen's gracious offer."

"Yes, with good reason. When I met with her in the conservatory, she asked that I watch over the girl." Tyg rubbed at her forehead as if she endured a terrible headache. "Apparently, she had a dream about this little Nor you dragged back to Tirnan."

Cyn leaned across the table. "Callum mentioned the queen has been babbling nonsense."

"It would seem so," said Tyg. "She spends more time dreaming than she does governing, and then there's Aygriel. I fear her influence. Innes listens to her without question. Mark my words, she will be trouble when the queen crosses."

"Cree's will is all that matters," said Callum. "Aygriel is wise enough to know that."

"Would Cree have willed such a weak ruler as Innes?" Tyg's voice became venomous. "The elemental fae have been left unchecked, and there is talk of the outlying sylvn clans gathering their strength, attacking merchants, and stealing from our villages. This is no time to dwell on such ridiculous notions of peace. Innes has left the farthest reaches of Mysanhal unguarded while we run petty errands. We should be securing our borders, not overseeing the resettlement of the Cedar Clan."

"You are too hungry for battle, my dear. This peace is welcome. The fae of Mysanhal are glad for it. It is diplomacy that has strengthened Mysanhal, not war," said Callum.

Her fingers curled tightly around the empty mug, and her words came out clipped. "The fae of Mysanhal have grown ignorant. The sylv have never wished for peace. Have you forgotten why King Odharan began the war?"

Callum sighed. "I haven't forgotten at all, but the sylv have no strength left. Their country was laid to waste. Their god is dead. The outlying clans are starving, and they have no one to blame but themselves. It takes but a few Yewolyn mages to put them back in place." He spoke with unyielding calm even as his wife seethed. "Besides, the smart ones have pledged their fealty to Mysanhal and live good lives within our borders. There is no reason to provoke them."

Tyg shook her head and went on, her voice rising. "I don't think they would agree. They live in filth. Eventually, the sylv will grow restless. The queen might have allowed them into Mysanhal, but she has done little to ensure their loyalty."

"We have given them refuge."

"Refuge from what?"

"The Wastelands, of course."

"*We* created the Wastelands. We have given them refuge from *us!* We should have finished what we started, but no, Innes ended the war prematurely. Because of her, the sylv are still a threat. They should have been stamped out along with their god."

"Tyg, my love," said Callum with a nervous laugh. Her raised voice had turned a few heads.

Cyn lifted his mug and downed the rest of his ale in a few gulps. Then, he slammed it against the table and said, "Enough of this. It's no time for such grim discussion. Let us celebrate our return!"

Tyg's stony expression did not falter, and Callum reached out to touch her arm. "You are wise to be concerned," he said. "Your counsel has always been heard. If a greater threat arises, our Yewolyns will be there to meet it. Let us discuss these matters tomorrow, though."

"Very well," she said, pulling her arm away. "Tomorrow."

Talk of politics and old enemies quickly faded into reminiscing. By the time they emptied their last mugs, all three could barely walk straight. Even Tyg's mood had lightened. They leaned into each other as they made their way along a cobbled road, not caring if they woke everyone up with their boisterous chatter.

Once they turned a corner, they parted ways. Callum wrapped his arm around Tyg's waist and said, "You're almost too sweet when you've had this much."

"Too sweet?" Her head wobbled back with a laugh. "How could I be too sweet?"

"I'm used to my wife's sharp tongue is all."

She jabbed at his side. "I'll show you a sharp tongue."

The playful threat reminded him of the early days of their courtship and how he did in fact love her once, in the silly, thoughtless way a young dren would. He stopped in front of their home. "Truly, if you don't wish to have a human in our house I—"

"You said it yourself. The dust needs dusting." She unlocked the door with a spell. "The girl will be useful."

Callum heard the rush of feet retreating down the hallway as they stepped inside. Perhaps the girl had some fear in her after all. Amused, he called for her, eager to test out the name. "*Ora*! Draw us a bath."

"What? A bath?" Tyg rubbed at her forehead. "It's late, Callum."

"That hardly matters. A bath sounds refreshing. And perhaps *you* can show me that sharp tongue while we're at it."

As Ora crept back down the hallway, Tyg shrugged away, once again her normal, bristly self. In no mood for his drunken, boyish romance, she headed for the stairs. "I'm going to sleep. No need to draw a bath, Ora."

Before the girl could return to the spare room, Callum beckoned for her. "Come. Get me some wine," he said.

She went to the kitchen and began to rummage around. While he waited, he bent before the hearth and used a spell to light the fire. Then, he slid down onto the rug and slouched against the chaise to watch the flames. The pleasant buzz of ale made his body feel numb, and the warmth of the fire lulled him. He felt his eyes growing heavy, but then he heard soft footsteps approaching. In his stupor, he had almost forgotten about the girl.

Ora crouched beside him and held out the bottle. With her other hand, she had bunched up part of her layered skirt. "I couldn't find a cup," she said.

"No matter." He ignored the wine and lifted her chin just as he had in the Great Hall. "You are pretty, especially for a human."

"Do not touch me," she said between clenched teeth.

"You have—what's the Norrish word? Mettle?" He let go of her chin and traced the pearly-white scar on his forehead with his thumb. "Quite a lot of blood for nothing, don't you think?"

She set the wine beside him but did not stand back up. "What would you have done?"

"I would have made sure my enemy was dead."

"Would you bring your enemy into your home?" she asked, voice quiet. The change in tone made Callum pause.

Firelight and disdain danced in her black eyes. He knew her intention before she ever moved. Still, the girl was swift. She drew back the hand she had been holding her skirt with, and he saw metal. As she drove the knife toward his chest, Callum caught her wrist. In an instant, he had twisted the blade against her throat.

"Oh, you *are* fearless. If you were born fae, I'd make a Yewolyn of you," he mused. "Do you have any idea how many battles I've seen?"

"It doesn't matter. If I had a silver blade, all those battles would mean nothing."

"I have lived five of your human lifetimes, but I have not spent that time learning spells. No, that's Tyg. I prefer to fight without relying on magic, so if you think silver frightens me, you are mistaken. And if you think a—" He gave a short laugh and pressed the knife harder against her throat. "A dull blade like this is your best weapon against a Yewolyn, you are a fool."

"You're right," she said, lifting her chin away from the cold metal. "It is dull."

Half-grinning, he withdrew the knife. She scrambled back from him at once. "No wonder the queen has Tyg looking after you. You're a fiendish little thing."

She glared in answer.

"Don't look so angry. There is no finer place in all the Ether than Mysanhal."

"The Ether?" she asked.

"Yes, the Ether. Where else would our realms exist? Or did you think we fae lived in the same world, cowering in the shadows? You humans really do astound me with your ignorance." He got to his feet and trudged toward the stairs. When he reached the banister, he paused. "And Ora … no more knives. Dull or not."

SEVEN

ORA tossed and turned in the dusty little room, thinking of Hademar and her family. Her mother would be sick with worry, and Uncle Lupin would be searching the Hy Borea for them. He would be the only one to suggest fae were involved. All the other men of Fel would likely credit their disappearances to a mountain lion or a sinkhole. How long, she wondered, would it take before they declared the Widogast siblings dead? Her heart ached for the small, familiar world she had been taken from. This was not the adventure she had longed for.

As early morning light pooled across her bed, the door to her room swung open. Tyg snapped at her to get up. She pulled on her shoes and followed the dren to the front door. There, Tyg paused and met her gaze.

"Do not stray from me," she warned, and then opened the door.

They walked across the plaza and began to wend through Tirnan's cobbled streets. Tyg took Ora to an open-air market, where she paid a clothier for less frilly attire. Ora stood in the corner of the stall, her eyes drinking in all the spectacular silks and patterns. Compared to Norrish dress, fae cloth was rich and colorful. It reminded her of the people of Galgoa, the desert country south of Nor. Though she had never been there herself, she had met a couple of Galgoans while visiting Port Besil with her uncle.

"There you are," said Tyg, handing over an undyed linen smock. "We'll get rid of that ridiculous thing you're wearing."

Ora did not know whether to speak or keep her mouth shut, but Tyg pushed her out of the stall without a word more. She hugged the smock against her chest, happy that she would be rid of the layered skirts. Still, she could not, would not, feel grateful toward Tyg.

They ascended another set of stairs, and Ora's stomach growled as the homey smell of fresh baked goods met her nose. They stopped at a stall for warm flatbread stuffed with spiced sweet potatoes. She devoured the meager breakfast as Tyg pressed on.

"Where are you taking me?" Ora asked as they crossed yet another plaza.

"To an Elder. Valor Marigen finds interpreting your language exhausting."

Confused, Ora stumbled over her words. "I can't speak your language. I can't learn it overnight."

"Of course not. We'll be needing an enchantment."

The idea of more magic made Ora's skin crawl. Still, she hurried alongside Tyg at a brisk pace. The streets of Tirnan had become crowded and noisy. Strange fae brushed against her. Those who bothered to look at her did so with haughty glances. The rising summer heat, the swirl of bright skirts, the smell of spices, and the foreign words made her head spin.

Tyg stopped at a corner building with a bright blue door and stained-glass windows. She knocked a few times and then waited. Ora had her back turned to the dren, still taking in all the unusual sights and sounds of Tirnan. When she felt Tyg's hand tighten around her shoulder, she sucked in her breath.

"Hurry up," said the Yewolyn.

The door had opened to reveal an old elven man no taller than Ora. His long, gray beard was braided and tossed over his shoulder. He wore what looked to be a green bathrobe and seemed, overall, disheveled. As he stepped aside, he waved them both into a dimly lit shop filled with odd instruments. Some ticked and hissed, some caught the sunlight in an array of rainbow spots, some hovered impossibly a few inches off the shelves. They created a cacophony of soft whispers, and Ora sensed the same energy she felt when touching the fae books crackling in the air of the strange shop.

Tyg spoke to the shopkeeper in fae, and they both looked at Ora. She backed herself against the shelves, nearly knocking a large crystal orb from its stand.

"Come here, come here," said the elf, waving her closer.

She cautiously stepped toward the Elder and stood in front of him. He took her face in his calloused hands and turned it, first one way and then the other, to study her ears.

"Elder Kavyn is a master of enchantments and charms. He will see to it that you understand the fae tongue," Tyg said.

"It's a complex enchantment you're asking for," said Elder Kavyn, not bothering to slip back into the fae language. "It will be costly, of course."

"How much?" she asked. When he told her the price, Tyg cursed under her breath but relinquished the coins. Then, she leaned on the edge of a display table covered in dusty trinkets and crossed her arms. "Get on with it."

He pocketed the coins with a smile and took a seat behind his desk. "Sit right there," he said to Ora, indicating the chair across from him. He put on a pair of wireframe glasses and began rummaging through the drawers.

"If you're a master of enchantments, why do you need glasses?" Ora asked.

"You are quite observant." The elf laughed. "Enchantments require an object to work properly. I can no more enchant my eyes than enchant your ears. Not without certain consequences, at least. As for these glasses, they are quite powerful. They allow me to see even the most minute details."

"She doesn't need a lesson in enchantments," Tyg snapped.

"Of course not," he said. "Forgive me, Magus Marigen."

As he spoke, he produced a gold chain, then a polished, white crystal pendant. For all the supposed complexity of the enchantment, it took mere seconds. He held the crystal between his hands and muttered a stream of fae words, his eyes fixed on Ora. She squirmed in the chair, uncertain of what the elf was up to. Finally, he snaked the pendant onto the chain and held it out to her.

"Put that on. You shouldn't have any trouble with the fae tongue as long as you wear it," he said.

She took the pendant and glanced at Tyg. The dren only scowled, and Ora quickly pulled it over her head. The weight surprised her, and the crystal felt warm against her chest.

"Simple enough," said Elder Kavyn as he dusted off his hands.

Tyg frowned. "I thought you said it was a complex enchantment."

"It is!" he snapped. "It took years to master. Transforming language into a deeply felt understanding that transcends mere speech is no small task. It requires not only an understanding of sound but a strong grasp of how a mind turns and how culture inflicts itself upon the meaning of words. It requires a shifting of perspective, not just *simple* translation."

The dren rolled her eyes. Though Ora knew they were not speaking Norrish, the words rang clear in her mind. Dazed, she said, "It works." As soon as the words fell from her lips, she drew in a sharp breath and clasped her hands over her mouth. Her tongue and lips had formed words in an unfamiliar way. Ora had spoken fae.

"Of course it works! An elf dedicates his life to an art, and this is all the respect he gets? I should start charging more. Honestly." He went on grumbling to himself as he shooed them both out of the shop.

The voices whirling around her were now clear, and she realized she had been a topic of conversation more often than not. Someone called her a smelly little human as they passed, making Tyg smirk. Ora wrinkled her nose at the insult. If she had not been within inches of the Yewolyn, she might have been bold enough to shout an insult back.

They eventually came to an enormous stone building not far from the palace. The large double doors had noble cliff elk engraved into the wood. Ora's eyes lingered on them as they passed through the doorway, and she had to hurry her steps in order to stay close to Tyg.

Inside was a flurry of activity. Yewolyns passed through the main hall with stony faces. Others sat around tables speaking in low voices. She could hear swords scraping against each other, shouting, and floorboards creaking above them. Tyg walked swiftly past her fellow Yewolyns and stepped into a portico surrounding a large courtyard. The sounds of combat amplified as the door closed behind them. A few dozen dren warriors practiced hand-to-hand combat, swordsmanship, and archery on the dusty, blood-splattered earth.

The flash of metal made Ora yearn for the silver sword her uncle had gifted her only two days before. Would he find it in the brush and guess what had become of his niece? Without meaning to, she paused to watch as two Yewolyns wrestled to gain control of a knife. One drew his fist back and struck the other in the face with a sickening crack. Blood flooded from the dren's nose, but neither slowed in their movements.

"A Yewolyn who struggles more in training sheds less blood in battle."

It was Callum. She turned to see a proud smile upon his face. Unamused and bitter, she said, "Your training does not take into account small river stones and Norrish girls with good aim."

"Perhaps not." His smile became a smirk, and he lifted the crystal that hung from her neck. "I see Tyg took you to Elder Kavyn."

The Magus had retraced her steps by then and did not share Callum's good humor. Despite her impassive expression, Ora did not miss the cruel gleam in Tyg's eyes. "Come, Ora," she said. "There is work to be done."

Tyg led her through a door on the far end of the training yard. They passed through a sunlit hallway and into a small, dusty courtyard. In the center stood a stone fountain with four metal spouts. A dren, who looked to be Hademar's age, held a pitcher beneath one of the free-flowing streams of water. When he noticed the Magus, he snapped to attention.

"Magus Marigen," he said. "Well met."

Tyg gave Ora a push forward. "This is Ora. Put her to work."

"Yes, Magus."

"Return her to me before the dinner bell," Tyg said. Before she left, she added, "She's been to Elder Kavyn. No need to trouble yourself with human tongues."

"Yes, Magus."

Neither the dren nor Ora moved until the Magus disappeared into the hallway. Both sighed. Their shoulders fell. For a few brief moments, they stared at each other.

"I'm Renna," said the dren. When Ora did not speak, he tapped the side of the pitcher. "Well, come with me then."

Ora followed him through a set of open doors that led to a kitchen. A savory smell curled up from the cast iron pot that sat atop a clay oven in the corner. Skillets, pots, and bundles of drying herbs hung from hooks on the ceiling. A long wooden table with barrels tucked beneath it sat against one wall. A sack of open flour spilled across one end. Bottles of wine, tin boxes, and baskets of bread and fresh fruit crowded the shelves on the opposite wall. Ora could picture her ma bustling about the space, and a pang of homesickness pricked her heart.

"I was just about to make bread," Renna said, pushing back thick, black hair from his forehead.

"Do you cook? For *all* of them?"

"You mean all of the Yewolyns?"

"Who else?"

"Of course. An enchanted pot can feed an army," he said.

"Are you a Yewolyn?"

The dren laughed. "No, I prefer ladles to swords. Now, why don't you change and help me with the dough."

Ora glanced around. "Change *here*?"

"Ah, you humans are strange about that, aren't you?" He went to the doors and pulled them shut. Then, he cast a spell that produced a glowing orb. It rose above their heads and filled the windowless kitchen with light. "Better?"

"Yes," Ora said and began to unfasten the belt around her waist. As she struggled to pull the layered dress over her head, she heard Renna's muffled voice through the fabric.

"Would you like some help?"

"Ah, no, no!" She wriggled free of the skirts only to discover that he sat atop a barrel watching her. Blood rushed to her cheeks, and she held the dress against her chest.

"Sorry!" Renna covered his eyes. "I heard Valor Marigen brought back a human, but I didn't think the Magus would bring you here. She's … well, how do I put it? Not fond of humans?"

"I noticed," said Ora as she draped the layered dress across a stool. She lifted up the skirt to retrieve her mother's handkerchief. The linen smock did not make it any easier to hide the bright, yellow square of cloth. She tucked it beneath the smock at her waist and then grabbed the belt to hold it in place.

"I'm dressed now," she said as she smoothed out the fabric.

"Good!" Hopping up from the barrel, Renna snuffed out the light with a spell and then flung the doors open once again. "Come here, Ora. I'll show you how we make bread in Tirnan," he said, waving her over to the long table. He pushed a wooden bowl toward her. "Leftovers from yesterday. Try some."

Ora lifted a cold, flaky piece of flatbread from the bowl and nibbled at the edge. Salt and oil melted on her tongue. "*This* is bread?" she asked, thinking of the fluffy buns her mother baked. "Is it … deflated?"

A twinkle of amusement in his eyes, Renna shook his head. "No, not deflated, but it is better hot."

He instructed her with the utmost patience on how to form flour and water into a firm dough. As she attempted to emulate his efforts, Ora's mind wandered. It would be easier to sneak away from Renna. Much like Wynn, this dren had a warmer, less threatening demeanor.

"Why does she hate humans?" Ora asked without looking up from the dough forming beneath her hands.

"History, I suppose."

"Did something happen?"

"Ha!" The question made Renna take pause. He peered down at Ora's work. "More flour than that."

"Well?" said Ora as she sprinkled more flour into the mixture. "Clearly something happened."

"I thought you were joking." Renna's brow wrinkled. "Tell me, what do humans say about the fae in their histories?"

"We think you're nothing but stories. Well, most of us. My uncle doesn't."

"I forget. Lives are shorter in the human realm. To you, it's ancient history, but our great grandfathers still pass down what happened in Himil."

"Himil?"

"That's what we call the human realm. We were once friends to humans, but you grew to envy our magic. When humans realized they could not possess such power for themselves, they tried to destroy ours. We call it the Silver War. Many fae had magic sliced from their veins."

As Renna told this story, Ora kneaded the bread with increasing forcefulness. "Perhaps if you didn't steal names and turn us into pigs, we would have stayed friends. Magic is horrible." To her surprise, she felt a gentle touch on her arm, and she lifted her head to meet the dren's gaze. Like Tyg, his eyes were bright blue.

"Magic is a tool, just like a knife. There are many ways to use it. It does not become a weapon without intent," he said.

She scowled and went back to kneading. "Magic is *not* just like a knife. You must drive a blade into someone for it to hurt. A spell can take all you have in just a few words." She paused to dust more flour onto her hands. "You're frightened of Tyg too, aren't you?" she asked but already knew the answer.

"It's true. She does frighten me," Renna admitted, then lowered his voice. "Ora, listen. Magus Marigen sees utility in violence. It's how she rose to her position, and it's how she maintains control. Be wary around her. I do not know why she wishes to keep you close. Tyg would sooner welcome a family of sprites into her house than a human, bound or not."

The warning made Ora all the more uneasy, but she did not want him to notice. Quick to change the subject, she said, "Tyg told me not to stare at sprites. What's so bad about them?"

"You don't want to draw their attention. They'll follow you home. Steal odds and ends." Renna wiped his hands off on a rag. "You still need more flour. Let me show you."

Ora stepped aside so the dren could fold more flour into the dough. "I've never been very good at making bread," she said as she tried to pick the sticky goop from her hands.

"You'll learn with practice."

She watched him for a while. Sunlight streamed through the open doors and warmed her back. The kitchen felt tranquil, a far cry from the training yard. "Renna, can I ask you something?"

He formed the dough into a ball and set it aside. "Yes, of course."

"Why are you here?"

"It's how I make my living."

"But why work for the Yewolyns? Couldn't you work in the palace or somewhere else?"

"My older brother is a Yewolyn. He got me this job. Of course, he'd probably like it better if I joined the ranks, but I never liked combat." He rubbed at the back of his neck, leaving behind powdery, white smudges. "He was there, in the Hy Borea."

A knot tightened in Ora's stomach. She edged away from Renna. "You aren't the Valor's brother, are you?"

"No. My brother is Cynaca. Most call him Cyn."

"If he was there, then you know what happened." A cold edge clipped her words, and the dren winced.

"Yes, I heard what happened to your friend. I truly am sorry, Ora. No one should suffer a transformation. It was a—"

She cut off his words. "Tyg changed my brother."

"Your brother?"

Silence stretched between them. She did not know what else to say, though a hundred thoughts clouded her mind. She could tell by the pained look in Renna's eyes that he wished he could help her, but she also knew he would not. His brother was a Yewolyn. He made their bread. He was fae.

When he spoke again, his voice sounded distant. "You cannot return to Himil without magic. There is no other way to cross the Ether."

Tears burned in her eyes, and she wrinkled her nose to stop them from falling. "I must find a way."

"You know I cannot aid you."

"I know. I—"

"But," he said, placing his hands on her shoulders. "I will not stop you either. It is my job to put you to work. I am not your keeper."

"Thank you," she whispered.

A shadow stretched across the kitchen as a Yewolyn appeared in the doorway. "You soft-hearted fool. You're not making friends with humans now, are you?"

In an instant, Renna's expression shifted. He turned away from Ora with a frown, carefully placing himself between her and the Yewolyn. "What brings you to my kitchen, Cyn?"

Of course. They could not look more alike. Each had blue eyes, the same straight-cut nose, and a square jaw. But Renna appeared small and wiry compared to his stronger, warrior brother.

"Food, of course." Cyn grinned and sauntered in to stand before the shelves. He took a plum from one of the baskets, then leaned against the end of the table to eat it. "Come on, Ren. Let me have a proper look at her."

Renna's shoulders tensed, but he stepped aside all the same. Behind him, Ora had been seething. Her hands were curled into fists and a furious gleam lit her dark eyes.

"Doesn't she look docile," Cyn said around a mouthful of plum. "Are you certain you can handle this little Nor?"

"Her name is bound, isn't it? What harm can she do?"

Having devoured the plum in a few bites, Cyn tossed the pit into a bowl of scraps and approached Ora. "You looked like a little beast last I saw you, all covered in mud."

"Only because I was flung into a mudbank," she said.

"And here I thought all you humans lived like pigs in that wretched forest."

"Cyn," Renna said, but his brother ignored him.

"Your friend is fortunate that his arrows missed Pyri's heart, or he might have been the pork in our stew."

Ora's eyes slid to a nearby knife. She did not care if Cyn was Renna's brother. Hatred rushed through her blood, a dark venom that dissolved her senses. She wanted to lash out, to fight back. What did it matter if she was smaller? She could take them by surprise. She felt her fingers twitch at her sides, but Renna spoke again.

"Don't taunt her, Cyn. They were not her arrows. Valor Marigen bound her name and brought her here. That is a suitable punishment, is it not?"

The drens' eyes met, and Cyn shrugged. "You know I am not one to question Callum's judgement," he said. "But if she gives you any trouble …"

"She won't."

"Don't let Tyg catch you being soft on her, Renna. You know it would anger her," Cyn said and at last left the kitchen. They watched as he turned down an open corridor.

"You look murderous," Renna said.

She crossed her arms. "Wouldn't you if I told you I wanted to make pork stew out of *him*?"

"Depends on the day. Now, let's get back to work."

Renna sent her to sweep the main hall while he finished the bread. She was happy to be alone with her thoughts. It gave her a chance to study the layout of the lodge and the cadence of activity. The Yewolyns took little interest in her aside from a few curious glances. She imagined they shared Renna's uncertainty about why their Magus had brought a human to their lodge to begin with.

Being so close to the large, front doors agonized Ora. She swept slowly, shoving the broom beneath tables and into forgotten, dusty corners in the hopes that she might find a moment alone if she took long enough. But there always seemed to be someone new passing through, and she eventually had to return to the kitchen.

Though he did not send her out a second time, Renna kept her busy. She peeled dozens, maybe hundreds, of potatoes and scrubbed countless dishes. By the end of the day, she felt no closer to escape than she had when she awoke. Just as Tyg had requested, Renna returned her to the Marigens before the dinner bell. When they came to the door, she gave him a pleading look.

"Try to stay out of trouble till tomorrow, alright?" Renna whispered, then knocked.

The door opened, and Callum waved her inside. "We're almost finished. Sit over there." He pointed to a bench along the back wall.

A large wooden table took up most of the space. A map stretched across it, each corner held down by a brass weight. Tyg and another Yewolyn stood over the table, arguing vehemently between each other.

"It's a waste of resources, Marigen!" the other bellowed. His hand was curled around the golden hilt of a claymore. A deep rumble reverberated in his words, and along with his enormous stature, he reminded Ora of a bear. She carefully skirted behind him to sit down, and Tyg's narrowed eyes followed her. "They're probably half-starved and harmless."

At those words, the Magus's eyes latched onto the ursine Yewolyn. "Half-starved means they're desperate, and desperation is precisely what leads to trouble." She dug into her pocket and produced a marble-sized, metal ball that hung from a chain. The dull copper necklace was turning green with age. She dropped it onto the map. The bear dren's eyes widened, and he leaned forward to study it.

A charge blossomed in the air, and Ora felt the hairs on her arm stand on end. She felt certain the necklace held power. Despite wanting to appear disinterested, she could not help but sit forward.

"Where did you get that?" Callum asked.

But rather than answer, Tyg became alert and held up her hand. "Do you hear that?"

They all tilted their ears toward the device. A soft hiss came from the necklace. Then, a click. And eight, delicate metal legs sprung from the side of the copper ball.

With a roar, the bear-sized dren brought his fist down on it. The force of the blow shook the room. When he lifted his hand, the orb had broken free of the chain and was rolling toward Ora. As it dropped onto the floor with a soft thud, she bent down to get a closer look. The legs unfurled a second time, but Tyg was already looming over her.

"Move, Ora."

She shifted to the far end of the bench just as the Yewolyn Magus cast a spell. A glitter of lightning danced across the surface of the orb. The legs shivered, then became still. As Tyg stooped to pick up the metal ball, she shot Ora a puzzled look.

"A scout brought it back this morning," she said and returned to the table. "It is a sylvn device, and apparently, it's still in working order, which means—"

"Clear them out," Callum said, his expression grim. "Take three of your mages."

"I can spare a few swordsmen," said the bear dren.

"There's no need, Gallant Myrdah. It will be swift work for our mages."

The giant dren looked defeated, but he did not argue. It was only after he left that a triumphant smile spread across Tyg's face. "What did I tell you?" she said.

"You didn't tell me about the scout."

The Magus's smile turned into a sneer. "Someone has to keep an eye on the borders."

The dinner bell rang out. Callum hunched over the table, his palms pressed against the wood. As the bell faded, he began to slide the weights off the corners of the map. "Take the girl back. I must send word to Queen Innes. She will want to know of this. I won't be far behind you."

Tyg pocketed the copper necklace and said, "Let me deliver the news personally. She will want to see the sylvn artifact."

"Very well," he said as he rolled up the map. "But before you go, Magus, I must request that you do not send anymore scouts without direct orders."

"Understood, Valor Marigen."

EIGHT

THE sun had just set. Tirnan's streetlamps sparkled beneath the lodge like pale, blue stars. A full, golden moon loomed above the city, and crisp air swept down from the mountains. Once the doors closed behind them, Ora drew in a deep breath and asked the question that had burned in her mind since the copper ball sprang to life. "What *was* that thing?"

"You are not to ask questions," Tyg said as they descended the stone steps.

Ora hurried to catch up to the Yewolyn and fell into pace at her side. "Why did it come toward me?"

"You insolent girl, I should be asking you that."

"Me?"

Tyg ignored her. Once the lodge was no longer in sight, the dren turned down a staircase that led to one of the many riverways in Tirnan. Wedged between the crashing water and a long, retaining wall, the path they followed had no streetlamps or storefronts. Even the moonlight did not reach the deep shadow cast by the wall. As Ora peered along the dark pathway, the thought struck her. Tyg wanted to be hidden.

Still, the dren's sudden movement startled her. Before she could run, Tyg had her pinned against the wall with an arm across her throat. The tip of a blade pricked her side. She did not dare struggle.

"Who are you?" Tyg growled.

"I'm just a Nor from Fel."

"Did you wake it?"

"Wake what?"

A frantic pitch crept into Tyg's words. "I've known Gallant Myrdah my entire life. That idiot can hardly cast a spell. And Callum? He doesn't trouble himself with sylvn artifacts. It had to be you."

"Casting spells? Are you—" Ora almost accused the dren of madness but swallowed her words. She could not stop her voice from quivering. "Magus Marigen, humans cannot use magic."

Fuming, Tyg withdrew the knife and gave Ora a harsh shove against the stone before pulling back. "You're right. Humans can't."

Ora pushed herself away from the wall, remembering how the Yewolyn first woke her in the palace. "You think I'm something else. That's why you asked if I was born to human parents, isn't it?"

"We'll settle it now," Tyg said. "*Ayluma.* It's a simple spell for light. Even a child can manage it. Cast it. Now."

"You want *me* to cast a spell?"

"I want you to prove that you can't."

Shaking, Ora lifted her hand and squeezed her eyes shut. Before she could utter the spell, Tyg grabbed her wrist and turned her hand so that her palm faced up.

"Do it properly," the Yewolyn said.

"Ay—luma?" Ora mumbled. A breeze tugged at her smock, and cold spray from the river wet her cheeks. When nothing happened, she opened her eyes.

"Say it with intention," Tyg ordered.

"I can't."

"If you can't, there's nothing to fear."

Once more, she held up her hand. "Ayluma!" she shouted. Warmth spread through her palm, and she waited, terrified that the spell had worked. But the world around them remained dark. Relieved, she lowered her arm.

Neither of them moved. Ora's entire body felt taut, ready to spring if the Yewolyn came after her a second time. Even if escape meant jumping into the river. But when Tyg raised her hand, it was a simple gesture to motion for Ora to follow. Silent and tense, they returned to the cobbled streets and lamplight.

Once they reached the palace, they were greeted by Wynn. Ora's legs wobbled with relief at the sight of the familiar fae. However, Wynn paid her no mind. She nervously informed Tyg that the queen was busy entertaining guests. The Yewolyn regarded the thachwing with an icy gaze. "Then I will join them," she said. "I assume they are in the main dining hall?"

"Yes, Magus," Wynn said and stepped aside.

They made their way through several corridors before reaching the dining hall. A savory aroma spilled into the hallway. After a day of working alongside Renna, Ora's stomach growled at the idea of food.

The royal spread was even more impressive than the smell. Every inch of the table was covered with food—roasted pheasant, pork, steaming pies, flatbreads, thick gravies, nuts, cheeses, mushrooms, berries. Half a dozen fae, Queen Innes included, sat around the feast, but none of them were eating. All their heads were turned toward one dren, whose energetic and charming speech had spun them into trance.

"One does not easily escape the attention of an angry fire imp. They are persistent creatures, driven by a destructive desire. But, you see, that is precisely what you must use against them if you wish to retrieve their heart." The dren's eyes twinkled as he spoke, and he held up what looked to be a jagged, black stone. The surface glittered as he turned it to catch the lamplight. His audience gasped in awe. "I woke the little bastard with an ember. Oh, he roared to life! Set half the forest to flame trying to come after me. He didn't notice that I was—"

Tyg cleared her throat. The storyteller lowered the stone, and the dinner party turned their attention to the Yewolyn. "I apologize for the interruption," she said with a slight bow to the queen. "Wynn mentioned that I might be able to join you for dinner."

"Magus Marigen! Of course, of course. Have a seat," Queen Innes said, still giggling from the tale. "Oh, and you brought the girl! She's been on my mind today. Please, let her eat with us."

Mortified by the queen's request, Ora glanced up at Tyg. She did not want to linger anywhere near Innes, the only fae who knew her true name. The idea that her secret could slip out and fall into Tyg's hands made her stomach churn. But the Yewolyn only gave the slightest of nods, and they sat down beside each other at the table.

"You are Ullkyrin elves," Tyg said, having a look around the table. "Well, most of you."

For the first time, Ora noticed the guests did not dress in the bright silks the fae of Tirnan favored. The women wore white cotton dresses, cinched high on the waist with belts made of hammered gold plates. The men donned tunics of the same material. The sides of their heads were shaven, and their long flaxen hair was braided back from their broad, sun-kissed faces. The dark-haired dren storyteller stood out among them, though he wore the same style of clothing.

"My friends, this is Magus Marigen. She is our most talented war mage and one of our finest Yewolyns," Innes said. Then, she began to gesture to each of her guests. "Magus, we are honored to have guests from Ullkyrin for a holiday in our mountains. This is Lord Cyprian of Ullkyrin and his wife Tola. They have brought along his cousin, Jarek, and his wife, Palegia. The dren is their dear friend—I apologize, what was your name?"

"Maol, Your Highness. Maol Becanan." The dren winked at Tyg as he introduced himself. "It's a pleasure to meet you, Magus Marigen. Now, I must ask, who is this girl of yours that has been on Queen Innes's mind?"

"Ora," said Tyg.

With all eyes on her, Ora shrank back against her chair, but Maol was persistent. "And what is so interesting about her?"

It was Innes who answered. "We do not often bring humans into Mysanhal, but Valor Marigen caught her name. She is Norrish. Quite pretty, don't you think?"

"Ah, I see," said Maol. "You've only just arrived in the fae realm, haven't you?"

"I didn't arrive. I was stolen from my home," said Ora.

The Magus glared down at her as if she had spat on the table. "I apologize for her ill manners. She is … *spirited*."

Nervous laughter trickled from the elves' lips, and Innes shifted the topic of conversation. They began to discuss the beautiful gardens and bathhouses of Tirnan. Though stunning, Tirnan was vastly different from Ullkyrin's capital. The company spoke at length about the beauty of their royal city, which sat on a rocky coast far to the south. The mention of ocean air made Ora long for home all the more, and she hardly touched her food after that.

Once Queen Innes's guests had their fill, she rose and invited Tyg into a parlor so they could speak in private. "Stay here, Ora," the Yewolyn said, her words sounding more like a warning than a command.

With the queen absent, the Ullkyrin visitors dispersed to wander the palace gardens. Only Maol remained at the table, still sipping wine. He eyed Ora and tilted the glass toward her. "Tell me about Nor."

"I don't want to talk about my home."

"Then tell me about you."

"I don't want to talk about myself either."

"You are a horrible dinner guest, you know that?"

Ora crossed her arms. "I am *not* a guest."

He tapped at the table, seemingly lost in thought. "Does she have another half?"

"Another half?"

"Yes, is she . . ." He waved his hand about as if trying to conjure the right word. "*Coupled* with another?"

"You're asking about *Magus* Marigen?"

"She's a powerful dren, Ora. You can't blame me for wondering. So, tell me, is she taken?"

"Yes, she's the Valor's wife."

"Fascinating. I would not think it proper to let a Magus marry a Valor." He poured himself more wine, and Ora began to laugh. "What do you find so funny?"

"I haven't known Magus Marigen long, but I'm certain that she will not fancy *you*."

"Ah, but you haven't known me long either." He reached across the table and took up Ora's glass. "Wine?"

"Me?"

"Of course." He filled the cup to the brim and held it back out.

Her laughter faded, but she accepted the wine all the same. Cautious, she smelled the burgundy liquid. The scent of alcohol made her head spin. "I've never had wine," she said.

"Ullkyrin wine is the finest you could wish for. Try it!"

The dren's insistence made her feel even more uncertain. She set the glass on the table. "What was that stone you were talking about when we arrived?" she asked, hoping to distract him from the full glass before her.

"You mean the imp heart?" He dug it out of his pocket. "Go on. Take it."

As he dropped the stone into her hand, she cried out in surprise and let it fall onto the table. "It's hot," she said, picking it up more carefully. "What's it for?"

"Imp hearts have unique properties, but they aren't easy to come by. I'm sure it will fetch a fair price if I find the right fae to take it off my hands," he said.

"So, you want to sell it?"

"I am a merchant by trade, my dear."

"Then why are you travelling with the elves?" she asked, placing the heart back on the table before him.

"You ask a lot of questions."

"Why shouldn't I?"

"I suppose you are in a strange, new place, aren't you?" Maol stood and walked around the table to sit beside her, the wine glass still perched in his hand. He leaned in close to her, his face looming before her own. "Look carefully, *Ora*, and do not speak of what you see to anyone."

Disgusted by the scent of wine on his breath, she leaned away from him, but as she studied his face, she saw a glimmer across his skin. Her uncle had told her many times that the fae could conceal their identity with glamour magic. The longer she gazed at him, the more the effect of the magic began to fade until she no longer saw a dren. Instead, to her horror, a strange being sat before her. His skin was weathered and old. His eyes were the color of red embers. And sprouting from his head were two goat-like horns.

"What are you?" she whispered.

"Not a fae. A faun. Well, *the* faun as far as I know. I am one of the delightful bastard sons of Cree," he said, voice bright with verve. As he leaned back in the chair, the glamour settled into place, and he became a handsome dren once again.

She frowned. "You truly expect me to believe that you're the son of a fae god?"

"I do, but let's keep that between us, Ora. I have far more fun when I blend in," he said. "Anyway, you are not what you seem either, are you?"

Tired of insisting on her humanity, she instead asked, "What makes you say that?"

"Because you exude a certain energy, dear girl. It's such a shame that you are name bound. What's that like?"

Before Ora could answer, she saw a streak of black fur out of the corner of her eye. The cat she spotted in the courtyard the day before had jumped onto the table. Its bright green eyes swept over her, then it bit into a leftover pheasant wing.

"Ora!" Tyg burst back into the dining hall. The cat leapt down from the table, taking the wing with it. "Come. It's time to go."

"Ah, the lovely Magus Marigen." Maol rose to his feet and gave an extravagant bow. "It was a pleasure to meet you. May we cross paths again."

This time, Tyg did not tolerate his flirting. "I am the Yewolyn Magus, not a harlot. Remember your place before I find a reason to gut you."

NINE

THE Marigen house had fallen silent at last. Ora stood before the door in the spare room. Fear amplified every small sound. The phantom popping and cracking of the house. Faint voices somewhere outside. Her own breath. It all made her heart go wild. She reached out to turn the knob. It clicked. She waited. When nothing stirred, she swung the door open.

The dark hallway felt endless. Each step stirred a new doubt, a new reason to turn back. If Tyg found her, would she be angry? Would she believe one of the handful of lies Ora had prepared? That she was thirsty. That she needed to pee. That she heard something in the parlor. Still, the Yewolyn's threats stalked her like a hungry beast, always at the edge of her awareness. She reached the parlor and lingered next to the banister. Embers still pulsed in the fireplace, and the full moon shone bright through the window.

She had intended to find a knife, a tool, a weapon. Whatever it took. Perhaps she could wedge open the window in the spare room without the enchantment searing her hands. If that didn't work, there was Renna. Even though she liked him well enough, she imagined the amiable dren would be easy to threaten with nothing more than a dinner knife or shard of glass.

But, before she could reach the kitchen, the bookcase made her take pause. The letters were still in fae, foreign to the Norrish alphabet, but the words along the spines leapt out at her. She could read them. Stunned, she lifted the pendant up and studied the crystal. It had to be the Elder's enchantment.

She ignored the prickling at the back of her neck and stood before the countless volumes of fae history, military tactics, and poetry. She skimmed past them all. Tyg was a respected mage. She had to have books on magic.

Finally, her eyes fell on a row of promising titles. Her lips silently formed each word: *The Fundamentals of Conjuring Flame, Burraus Fygin's Contemplations on Arcane Battle, The Mage's Companion to Subjective Reality, An Expanded Appendix to Torsyn's Encyclopedia of Spells, The Transformative Arts and … Reversals.*

She slid it from the shelf. A rush of energy shot up her arm, and she remembered the book she had hidden beneath the mattress. Careful not to make a sound, she snuck back to the spare room and opened the curtain to let the moonlight in. Then, she lifted the mattress to retrieve the other book.

"*An Introduction to Spellcasting,*" Ora whispered as she tilted the cover toward the light.

She set aside *The Transformative Arts* and sat beneath the window to open the spellcasting book. The crisp, old paper cracked as if it had gone untouched for countless years. She thumbed through the pages, looking for anything related to enchanted doors or travel between worlds. When nothing jumped out at her, she returned to the beginning.

Spellcraft is an ancient art that requires many years to master. A new mage must learn certain fundamentals before attempting even the most basic of spells, lest they should suffer the grave consequences of a failed casting. One must also be patient when beginning their studies. Some spells and schools of magic take years to master.

Ora lowered the book into her lap. How could she escape and help Hademar if it took years to master magic? Fighting back a wave of hopelessness, she gently closed the book and picked up *The Transformative Arts and Reversals*. The introduction contained a similar warning, as well as a terrifyingly detailed story of a transformation gone wrong. The last line filled her with dismay.

The poor mage became a half-beast and was exiled to the mountains, where he is said to stalk the old forests in eternal suffering.

The first chapter contained strange illustrations of transformations with detailed anatomical descriptions. Despite her best efforts, she could not pronounce or understand many of the words, even with the help of the enchanted amulet. It was dizzying to think that Tyg had mastered the art well enough to change Hademar. She wondered how easily her brother could have been made into a creature much worse than a brush pig.

Frustrated and even more frightened of Tyg, she snapped the book shut. Even if she could learn the simplest of spells, it still might not be enough to help her escape. She had no idea how to get back to Nor. *If* she did, and *if* she could find Hademar in the Hy Borea, she doubted that she stood a chance of changing him back. Would she have to care for her brother as a brush pig for all his years? What would she tell their mother?

Determined to press on, she returned to *An Introduction to Spellcasting*. Soon, she realized the book contained no spells at all. It went on at length about breathing correctly and the importance of pronunciation and intent. She found herself rereading the same lines again and again.

As Ora's eyelids grew heavy, she became more fascinated by the sensation of energy that spread through the pages to her fingertips than the contents of the book itself. It felt the same as the crystal pendant or the warmth that blossomed in her palm when she tried to cast light.

Had it been her imagination? Magic had no place in the human realm beyond myth and stories. The idea that she, a Nor, could summon anything with a single word frightened her, especially after reading such grave cautionary tales. If the warmth meant something, if she could use magic, then why had the spell failed? If it was a failed spell, why had no harm come to her?

With a hundred new questions and the book still open in her lap, Ora at last fell asleep, and her dream formed as it always did.

First, a sky glittering with thousands of stars, then a land of hard earth and hidden spaces. Ora sat on the edge of a cliff, looking out over the quiet nightscape. She let herself forget that she was sleeping, content to pretend she had always been part of the dark land.

She could have sat there for hours, but in the distance, a faint, reddish glow ignited. Entranced, she lowered herself over the edge of the cliff and climbed down the rocky face. When she reached the bottom, she began to walk.

And walk.

And walk.

Time and distance did not seem to matter. She might have wandered for days or mere minutes. The flame remained a constant beacon, guiding her across the hard desert like a sailor's polestar. Something waited for her there, and she longed to reach it.

Not until she drew close enough to see the source did she understand. The light before her was not a camp or a pyre but a living thing, a falcon made of flames rather than feathers. This was the symbol of Farig, the wise hunter and god of Nors. It perched atop a rock, watching her with a tilted head as she approached.

"Farig, why you have come to me in a dream?" she asked.

The falcon stretched its wings, a brilliant display of flickering light. It pushed itself off of the stone. Its burning form rose into the air, but then, it snagged. A chain extended from one leg to an anchor in the rock. It was trapped.

Uncertain of its meaning, she watched the bird fight against the chain. Perhaps she had been wrong to assume it was Farig. A god would not be tethered to a rock.

The falcon let out a loud cry. The sound hung in the air, desperate and forlorn. She knew then that she must free it.

Ora pulled herself onto the top of the rock and reached out toward the falcon. Furious, it beat its wings harder. Determined to help, she took hold of the chain and gently pulled the falcon toward her. She expected to feel the heat of flames but instead the cool rush of wind stirred by its flight washed over her.

She lifted a shaking hand to catch hold of one leg. It twisted against her, and its talons dug into her skin. She cried out in pain but did not let go. The unexpected strength of the bird made her blood surge. In the struggle, Ora lost her footing and tumbled from the rock. She maintained her grip on the falcon, dragging it to the earth with her. Quick to gain control, she pushed its sharp beak back with her arm and began to work at the chain link attached to its leg. She dug her nails into the metal joint, grinding her teeth as she tried to pull it apart.

"Come on," she growled when it did not budge. The falcon fought against her, its talons scratching at her hand and its beak tearing at her sleeve. Frustrated and angry, she at last shouted, "Just open!"

At her words, the chain gave and crumbled apart in her hands. Before she could make sense of what had happened, a great force knocked her back. The falcon shot up into the night. Panting and covered in blood, she stood and watched as its form streaked against the night sky. At first, her heart soared with it, but then it dove toward her, a blur of light as quick as a shooting star.

She shielded her face with her arms. As the falcon struck, she fell. The certainty of earth rose up to meet her. The flames and the talons pierced her chest. She gasped, and her eyes flew open.

Bright light clouded Ora's vision. Had she woken? Was it morning? She sat up straighter, having forgotten where she fell asleep. The book slid off her lap, making a soft thud against the wood floor. But the sound was not what made her breath catch.

Above her floated a glowing, white orb. Pulse drumming in her ears, she reached up to touch it. Just as her fingers were about to brush the orb, the floorboards creaked.

One of the Marigens was awake.

In a panic, she kicked the books under the bed. Then, she tried to grab hold of the orb. It drifted just out of reach and bumped against the ceiling. The stairs awoke, snapping and cracking beneath heavy steps.

"Come on," she muttered and climbed on top of the bed. Each time she stretched her hand out toward the orb, it floated away as if her touch repelled it. Frantic, she whispered to the light, "How do I get rid of you?"

The footsteps had reached the hallway. Ora picked up the pillow and flung it at the orb. The light snuffed out. There came a soft knock. She turned, cold fear spreading through her veins.

"Ora, let's go," said Callum.

Confused, she glanced out the window. The sky had turned a deep shade of blue, the first light of dawn. "I'm coming," she said and leapt down from the bed. Before she left, she tucked the books back beneath the mattress.

TEN

RENNA smiled when he saw Ora standing in the kitchen's open doorway. He sat on a barrel with a half-eaten pear in one hand. "You look like you slept poorly," he said and snatched another pear from the wood bowl beside him. "Breakfast?"

Stomach growling, she gave a quick nod, and he tossed the pale-yellow fruit over. The first bite was so sweet and juicy that she could not help but close her eyes a moment to savor the taste. She grew up eating burberries, fog apples, thimble grapes, and countless wild mushrooms. None could compare to the spectacular, sugary fruit of the fae realm. Without pause for breath, she devoured the rest of the pear in a few giant bites.

As she swallowed the last bite, Renna said, "Magus Marigen left this morning. You can breathe for a few days."

Still dazed from a night of books and unexpected magic, she shook her head. "Days?"

"Yes. She took three mages earlier this morning. They're clearing out some rebels."

Ora pulled her sleeve up over her hand and wiped pear juice from her lips. "There's still Callum," she said. "I don't think I'll breathe, as you say, until I'm back in Nor."

"Ah, still set on that, aren't you?" He jumped up from the barrel and grabbed a large basket. "Come on, Ora. We're going to gather plums."

Though she chose a smaller basket, Renna did not complain. They set off across the courtyard and followed a walkway between plain, gray-stoned barracks. A few Yewolyns hurried past, late for training and looking panicked. Beyond the living quarters, the grounds stretched for several green acres to the wall surrounding the complex.

As Renna led her across a footbridge over a shallow stream, Ora caught sight of a round slab of stone with glyph-like carvings swirling toward its center. It looked similar to the circle she spied in the palace grounds.

As they began to skirt around the edge, Ora felt a strange, old power rising from the stone. It resonated through her body. Her heart fluttered. "Renna—" she began.

"*That* is a crossing," he said without slowing his pace. "You have to know the words of passage to use it, but even that's not enough. To cross the Ether, you must be a practiced mage. It takes focus to direct that much energy. A simple turn of the mind, and you could end up in an unknown land. Do you understand?"

They pressed on, giving Ora little time to study the circle. "I understand," she said. Her grip on the basket tightened. "You mean I can't go alone. I will need help."

He glanced back at her. "That's exactly what I mean."

They had come to a small grove of plum trees. Ripe fruits had fallen from the branches and were scattered across the ground. Wasps drifted between decaying pieces, dipping down to nibble at the sweet rot. Renna picked up one of the foggy, violet plums and bit into it. "They're perfect this time of year. Help yourself. Just make sure you fill the basket before we go back."

Ora balanced the basket against her hip. "Do you know how to use the crossings?" she asked.

Renna spoke between bites. "No. I do not. Yewolyn mages study words of passage, and they won't help you. That mostly leaves merchants and treasure hunters. But they're unreliable and often poorly studied. Plenty have been ripped to shreds in the Ether. What *you* want is a wayfarer. The thing is, they're pricey."

"How pricey?"

"Well, do you have anything that you cherish?"

Ora's hand went to her waist. The yellow handkerchief was the only piece of home that she had, the only thing she owned in the fae realm. "I think so," she said.

"Whatever it is, you'll have to hope that it makes do. But, Ora, there's another problem to solve. How do you plan to reverse the transformation spell cast upon your brother? What use is it returning to your home if you cannot change him back?"

She hesitated to answer. Without a mage to aid her, Hademar would likely be a pig forever. Even if she had woken up to a mysterious orb of light, it did not mean she was capable of casting more complicated spells. It had to be a fluke, a side effect of spending time in the fae realm. She squeezed her eyes shut and drew in a deep breath. "I can at least look after him. Ensure he isn't hunted down for someone's dinner."

Renna's expression became grim, and he nodded. "Very well. There's a small crossing in the market district. You might chance upon a willing wayfarer there."

"Thank you," Ora said, her voice soft.

He ignored her and bent to start gathering the plums. "Come on. Get to work, Ora. I didn't bring you out here just to chat."

Suspecting that to be a lie, she smothered a smile and began to fill her basket. They worked in silence alongside each other. Ora wanted to hate Renna because he was a dren and a Yewolyn's brother, but he was also kind. She looked up once to study him. He was bent over, eating another plum, and had started humming to himself.

"What's that song?" she asked.

"Would you like to learn it?"

"No," she said, as swift and pointed as an arrow.

"Then teach me a Norrish song."

"You'll have to find another Nor, one more willing to sing for you," she said.

Most of the songs she knew were the ones Lupin loved. He would drink and then dance through Mathilde's inn, bellowing ballads and tales until Mathilde herself stormed out to quiet him. Thinking of this, Ora smirked. "I do know one about how awful the fae are. How they steal babies and leave hideous changelings behind. Maybe you'd like that one?"

"Oh sure, we have the same sort of songs about humans. How they steal our magic, leaving their victims hollow and forlorn." He sat on a stump to wait for her to finish filling her basket. "You know, changelings aren't real."

"No?"

"Of course not. That's just a story."

"Well, our silver blades *are* real. I had one too." She straightened, her fists against her hips. "And if I had it now, I would drive it through any fae standing between me and—"

"Ora! It's terrible thing to do. Silver is poison to us."

"So is name binding."

At a stalemate, they both stared hard at each other. Then, Renna muttered, "You're right."

The fight drained from Ora's blood. Her shoulders fell. "I'm sorry, Renna," she said.

"You have nothing to be sorry for. But you should know, not all of us fae share the same opinion on name binding." He lifted up his basket of plums and tilted his head toward the main lodge. "Let's head back."

Renna was quick to forget their short-lived quarrel. He showed her how to prepare the plums for wine and distracted her with comedic stories of failed romances, drunken nights with friends, and his childhood with Cyn. To her relief, he did not pry her for stories of Fel. She did not think she could bring herself to speak of home or family.

When Renna and Ora parted for the day, she once again wished she could stay with the affable kitchen master. He had managed to soften her anger, but as she stepped into the Valor's quarters, it all flooded back.

Callum did not bother looking up from a letter in his hands as she shut the door. She stood in front of him and waited. When he at last finished, he folded the letter in half and tossed it aside.

"Now, what to do with you?" he said, studying her from the other side of the table.

"I have a few ideas."

"Is that so?"

"Returning me to the Hy Borea would be a start."

"Had it been up to my wife, you would have shared your brother's fate. Instead, I brought you here and bound your name to Mysanhal. You should consider yourself fortunate," Callum said and rose to his feet.

"So I've been told."

Amusement tugged at the fine lines that creased his face. He did not possess the same permanent malice as his wife, and in his golden eyes, Ora saw nothing but mirth. "I must admit, I enjoy your boldness," he said.

"You enjoy it because you do not see me as a threat."

"Of course not. You're thin as a willow branch and bound to do as I say." He motioned to the door. "Shall we? Or must I bother with your name?"

Walking alongside Callum was different than being with Tyg. He would linger at street stalls to talk to merchants, kiss the hands of beautiful dren women, and receive gracious offers to dine with well-dressed lords and their wives. Ora despised the way the people of Tirnan revered him. She stood behind him, glowering, as he chatted with old friends and acquaintances. Soon, she realized they had been drifting through unfamiliar plazas and streets. They were not returning to the Marigen house right away.

Eventually they came to a yellow door. Hanging above it was a sign that read: NO MAGIC & NO SPRITES. It led to a narrow staircase that descended into a crowded tavern. To Ora's great disappointment, she saw Renna's brother lift his chin at Callum from the far side of the room.

They did not have to push their way through the crowd. In the presence of the Valor, the fae parted and bowed their heads in a respectful greeting. When they reached the table, he clapped Ora on the back. "Sorry, had to bring her along. Running late."

Ora sat beside the Valor, resentful and silent. Cyn eyed her. "Should I order her one as well? She looks ready to murder someone."

Callum laughed. "Why not?"

"Kyrjac!" Cyn shouted over his shoulder. The elven barkeep lifted his head up from a conversation. "Two more here!"

"I don't want one." Ora crossed her arms. "I'm not here for the fun of it."

"Does she talk like this around Tyg?" Cyn asked.

"Clearly not," said the Valor, leaning back in his chair.

"I imagine you find it amusing."

"I do, as a matter of fact. She'd make a fine Yewolyn were she a dren. She even tried to stab me that first night."

Cyn's brow rose in surprise. "This little thing?"

Glad to have taken him off guard, Ora gave a self-satisfied smirk. "I did, but the blade was dull. You'd think a couple of Yewolyns would keep their knives sharpened."

Both looked down at her, and she could not tell if they were impressed or taken aback by her words. Before either could speak, Kyrjac slammed two more frothing mugs of ale on the table before them. "Who brought the human?" the barkeep asked.

"I did," said Callum. "Is there a problem?"

Kyrjac glanced at Fyn in the corner. The old elf gave a nod. "Suppose not," said the barkeep before ambling away.

"I admit, I am more inclined to agree with Tyg. Why not turn her into a pig as well?" asked Cyn.

"It's not often we have good reason to bind a human's name, and her brother shouted hers loud enough for all of us to hear, didn't he?"

The turn of conversation made Ora dig her nails into her palms beneath the table. If only she had silver.

"Seems a waste. You can clean a little piglet up all you like, but it won't change her nature," Cyn replied before tipping his mug back.

Ora's mind churned with dark thoughts. Perhaps she had been wrong to focus her hatred on Callum. Compared to Tyg and Cyn, he was far more discerning. She glared at Cyn and wondered how he could possibly share the same blood as Renna. Part of her wanted to fling the ale in his face. A buzzing ignited in her veins, spreading along her arms to the tips of her fingers. Her eyes flickered to the mug, but she drew in a deep breath instead, trying to hold back her sour words. As she exhaled, she relaxed her curled fists.

The air shifted. She felt it like a cool gust of wind or icy water sliding across her skin. Then, the chair Cyn sat in flew back. The Yewolyn dropped to the floor, mug still in hand. Ale spilled all over his shirt, and worse, his elk cloak. Beneath the table, Ora's hands shook. She felt a prickle of energy still dancing across her fingertips.

For a moment, she felt faint, and the world appeared clouded, the lamplight dimmed. It had to be in her head. How could she cast a spell without meaning to? No. It couldn't have been her. Someone must have played a prank on the Yewolyn.

Cyn jumped to his feet, his eyes wild. "Was it you?" he shouted and pointed at a rough-looking thachwing who was missing one of his wings as well as the tip of an ear.

The fae man turned and growled, "What if it was, Yewolyn?"

Before either could make a move, Fyn roared from the corner, "No magic in my alehouse!"

The old elf's words did little good, but Ora's eyes were not on Cyn as he drew his fist back. A few tables away, a dren man had settled his gaze on her. He was not a Yewolyn. He wore plain, dark clothes and had long, uncut hair and an unshaven beard. The look in his eyes confirmed what she feared. She had used magic. Right beside the Yewolyn Valor. Right in front of everyone. Why had no one else noticed?

As she rested her hands on her knees, she heard the sickening crack of Cyn's fist connecting with the thachwing's jaw. All at once, chairs and tables shifted. An explosion of shouting, swinging fists, and wrestling bodies ensued. Beside her, Callum drank his ale. No one dared to pick a fight with him.

Ora searched the mess of bodies for the dren man. He had vanished. The panic must have shown on her face because Callum leaned close and said, "Don't worry. It'll settle down as soon as Fyn has—"

"Enough!" The old elf climbed on top of his table and stood with his hands outstretched. "I'll set the lot of you on fire if I have to!"

Every fae in the tavern grew still. Some stared down at their feet as if they were children caught performing a small act of disobedience. Others shuffled back to their tables, picked up their chairs, and grumbled under their breaths. Cyn wiped his bloodied lip on his sleeve as Fyn's squinty eyes fell on him.

"I don't much care if you're a Yewolyn. One more antic like that and you'll never be welcome back here." With that, old Fyn hopped down from the table in a surprisingly nimble movement.

Still searching for the dren, Ora did not notice when Callum stood up. He touched her shoulder, and she flinched. "Come, Ora. I think it's time we leave."

Indeed, Cyn's angry outburst had caused many glares to slide their way. The Valor left a stack of coins on the table and nodded at Cyn. As they passed through the tavern, all remained tense and watching. A few chairs had been broken. Glass crunched beneath their boots. At the door, Callum turned and said, "Apologies, Fyn. I will repay you for any damages tomorrow."

The old elf gave an approving nod.

Cyn trudged up the stairs ahead of them. When they stepped into the street outside, Callum suddenly lurched toward the young Yewolyn and pinned him against the wall.

"Thirty lashes tomorrow, and *you* will be the one paying for whatever you broke. Understood?"

"Yes, Valor Marigen," Cyn said, his expression stony.

"Do not act so foolishly again. When you wear an elk cloak, your reputation is not your own." Callum pulled him back from the wall and gave him a push down the street. "Go. Before I make it twice as many lashes."

Ora could not help but feel pleased as Cyn ambled away, his head bent. Served him right. A smile crept into place, and she had to turn her head to be sure the Valor did not notice. It was then that she saw the long-haired dren farther down the street. He was leaning against a wall with a pipe in hand, the red ember glowing as he inhaled. Though he stood in shadow, she knew his eyes were fastened on her.

As she followed Callum along the narrow passage, she could not help but glance over her shoulder several times. The dren still stood in the same spot, and aside from lowering his pipe, he did not move. She kept expecting him to call out to Callum, to tell him what he had witnessed. And then what? Would they imprison her? Kill her? These fears followed her as they turned the corner and made their way back to the Marigens' townhouse.

Despite the mysterious dren, Ora took consolation in the fact that she could use magic. It meant she stood a chance of helping Hademar. Still, it was a grim hope. She could not risk casting a spell in front of another fae, especially Tyg. But how could she be sure it would not happen again? She had no idea how to control the power that flowed through her veins.

She had to leave Tirnan as soon as possible, and it had to be before Tyg returned. Callum thought she was name bound. He did not watch her as closely. All she needed was a chance to sneak away, and she would find a wayfarer and cross the Ether.

That night, Ora sat beneath the window with *The Transformative Arts and Reversals* propped against her knees. She turned page after page, skimming each for anything pig-like. At last, she came to a section titled *On Porcine Character and Anatomy*, beneath which was a diagram of a boar with huge tusks and large, fuzzy ears. It was nothing like the brush pigs of the Hy Borea, but surely it was similar.

There was a note scrawled in the margin. She turned the book so she could read the pointed, narrow letters. *Try Casyan's visualization method to enhance effect. Proven by Auldymere.* It might as well have been gibberish. She rubbed at her eyes, wishing the answer could be simple.

She turned a few more pages, trying to discern where the writing on pigs ended. Then, she tore out the entire section, folded the pages in half, and tucked them beneath her smock with the handkerchief. At least she could take the chapter with her.

Home haunted Ora through the night. The longing in her heart felt like a rope pulled by a distant hand. She wished she could wrap her arms around her brother, kiss her mother's cheek, curl up before Lupin's fire. She craved the scent of sea wind and the damp, dark Hy Borea. She wanted to tilt her head back, breathe in the air of storms. Run her hand along a mossy rock. Search tide pools for treasures. Climb into the thick branches of an ancient pine.

With these thoughts, her determination to escape grew. She held her palm open in the moonlight and thought of how she wrestled with the burning falcon. If the cliff elk had been a warning, then surely Farig's messenger bode well.

ELEVEN

THE house had been built into the crest of a hill covered in rolling, green grass. Sheep grazed in the surrounding fields, and a lone shepherd walked among them with a wooly dog at his side. In the distance stood the ethereal peaks of the Sylamor Mountains, but the peaceful scene was lost on Tyg as she approached the quaint home. She lowered the hood of her elk cloak and knocked on the door. Behind her stood three Yewolyn mages, still in their elk forms.

On the second knock, the door burst open. An elderly thachwing stared up at her, his eyes watery and sunken. "It's about time," he said, voice gruff. He opened the door wider. "Have a look. They took everything they could carry."

The house was barren. A few dried bundles of herbs hung from the ceiling, a broom leaned in one corner, and a wood table and five chairs were tucked beneath the window. A thachwing woman and her young son, maybe six or seven years old, sat on a rug before the fire. In truth, Tyg could not tell if they had been raided or if it was the simple homestead of a herding family.

"No injuries?" she asked.

"My husband," said the thachwing woman without turning to them. Her voice had a ghostly, distant quality, and her next words sounded strained. "Shot through with silver."

"I'm sorry we could not be here sooner." The Yewolyn Magus stepped to the side. "Can we speak more privately?"

The old man shuffled outside, his body heavy and slow. Then, he closed the door behind him. "We are glad you came."

"We wasted no time. I understand you caught one," Tyg said. "Where is she?"

"The barn, of course. Don't want her anywhere near us." He pointed out across the field to a small, weathered barn that leaned from years of neglect. "Over there. Just a simple trapping enchantment."

"Simple but effective. Well done." She presented a small purse of coins. "Consider this a token of gratitude. I am sorry it cannot be more. You have served Mysanhal well."

"Thank you," he said, his gnarled fingers curling around the pouch.

Tyg nodded to her Yewolyns, and they walked through the soft waves of grass toward the barn. When she had presented the sylvn device to Callum and Gallant Myrdah, she lied about the scout's report. They would not have agreed to go after one sylv. It had to seem like a greater threat. But they did not understand. The one could lead to many. For months, she had been paying for leads in secret. Most rumors turned out to be dead ends, but now, she finally had a promising one.

When they reached the doors, Tyg broke the enchantment with a spell, and they filed inside. Sunlight dappled the muddy ground and straw below. The wind made the beams creak and moan.

She signaled for her Yewolyns to begin searching. As they lowered their cloaks, she called out, "You are under arrest by order of High Queen Innes. Come peacefully and no harm will come to you."

A voice rang out from behind her. "Magus Tyg Marigen, I've heard so much about you."

Tyg turned, already lifting her hands to cast a spell. But as her eyes fell on the sylv, she froze. This was no starving outlier. Silhouetted in the opening of the barn stood a sylvn girl with one hand held delicately before her as if prepared to thread a needle. The sun shone bright behind her and lit up her fine, white-gold hair. Tyg could not quite make out her face, but she could make out the three dart-like pieces of silver that floated just inches from the sylv's hand.

"Lower your hands, or I will let them loose," said the sylv. "All of you."

Without looking, Tyg sensed her mages' uncertainty. Still, she let her hands fall to her sides and nodded for them to follow. "There are four of us," she said. "*If* you manage to kill three of us, what then?"

"Then we're evenly matched."

"You were trapped in a barn by herding thachwings, and you think we're evenly matched?" Tyg took a step toward her. "There is no scenario where this ends well for you."

"I'll take my chances." The girl flicked her hand. The metal darts shot toward them.

Tyg shouted a deflection spell. The darts dropped to the earth before they could pierce any of the Yewolyns, but the sylvn girl had vanished.

"Magus Marigen, look!" The nearest mage pointed to the fallen darts. Each had unfurled four narrow wings, which appeared to be made of glistening, metal threads. They buzzed into the air and flitted toward the entry.

"Follow them," Tyg said.

The devices zipped around the barn. The Yewolyns chased after them and spotted the girl running toward the woods in the distance. They lifted their hoods. As cliff elk, they were swifter. They sped past the winged darts just as the girl reached the tree line.

They had only sprinted a few yards into the woods when they found the girl standing atop a stone outcrop. She held her hand out before her, claw-like and shaking. Tyg lowered her hood, a spell already on her tongue. The force of the casting knocked the sylv from the rocks, but Tyg heard three more dull thuds. She turned to find her mages rigid on the ground, the silver darts protruding from the backs of their necks.

Fury gripping her heart, Tyg stormed to the other side of the outcrop. The girl was pulling herself through the damp leaves. Blood spilled from her crooked calf where bone had broken through the skin. With a sneer, Tyg stepped toward her and pressed her boot into the hideous wound. The sylv howled in pain, her scream splintering the otherwise still air.

"Stop!" she cried. "I beg of you! Stop!"

"You have killed three Yewolyn mages." Tyg's voice shook with rage, and she dug her boot in harder. "You deserve every bit of pain that you are about to experience."

When the girl's cries faded to strained sobs, Tyg dragged her to a nearby tree. She tied the sylv's wrists and flung the rope over a branch. Then, she pulled the girl to her feet, causing her to shriek in pain once again.

"Where did you get the silver?" Tyg asked as she tied the other end of the rope around the trunk.

The sylv let her head fall back and stared at her wrists. She mumbled something. Her fingers twitched.

"Answer clearly or I will—"

But before Tyg could finish her sentence, a silver dart hissed past her ear. It lodged into a nearby tree. The damn sylv was casting a spell. Furious, she drove her fist into the girl's stomach, and her jaw gaped open in a desperate gasp for air. The Yewolyn Magus waited until the girl could breathe again.

"That's it, catch your breath," she crooned. "I still need answers."

The girl spoke, her voice gravelly. "There are more."

"What? More darts?" Tyg scoffed. "Go ahead, you sylvn swine. Let's see if your aim is any better."

"No. There are more sylv."

"Yes, and you will tell me where they are."

"Don't worry, Magus Marigen. They will find you."

In a swift movement, Tyg drew her knife and pressed it against the sylvn girl's stomach. "Or you could save us all time and tell me where they're hiding."

A breathless, shaky laugh trickled out from between the girl's lips. "To think, all of this over a child's toy."

"A toy?"

"That little necklace."

Only then did the realization sink in. The girl had baited her. It had been staged. The captured sylv, the barn, the chase. It all started with the little copper ball brought back by her scout.

"You wanted me to come here," Tyg said. "Why?"

"To kill you, of course."

Furious that she had been drawn into a trap, Tyg slid the blade into the girl's gut. "It seems you have failed," she said as she withdrew the knife. The girl gasped and looked down at the blood flooding from the wound.

Tyg turned away from the dying sylv. The thachwing traitors would pay for helping the sylvn girl. She raised the hood of her cloak and flew back across the rolling green fields. Once she reached the herders' door, she flung it open.

As soon as she stepped inside, something felt off. The house was quiet and cool. The fire had been snuffed out. Dust swam in the sunlight. As for the thachwing family, the woman and child were slumped by the hearth. The old man had collapsed on the floor.

Tyg stepped toward the thachwing man and nudged him with her boot. It made a soft rustle. The body collapsed, turning to clods of clay. The clothes hung over it, lumpy and damp. Only then did she realize what it was. *A golem.*

It had been at least a dozen years since she encountered one, longer since she came across one so convincing. The girl could not have created these. She was too young to have mastered sylvn alchemy. And who would have taught her? All the old sylvn masters had been hunted down and killed under Odharan.

But who else could it have been? The magic had faded with the sylvn girl's life, leaving behind three lifeless bodies of clay.

Skin crawling, Tyg stepped around what was left of the golem and opened the only door in the house. It led to a small bedroom, but it was empty and smelled of stale earth. The house had probably been abandoned for years.

She drew her knife and returned to the pile of clay and clothes. There, she crouched down and cut through the fabric. With great care, she parted the earthen clods until she found a foul-smelling bundle wrapped in linen. She sliced through the cloth and dissected it piece by piece. The contents did not surprise her—a tongue, an eye, an ear, and a braided cord of hair. She shivered, wondering what poor souls had been butchered to create the golems. The knife scraped against metal. The heart. She used the tip of her knife to knock the smooth, silver ball from the mess. It was no wider than her thumbnail, and she could just make out the steam rising from the surface. It was still hot.

Feeling numb and tired, Tyg sat down at the table. Such magic could not be allowed to return to the fae realm, but even if she went to Innes with the silver hearts, she doubted any action would be taken over one rogue sylv. Innes would call these golems incidental, then continue insisting to the fae of Mysanhal that there was nothing to fear, that these tragedies sometimes happened—it was no different from the occasional thief or murderous outlaw.

Before she left the cottage, Tyg gathered the three metal hearts. The brush of silver against her skin left red, burning welts. She hissed through her teeth and dropped each into a small silk pouch. "Damn the sylv and their alchemy," she growled.

If Innes did not see reason when she returned with the silver and news of three dead Yewolyn mages, she would hunt down the sylv on her own. Her mages would follow. They trusted her above all else. They understood the threat of magic that could give voice to mud and coax metals into living weapons. War could be waged in secret, and next time, she would not be taken off guard.

TWELVE

A Yewolyn rushed toward Ora. She had just finished mending worn tunics, a task that took her most of the morning. Still, she feared she had done something wrong, and she pressed a hand against her waist to be sure pages from *The Transformative Arts* had not fallen from her belt.

The Yewolyn sprinted past with a wide-eyed look of alarm. Ora edged along the passage, watching as the dren woman neared Callum's quarters. Intrigued by the dren's urgency, she did not notice Renna approach, and when he touched her arm, she drew in a sharp breath.

"Sorry, I didn't mean to startle you," he said. "I need your help."

Her gaze lingered on the Yewolyn, who now stood pounding at the Valor's door. "Something's happened," she said, turning to Renna. "What's going on?"

He shook his head. "I'm not sure."

The Yewolyn stopped banging on the door, and she turned to them instead. "Where's Valor Marigen?" she asked, her words rushed and breathless.

With an uncharacteristically bitter expression, Renna pointed along a passage bright with midday sun. "He's sparring with Gallant Myrdah."

The Yewolyn left without a word more.

"Please, let's hurry," said Renna. "I don't want to waste any more time."

The anxious pitch in his words made her forget about the commotion. They walked at a fast pace toward the kitchen. When they arrived, she was surprised to see the doors closed.

"Ora, do not mention this to anyone," he warned her and cracked open one of the doors just enough to squeeze inside.

Candlelight and flames from the stove lit the small space. The air was thick and hot. Hunched over on one of the barrels sat Cyn. He wore no shirt, and his head hung heavy between his hands. He did not look up as they entered.

"Clear off the table," Renna said.

She watched as he pulled a mortar and pestle from the shelf. "What's this about?"

"Do as he says, Ora," Cyn hissed without lifting his head.

Irritated, she stepped past the Yewolyn. It was then that her eyes fell on his back. The skin had been shredded by a cane, and blood glistened in the flamelight. Her stomach twisted, and she remembered the Valor's sentence.

So, this was what thirty lashes looked like.

She bowed her head in guilt, thinking of how she had relished the idea of Cyn's punishment the night before.

"A Yewolyn is expected to endure pain," Cyn said. "If you tell anyone of this, I will slit your throat."

Without turning, Renna said, "No need to threaten. Her name is bound."

Ora cleaned off the table in silence. Once she finished, Cyn slid off the barrel. He gritted his teeth, and with pained, slow movements, he laid himself across the surface. Renna had begun to grind at an herbal mixture, each strike of the pestle louder than the last. Anger sat on his shoulders, making his form square and rigid.

"Water," said Renna as he worked. "I need clean water."

This time, Ora did not hesitate. She grabbed a pitcher and slid into the courtyard. As she closed the door, her eyes fell on a dren who had just bent over to drink from the fountain. He was not a Yewolyn. His black hair was long, his clothes worn and plain.

A jolt of recognition struck her. It was him. The dren from the alehouse. The dren who saw her use magic.

She pressed herself against the door as if it would make her invisible. Why had he come to the lodge? Had he spoken to Callum?

He straightened. Water dripped from his beard. "Ah, it's you," he said, brow raising. "I wondered if I'd run into you here."

"What do you want?"

"I came to join the Yewolyns, but . . ." He tilted his head toward the training yard. "It seems there's a commotion."

Uncertain of what to say next, she waited for him to leave. He had come to drink water, and he was finished. Why was he still standing there? He scratched at his beard as if wrestling with a thought. Then, he held out his hand.

"You needed water, right?"

Ora hugged the pitcher against her belly. "I can get it on my own."

"I insist," he said.

Realizing he would not budge, she stepped toward him. He took the pitcher from her hands. As it filled, he spoke under his breath.

"In all my years, I have never seen a human cast a spell."

"I don't know what you're talking about."

With a crooked grin, his eyes flickered to hers. They were a stunning shade of green, as deep and dark as the Hy Borea's ancient pines. Like Maol, magic shimmered across his skin. Had the self-declared son of a god taken on a new disguise?

"You know exactly what I'm talking about," the dren said and held out the full pitcher.

But Ora did not take it. She stared hard at him. "You're using glamour," she whispered.

His smile faded. "How did you guess that?"

Before she could think of how to respond, the door opened behind her. "Ora, what's taking so long? It's just …" Renna's voice trailed off as he realized they were not alone. "Who are you?"

"Berengar Lyllwn," said the stranger. "I've come to join the ranks."

"You shouldn't be here."

Emboldened by Renna's words, she snatched the pitcher from the dren's hands and hurried back to the kitchen. When the stranger followed, Renna stepped around her, crossed his arms, and positioned himself in front of the doors. Ora peered through the crack.

"What's happening?" Cyn groaned.

She ignored him and watched as the bearded dren loomed over Renna. "You're the kitchen master, aren't you?"

"My kitchen is closed."

Berengar, if that was truly his name, looked past Renna and caught Ora's gaze. She leapt back from the door, almost spilling the water. He squinted into the dark kitchen, then said, "I'm a mage."

Renna did not budge. "Then you should come back when Magus Marigen returns."

"I know healing spells."

Cyn shifted and sucked in a sharp breath as he lifted his arm to catch hold of Ora's wrist. "Tell Renna to let him in," he said, his voice strained. She could feel him shaking. The sight of the gashes along his back made a needle-sharp sensation prickle across her skin. "*Ora*, tell him."

She pulled away and set the pitcher down atop a barrel before creeping back to the door. Renna was trying to turn the dren imposter away again. She tried to steady her nerves with a deep breath.

"Cyn asked that you let him in," she said, pushing the door open further.

"No. This is none of his concern."

"Renna, please." The desperation in Cyn's voice summoned another pang of sympathy from Ora.

"Let him help," she said softly.

Renna shoved a finger against Berengar's chest. "Breathe a word of this, and you will regret it."

"You will meet few dren who can keep a secret better than I."

The earnestness in his voice made Ora wonder if he meant to reassure her as well. Renna stepped aside, and Berengar brushed past her to inspect the wounds. As soon as the doors closed, he started singing, but the words were not fae.

Renna shook his head groggily and leaned against the table. "What sort of spell—" he began to ask, but then his knees buckled. He sank to the floor. Cyn's body relaxed.

An intense weariness crept into Ora's mind and tugged at her eyelids. She fought against it, thinking of how easily Callum sang her to sleep in the Hy Borea. She would not be fooled by the same spell twice. Blinking back exhaustion, she edged toward the stove. Out of the corner of her eye, she saw Renna's cleaver. It hung from a hook within arm's reach. It was not silver, but it was sharp.

She wrapped her hand around the wooden handle, and as she lifted it, the blade scraped against the wall. Berengar whirled around. The last word of the song hung in the air, as sweet and heavy as warm milk.

She brandished the cleaver, ready to strike if he made a move toward her or tried to cast another spell. "What did you do to Renna?"

"He's asleep." He gave a slight nod toward the cleaver. "You can put that down. I won't hurt you."

"Tell me who you are. I mean who you really are."

"*Ora—*"

"Do *not* use my name."

He held his hands up in defeat. "Very well. My name *is* truly Berengar, and I am no more a dren than you are an ordinary human girl. Will that do for now?"

"No. Why are you using glamour?"

"To disguise myself. Why else?"

"You're evading my questions."

As they spoke, he had been inching toward her. Determined to hide her uncertainty, she held her ground, but he soon stood within arm's reach. He gently took hold of the hand she held the cleaver in. "Give it here, Ora," he said.

Knowing she could not risk revealing the truth about her name, she swallowed the lump in her throat and loosened her grip. He drew the cleaver from her hand. Then, he reached around her and hung the blade back in its place. Each movement was slow and measured as if to avoid startling her.

"There," he said. "I find conversation much easier without sharp objects involved."

"And I find conversation much easier without magic."

"I wasn't directing that nodding spell at you. In fact, I had hoped we could chat."

Ora frowned. "I meant the glamour."

To her surprise, Berengar took a step back and said, "Very well, a secret for a secret."

The glamour began to fade. His hair turned ashen blonde. The sharp, angular features of a dren softened. His skin took on a darker, olive tone. Somehow, he seemed taller too. Only his eyes remained the same.

He was definitely not Maol.

"What are you?" Ora asked.

Rather than answer, Berengar shrugged, dug a pipe out of his pocket, and lit it with a spell. A sharp scent filled the kitchen as he exhaled. In disbelief, she edged closer and sniffed the air.

"That's mageweed," she said. She thought of Uncle Lupin, his smoky cabin, his stories. Her hand found its way to her waist, and she felt the hidden bundle beneath her belt. "You've been to Nor."

"Indeed, but that's not important." He spoke with the pipe between his teeth. "I would like to propose a mutual agreement between us."

Suspicious of the fae man, Ora narrowed her eyes. "An agreement?"

"Yes. You will relay to me anything you hear the Marigens discuss in private, and I—" Berengar blew smoke through his nostrils. "Well, what would you like?"

"Take me back to Nor."

"I'm afraid I can't do that."

"Then we do not have an agreement."

"In that case, *Ora*, I insist that you tell me anything the Marigens discuss in private."

"Why?"

"That's my business."

She considered refusing, but what did she care if this stranger spied on the Marigens? Besides, she did not want to give away the truth about her name, and he might be swayed to help her return to Nor later. "Fine," she said. "I'll tell you what they say, but I still want something out of it."

"As long as it doesn't involve returning to Himil," he said.

"Teach me a spell." She reached down into her smock, pulled out the folded pages from *The Transformative Arts*, and held them out. "This one."

Pipe still in one hand, he took the pages. As he unfolded them and skimmed through the first few lines, his eyes widened. "You want me to teach a little twig like you a transformation spell?"

"No," she said. "A reversal."

Small puffs of smoke rose from the corner of his lips as he studied the text. Then, his head snapped up. "Ask for something else."

Ora snatched the pages from his grip. "No. This is what I want."

"I will owe you a favor … when you think of something more reasonable."

"I think teaching me a spell is more than reasonable. You're asking me to spy on *Tyg* Marigen. She'll kill me if she finds out."

"You don't understand. That type of magic takes years to learn," he said and pointed at the pages in her hand. "You would have to learn the basics of alteration first. Even then, I don't have years to teach you."

"But you *can* cast this spell?"

"I can cast a spell akin to it."

"Then here is what I ask. Tyg transformed my brother into a pig. He's in the Hy Borea. Even if you will not return me to Nor, you can change him back, so he can at least go home." Despite her firm words, the idea that she would be stuck in Tirnan for the rest of her life felt like a clawed hand curling around her heart. The longing for her family swelled, and she felt tears gathering in her eyes.

Berengar became solemn. "I will consider it, little twig. That is as much as I can promise at this present moment."

Unable to bear talk of home and Hademar any longer, she sniffed and nodded toward Cyn. "What about him?"

"Yes, I nearly forgot. I suppose I should make this convincing." As he stepped past her, he ruffled her hair. Annoyed by the gesture, she ducked away and stashed the pages beneath her smock once again.

Berengar held his hands over Cyn's back. His chest rose with a deep breath. Then, he began to chant. His face became taught with concentration, and the words fell from his lips at a steady rhythm. Ora crept closer to watch as the flesh began to weave back together. It took longer than she imagined, but at last, Berengar stepped back from the dren. Though the deep gashes had scarred over, blood still caked Cyn's back.

With another spell, Berengar's glamour returned, and he looked indistinguishable from any other dren, aside from his uncut hair. He lifted the nodding spell next. Neither Cyn nor Renna seemed aware they had been under. They reasoned away the slumber. Cyn fell unconscious from the pain. Renna fell asleep waiting for Berengar to finish the spell. And that was that.

Rather than offer thanks, Renna opened the kitchen doors and said, "Magus Marigen will return tomorrow."

"Then I will return tomorrow," said Berengar as he stepped into the sunlit courtyard.

Not until he was out of sight did Renna meet Ora's gaze and say, "I don't trust him."

She shrugged. "I don't trust any of you."

THIRTEEN

DARK clouds drifted in from the east, where the Mysanhal foothills stretched into an infinite distance. Ora sat in the branches of a plum tree as Renna paced below. He had been agitated over Berengar, and she suspected part of him knew he had been put under a spell.

Lightning danced along the edges of the clouds. When a low rumble followed, Renna crossed his arms and tilted his head back to search the mosaic of sunlight, ripe plums, and spring-green leaves. Cool wind swept back his hair.

"Best get down," he said. "Sun will be gone in a blink, and that storm looks fierce."

She did not answer. Countless rooftops stretched below the lodge, but in the distance, she could make out the city's wall. Beyond that, glistening terraced farmlands, small orchards, and clusters of homes hugged the steep hilltops.

"Ora!" Renna tossed a plum at her.

The fruit struck her leg, and she peered down at him. "Where's the market district?"

"A little west of here. Did you hear me?"

"About the storm?" She scrambled down from her perch and leapt from the last branch. "Is Elder Kavyn's shop in the market district?"

"Close to there, yes. And before you ask, I don't know exactly where to find a wayfarer."

"I bet there's one near the crossing."

"A reasonable assumption."

"I have to leave before Tyg returns," she said. Berengar's deal had left her uncertain, and she would not rely on his whim to help her brother. Hademar could not wait.

"What's the point in telling me this?"

"You said you won't stop me."

"I won't as long as I don't know what you're up to. They lashed my brother for being a drunken idiot. What do you think will be done about the kitchen master who let the Marigens' human sneak away?" When she did not answer, his voice became dark. "And what do you think will happen to you if you're caught?"

"Don't try to scare me into—"

He cut her off as he turned toward the path. "Let's get back to the kitchen, Ora."

Like poison, a wretched notion seeped into her thoughts, and she lingered for a heartbeat. Her eyes darted across the plum-strewn earth. A rock would do. Renna would not expect it, and she could sprint across the grounds before anyone noticed. But then what? The doors to the lodge could not be farther from where they stood, and if she ran, it would arouse suspicion.

It was the wrong moment.

"I'll have you sweep the main hall tomorrow," Renna said just as she caught up to him. "During the morning drills so it will be empty."

Renna was giving her a chance. Guilt gnawed at her stomach for the savage idea that had tempted her. She said nothing but gave a slight nod to show she understood.

The evening deepened quickly as the storm approached. By the time they reached the kitchen, a pall of dark, indigo clouds roiled over Tirnan. Renna had fallen behind on preparing dinner, so he sent Ora to Callum's quarters alone.

She found the Valor speaking to a dreary group of fae in the passage along the training yard. There were three of them, all dressed in drab gray robes and shifting on their bare feet as if the ground unnerved them. Everything about them was gray. Their stringy hair, the colorless pallor of their skin, the strange feathers along their necks.

As Ora approached, she heard Callum say, "This news is urgent."

"There is a storm," hissed the tallest, his chin lifted so he could meet the Valor's gaze.

Callum looked to the sky but appeared unimpressed by the clouds. "You're sluaghs. Chaos is your friend, is it not?"

"For the right price," said another.

"Price?" Callum's voice became low, dangerous. "You are in service to the Yewolyns. Your pay is fair, and you will do as told."

They exchanged flustered glances, then hopped back a few feet. Their bone-thin shoulders quivered. Their limbs shifted. Between one breath and another, they became three shabby, gray birds and took off over the roof.

"Damn sluaghs," Callum growled beneath his breath. "Is Renna done with you then, Ora?"

"So it would appear."

"Watch your tongue."

Taken aback by his foul mood, she studied him. "Something happened, didn't it?"

"It is none of your concern. Come," he said.

They left the lodge and began to make their way toward the palace. This time, Callum did not stop to chat or flirt. He walked ahead of Ora in silence, his shoulders tense.

The first cold drops of rain fell just as they reached the palace. Wynn greeted them almost as soon as they stepped into the grand entry hall. The thachwing woman was much calmer and composed around Callum. She did not fidget with her skirt or wring her hands together. Instead, she smiled and beckoned them onward.

"Queen Innes was expecting you. She's in the conservatory," Wynn said. "She'll be pleased you brought the girl. She's so fond of her, you know. I don't understand it, but Her Majesty is … Her Majesty."

"Yes," said Callum, but he sounded distracted.

Wynn continued to chatter on about trivial matters. The queen's collection of Merinian ferns had caught mealy mites, a charming traveler—Ora assumed Maol—had decided to extend his stay at the palace, a painter had just put the finishing touches on a portrait of Her Majesty, and so on.

The door to the conservatory was made of thick, clouded glass and copper details. When they entered, the last light of day was fading, and ornate candelabras lit their way. The glass enclosure amplified the rain and thunder, but as they reached a circular opening in the lush flora, the deafening sounds became muffled.

Several trees with thick canopies and braided trunks arched over the space. Beneath their feet stretched a mosaic of rich blues, greens, and reds in lively floral patterns. The carefully laid tiles were polished to a brilliant shine that glistened in the candlelight. For all the opulence, it was the distinct charge in the air that caught Ora's attention. She wondered what sort of magic had been cast there.

The queen sat in a blue-velvet chair with a butterfly perched on her thin finger. Its wings were the color of dark, inky glade berries and kept a languid beat. She leveled her pale gaze on the delicate creature even as Callum bowed before her. Ora stood unmoving behind him with her chin lifted and hands clasped behind her back.

"Valor," Innes said, ignoring the girl's poor etiquette. With her free hand, she gestured to a golden tray on a table beside her chair.

It was piled high with what looked to be tiny, pink carvings of roses. "Have one if you'd like. They're butter sweets from Ullkyrin."

"A kind offer, but I have come to discuss more serious matters, Your Majesty," said Callum.

She looked up from the butterfly at last. "You have come to tell me there is an imposter among the Yewolyns."

The queen's words caught Ora off guard. She thought of Berengar, but he had not joined the ranks yet. How would Innes know of him already?

With an indifferent expression, Callum produced a small cloth bundle and unwrapped it to reveal a metal ball. "There *was*, yes. A sylvn golem."

The butterfly fluttered down from Innes's hand and found a new perch on the sword-like petal of a vivid red flower. The queen reached out and plucked the silver ball from the cloth.

"Your Highness—" he began.

"One can learn to ignore the sting of silver, Valor."

Ora felt her heart grow restless. She had not seen silver since arriving in the fae realm.

"Either your wife has taken care of our sylv problem, or the spell faded," said Innes.

A half smile pulled at the corner of Callum's lips, and pride warmed his words. "I have no doubt that Magus Marigen was successful."

The queen returned the silver ball to the cloth, which the Valor still held in an outstretched hand. He wrapped it and tucked the bundle back into his pocket.

A dainty sigh passed between Innes's lips, and she folded her hands on her lap. "She undoubtedly sees a greater threat."

"Your Majesty, I am quick to remind Tyg of the peace that you have nurtured in Mysanhal. She is loyal to your will and to mine. A Yewolyn does not act without orders."

Ora's eyes widened. She did not imagine Tyg would approve of her husband's words. The queen either did not notice or, once again, chose to ignore her.

"I do not mean to sow doubt between you, but please, Valor, be impartial in your judgement. You have always been discerning and wise, but when it comes to Tyg, I worry that you see only what you wish to," said Innes.

Callum bowed his head. "I understand your concerns, Your Majesty, but I assure you, I place Mysanhal before my own passions."

"Good. Then, you will tell me what you are so clearly withholding."

It was then Ora realized the Valor was gazing straight into Innes's eyes. A long, uncomfortable silence followed. Eventually, Callum shook his head as if waking from an afternoon nap.

"Magus Marigen has been sending scouts to Mysanhal's farthest reaches. The golem—it took the form of one of her scouts," he said. "My apologies, Your Majesty. I should not withhold such details."

"No need to apologize, my dear Valor." Innes stood, her long skirts sweeping across the mosaic tiles beneath their feet. "I do not want another war. Ensure that Magus Marigen does not meddle with the sylv a second time, and I will take measures to placate those who live within our borders."

"I will, Your Majesty."

"And Callum," she said and reached out to caress his face. He shivered at her touch. "Visit me more often. I much prefer discussing these matters with you."

He caught her delicate wrist and gently pushed her hand away. "Tyg simply wants to protect Mysanhal. She does not easily forget the sylv's atrocities. Surely you recall that it was a sylvn alchemist who killed her father."

"Yes. We all suffered great losses during my husband's wars, but that is precisely why I wish to avoid another." A deep sadness filled Innes's gaze, and Ora wondered if she too had lost someone dear to her.

"I understand, Your Majesty, but please, hear her when she returns," said Callum.

Innes smiled. "Of course, Valor, it is always beneficial to keep good company with those who have opposing intentions."

"Yes," he said and then bowed. "I will send word once she returns, Your Majesty."

"Good. Now, I wonder if you would allow me to speak to your human girl alone? I wish to see how she is faring."

Ora, who had been watching the exchange with increasing apprehension, flinched and took a step back. She had no desire to be left alone with Innes, who was proving to be far more manipulative and cunning than she first seemed.

"Of course, Your Majesty. I will wait in the Great Hall," he said.

The Valor left along one of the conservatory paths, but Innes did not speak right away. She returned to her chair and studied Ora, her pale gaze just as haunting and entrancing as it was during court. But something had changed. Ora did not find herself so easily drawn in.

"Fascinating," said Innes. "I sensed something had shifted, but even now, I cannot discern what it is. Cree has blessed us with quite the mystery, *Eudora*."

The sound of her true name made Ora's skin prickle.

"Tell me, what do you think of Mysanhal? Of Tirnan?"

It was not the question she expected, and she stumbled over her words. "I think—well, it's not …" She swallowed hard. "It is very different from Nor."

"Tell me of your parents, Eu—"

"I will tell you without need of my name," she said quickly.

"Plucky of you to interrupt your queen," Innes mused. "But go on. I will know if you are lying anyway."

"There is little to tell. My mother is Norrish and so was my father. I lived my whole life in the Hy Borea, in Fel, and I want to return."

"Your father *was*? He is dead, then?"

"He died of a wasting sickness while I was in my mother's womb."

"So you never knew him."

Ora's cheeks grew hot. "I know him through what he left behind."

"How sentimental," Innes said, voice as sugary sweet as the rose candies beside her. "Come closer, dear."

Ora stepped forward, but the queen was not satisfied. She took Ora's hand to pull her close.

"There. Now I can have a better look at you." Innes held Ora's chin between her thumb and index finger to turn her head every which way. "I wonder if you are part fae?"

Not long ago, the idea would have sounded absurd, but she had used magic. She could *feel* magic.

"How would you know?" she asked as the queen released her.

"There are ways to find out. Would you like to know what you truly are, *Eudora*?"

"Yes," she said. Her name had summoned the answer without her thinking of it. Furious, she bit down on her tongue. Despite her curiosity, she did not want the queen involved in finding out the truth. Besides, it did not matter if she was part fae or anything else. She was Norrish first.

"I will make preparations." Innes waved her away. "You may leave now."

"I didn't mean that," Ora said. "I just want to return home. I don't need to know what I am. It doesn't matter. Just—"

"I said leave, *Eudora*, and show some decorum. Bow to your queen."

She wanted to argue, but her body defied her will. She bowed, turned from the queen, and marched out of the conservatory. Only once she stood in the hallway did the force of her name fade. She leaned against the wall, breathless and dizzy.

"It's the last night," she promised herself. "You will be home tomorrow."

FOURTEEN

THE storms lasted through the night and into the next morning. When Ora made it to Renna's kitchen, she was soaked and shivering. The small courtyard outside the kitchen had turned into a giant puddle. Thunder made the earthenware pots shutter on the shelves.

He did not mention sweeping all morning. Instead, he put her to work with dishes, chopping vegetables, and scrubbing the kitchen floor. She grew impatient. Had Renna forgotten? Or worse, had he changed his mind?

She ground the scrub brush against the floor, angry with herself for trusting a fae. Renna had no intention of helping her. And why would he? They had only met days ago, and though sympathetic about her brother, he made it clear that aiding her escape was too great a risk. The least he could do was stay out of her way, but even then, she could not seem to find a moment alone. No matter where she went in the lodge, there was always a Yewolyn or two nearby.

Arms aching, she stopped and sat back on her knees to wipe sweat from her forehead. "Have you *ever* scrubbed this floor, Renna?" she asked.

But no answer came.

She twisted around. The kitchen was empty.

"Renna?"

Ora stood and crept to the open doors. The rain had stopped, but heavy clouds still loomed overhead. Most of the water in the courtyard had drained. She stepped outside to peer along the passage leading toward the main hall. It too was empty.

Had Renna meant for her to take this chance?

She could hear shouting and the clash of metal. The Yewolyns were sparring. To reach the main hall, she would have to pass by the training yard. But, if she appeared busy, who would stop her? They all believed her name to be bound. Still, her heart fluttered in her chest as she snatched up the broom and began to make her way toward the main hall.

The sounds of combat swelled as she walked along the training yard. The scent of blood and sweat soured the humid air. She spotted Callum on the other side, watching his Yewolyns. Ever since the day before, he had been pensive. Even now, he stood stoic and rigid with his arms firmly crossed.

Ora had sensed a change in mood among the Yewolyns as well. The golem, whatever it was, had made them tense. They spoke in hushed voices and slid wary glances between each other. More than once, she caught the Magus's name tinged with fear and speculation.

The Valor's golden eyes flitted toward her. She pretended not to see him and quickened her pace up the steps and through the doors.

For once, the main hall was empty.

Relieved, she set aside the broom. Just as she did so, the front doors opened.

"Ah, little twig!" Berengar strode lightly toward Ora. His cheerful greeting was jarring, and she gazed at him as if he had appeared from thin air. "What? Didn't think we'd meet again so soon?"

Determined not to miss her chance, she balled up her fists and stormed past him. When he tried to catch hold of her arm, she wrenched away. "I don't have time for you," she growled.

"I think you'll find that you do, *Ora*."

"Funny, I'm simply not convinced."

Berengar's lips parted as if he might speak, but he shook his head in disbelief instead. With a wicked grin, she pressed on to the front doors.

"Wait, wait, wait," he said, rushing to catch up with her. "You're not bound?"

By then, she had her hand against the door. "If you try to stop me, I will reveal your secret to Magus Marigen."

"And then I will reveal yours."

"She already knows about my name."

"What of your magic?"

"Why would she listen to a dren imposter?" She watched as his expression darkened and knew she had gained the upper hand. When he did not budge right away, she pressed him. "Well, is it worth the trouble?"

At an impasse, Berengar stepped back. "You've made your point."

As she cracked the door open, she paused. Why not cause some trouble for the Marigens before she left? She lowered her voice. "Last night, the Valor delivered news to the queen. There was a sylvn golem among the Yewolyns."

"Is that all?"

"No. Callum and Tyg do not see eye to eye, and Innes does not seem to trust her either. As for Callum, he was captivated by the queen and too easily swayed by her words. I don't know what to make of that, but maybe you do."

"I will have to ponder this. It's a shame I won't have you around." He smirked. "You're hoping to find a wayfarer, aren't you?"

"I am."

"You'll find one at Fyntolomah's."

"I don't know the place."

"You do. It's where we first crossed paths. Ask for Esi. Tell her Berengar sent you."

Ora held back a smile and thanked him. As the door closed behind her, she looked down on Tirnan. The rain made the city damp and dark, a sharp contrast to the shining grandeur she first experienced. It seemed far more fitting. She descended the steps and forced herself not to glance over her shoulder. A lie rested on her tongue should she be stopped, but as she set off along the cobbled street, she soon realized the fae cared little about a stray human.

Any time she reached a plaza, her pulse quickened. With so many fae swirling about, it was difficult to tell if she recognized any of them. She kept to the edges and moved as quickly as she dared. Unable to recall the exact route to Fyntolomah's yellow door, she followed a series of staircases and pathways that sparked familiarity.

As she navigated the city, she realized just how little she paid attention to where the Marigens led her. She wandered for well over an hour before she found the market district, and then, she walked down several narrow side streets before finding the yellow door.

Inside, the tavern was less lively than the night Callum brought her along. A thachwing stood behind the bar, red hair flowing over her shoulders in feathery wisps. Her eyes found Ora straight away.

"You, human girl," she said, leaning over the bar. "Come here."

As Ora approached the barkeep, she felt the patrons' eyes following her across the room. Was it possible that one would recognize her from the night Callum brought her along? Did it matter?

The fae woman had a warm voice, and when she spoke, it put Ora at ease. "What brought you here?"

She donned a clueless expression and said, "I was told to find someone called Esi."

"She's right over there. Is everything alright?"

It was not the question Ora expected, and she became flustered. "Yes, I—I think so?"

"Well, whoever sent you must be desperate. It's none of my business though." The barkeep slid back from the counter as she spoke.

"Thank you," Ora muttered and turned toward the table she had been directed to.

The wayfarer's back was turned, so all Ora saw at first was a pale, bald head. No, not just bald. Entirely hairless. Blue lantern light shone against her smooth scalp. The fae woman wore a black dress with a simple gold waistband and sipped a mug of steaming liquid.

As Ora sat down, she saw that the fae's eyes were entirely black, without the faintest hint of white around her irises. It was like staring into the space between stars.

"Berengar sent me," Ora said when the wayfarer did not acknowledge her presence.

"Berengar is a good friend." Esi smiled, revealing sharp little teeth. "What did you bring me?"

"I only own one thing." She reached down into her smock and tugged out the yellow handkerchief. "It is the last thing my mother gave to me."

"A piece of cloth from Nor, is it?"

"Yes."

Esi snatched up the yellow handkerchief, pressed it against her snub nose, and breathed in the scent. "I can almost smell the old trees. The pines."

"Will it be enough?"

"You have *nothing* else?"

"No."

"I have no patience for lies, little Nor. Give me the thing you wish so desperately to keep, and I will provide passage."

Feeling nauseous, she reached into her smock a second time. The pages she stole from *The Transformative Arts* had become wrinkled and soft beneath her belt. She smoothed them out against the table. "Isn't there something else you want?"

The fae woman shook her head. "Do you know how one becomes a wayfarer?"

"No," said Ora, her eyes fastened to the pages as the wayfarer lowered her hand down on top of them.

"It is not by choice. It is a curse, a punishment for using forbidden magic." She dug her nails into the paper and dragged it toward her. "The Ether is consuming. It hollows you out. One must feed it with … *meaning*, I suppose."

Page by page, Esi wadded up *The Transformative Arts* and stuffed the paper into her mouth. Ora watched in bitter silence as the wayfarer grinned and took the handkerchief. "This too," she said. "Because you lied to me."

The yellow square of cloth disappeared between her sharp, gnashing teeth.

"Will that be enough?" Ora asked again.

"Hm." Esi licked her lips. "My, my, that *was* important to you, wasn't it?"

"I have nothing else," she said, words clipped with anger.

"Good. I will meet you at the crossing."

"Where is it?"

The wayfarer hunched over the table. Then, she took hold of Ora's hand, dug her nail into her wrist, and muttered a spell. A map, or was it a memory, imprinted itself in Ora's mind. Every turn, every fountain, every shopfront. It was as if she had always known the route.

"I will be there within the hour," Esi whispered.

*****

Ora wasted no time in leaving the tavern. Her encounter with the wayfarer left her shaken and anxious. She tried to remind herself that the pages were useless without help from a practiced mage. At least she could return to the Hy Borea and ensure Hademar's safety.

She turned up a staircase that led to a crowded plaza and walked along the southern edge, which looked out over the mountains. Had she been allowed to explore on her own terms, she might have found Mysanhal's terraced farmland, waterfalls, and misty cliffsides wondrous. She would have been joyful at the idea of bringing back stories about running water, lamps lit by magic, and impossible architecture. Instead, thoughts of her brother and escape dulled the splendor. She spat on the stone beneath her feet. *Good riddance*, she thought.

She closed her eyes. The way to the crossing filled her mind. She was close.

The brush of fingertips against her shoulder made her flinch. Ora whirled around. A sting of panic shot through her heart. But it was only a dren in a layered silk dress. The woman withdrew her hand, a dozen gold bracelets tinkling against her thin arm.

"Sorry, I didn't mean to frighten you. Aren't you the Marigens' human?" asked the dren.

Ora glared and flatly answered, "Yes."

"Are you lost?"

The lie she had readied when leaving the lodge flowed from her lips. "Valor Marigen sent me on an errand. He forgot something at home."

"Really?"

She sensed the dren's suspicion and swiftly gave a nod. "Yes, I'm on my way now."

"And you stopped to enjoy the view?"

"I …" She glanced out at the mountains and clouds, unable to find the right words.

The dren shrugged. "Tirnan is lovely, isn't it? Perhaps I can walk with you. I've been wanting to meet you."

"You have?" Ora fought the urge to run. *You're close, you're close, you're close*, she chanted to herself.

"Oh, yes. I'm a dear old friend of the Marigens, you see. You can call me Alish."

"A friend of the Marigens?" Ora repeated, but she was already scanning the plaza for an escape route. She doubted Alish could outrun her in such a ridiculous dress.

"You must have tea with me." The dren looped her arm through Ora's. "Callum won't mind if you're a little late."

"He will," said Ora, slipping away before she could be led into the crowd. "He asked me to hurry."

"Just one cup of tea. It won't take—"

"*Ora.*"

A treacherous power charged the air. Ora felt the blood drain from her cheeks. Bound or not, the voice gripped her, made her freeze in place.

"Well met, Magus," said Alish.

Tyg's hand curled around the back of Ora's neck. "You may go, Alish."

"Pardon?"

"You may go."

The Magus's voice was pure venom. Alish took a step back, and then, with a parting nod, disappeared into the throng of fae.

"What are you doing here?" Tyg asked, turning the girl to face her.

Ora stared at the Magus. She thought of the lie she told Alish; she almost said it again. But something in Tyg's eyes glittered. Something predaceous. Something dark.

So, Ora ran.

As she shoved her way between fae, she did not bother looking to see if Tyg pursued her. That would mean slowing down. Stairways, plazas, markets, shopfronts, tea stalls—she hardly noticed a thing that blurred past. Though the fleeing human girl certainly raised brows and drew out a few annoyed curses, no one tried to stop her.

She descended deeper and deeper into the city without any awareness of the streets she chose. Her feet pounded hard against the cobbled road, and her breath came in painful, needle-sharp bursts. She did not think she could run anymore and at last stole a glance over her shoulder. When she didn't see Tyg, she ducked into an alleyway and pressed herself against the wall. She could feel her pulse in her ears, and her legs felt tight. She leaned her head back and tried to steady her breath.

"You have to keep going," she whispered to herself.

Having lost the Yewolyn, Ora became more cautious. At every turn, she peeked out before stepping into the open, and she slowed her pace to avoid attracting attention. The map the wayfarer had etched into her memory shifted and guided her toward the crossing.

It led her down a staircase alongside one of Tirnan's falls. Farther down the path, a bridge crossed the river, and beyond that, she could see another plaza with a stone circle in the center. She had made it.

Throat dry with thirst, she paused to crouch beside the rushing water and scooped some into her palm. After she drank, she splashed some of the freezing water against her face and neck.

The soft, almost inaudible scuff of a boot made her flinch away from the river's edge.

"Go ahead," said Tyg as Ora rose to her feet and stumbled back. "Make a run for it. I can assure you the outcome will be painful."

The temptation to flee overwhelmed Ora. How far could she make it? She glanced at the river and wondered where the rapids might carry her if she were to jump in.

Tyg sneered. "What use would you be to your brother dead?"

The words rang true. The tumbling water would drown her, or her head would be broken against the rocks. Ora shivered.

"Do you think I don't know what drives you? What makes you so defiant?" The dren drew closer as she spoke. "You can't even change him back. He's lost to you, Ora."

"You're wrong," she said.

"Don't be foolish."

She had to try. The crossing was just over the bridge. Ora turned to run. Almost immediately, her ears filled with buzzing. The faint sound was familiar, but before she could place it, she felt a force strike her side. With a strained cry, she crumbled on the shore. Spots danced in her vision, and pain coursed through her, making her claw at the earth.

"I warned you." Tyg's voice was just loud enough to hear over the roaring water. The dren crouched beside her, watching her writhe for a few long seconds before lifting the spell.

Relieved, Ora drew in a shaky breath and squeezed her eyes shut. It was the same spell Callum had struck her with in the Hy Borea, but his casting had not been as powerful. Pain still burned her skin and lingered in her veins. Tyg took hold of her arm, forcing her to sit up.

The Yewolyn leaned in to whisper against her ear. "If you try running from me again, I will toss you into the falls and claim that you slipped. Do you understand?" Ora did not answer, and Tyg tightened her grip. "I asked you a question, you idiot girl."

Ora's black eyes rose to meet hers. "The falls don't sound so bad."

"Get up." But Tyg did not wait for her to stand. She yanked the girl to her feet. For a heartbeat, Ora was sure the Magus had decided to toss her into the waters, but she was pushed toward the stairs instead.

The walk back to the Marigen household was a long one. Tyg's hand rested against Ora's neck, guiding her along the streets. Even if she wanted to try running again, she could not. Despair consumed her. She had been so close, and now, she had nothing to bargain with.

As they passed through the Marigens' front door, Tyg shoved her inside. "What did you have planned? Did you think you could find a wayfarer? You have nothing to offer."

Ora backed into the table. "I'm sorry," she said, not knowing what else to say.

Perhaps if Ora had not been handed over to a Yewolyn, a sorry might have sufficed. But Tyg hardly tolerated apologies from her subordinates. A human girl stood little chance against her wrath. The dren grabbed hold of her wrist and slammed her hand down onto the table. Realizing what the Magus intended, Ora pulled away at once.

"Please don't," she begged, taking a step back and holding her hand close to her chest.

"Place your hand there," Tyg said.

"But—"

"Place your hand there, Ora. Do as I say. Or would you rather it be two fingers? One for trying to run off and one for not doing as told."

Shaking, Ora lowered her hand to the table. She met Tyg's cold gaze and wondered if the dren could be bluffing. Maybe it was only meant to scare her. But then, Tyg drew her knife.

"I sharpen this blade every day. It can slice even a hair," she said and turned it so that it would catch the light. "Elves made it. They're so clever with metals." She brought it down in a flash. Ora's eyes flew shut at once. So sharp was the blade that she did not at first feel the pain or cry out, though Tyg would have cherished the sound.

Breathing heavy, Ora opened her eyes and looked tearfully down at her severed pinky. Blood spilled onto the wood. With a sneer, the dren lifted her pitiful, trembling hand and cast a spell that turned the blade red-hot. Tyg cauterized the wound without warning. This drew out a scream. She held Ora's wrist tight until her agonized cry faded into a whimper.

"Clean this up," Tyg said and left her to it.

FIFTEEN

WHEN Tyg arrived at the lodge, the Yewolyns had been eating their evening meal. After a day of training, they were covered in dust. Some were blood-stained and bruised. Others were triumphant and boasting. The banter faded as one by one they became aware of the Magus. A grim hush weighed upon them.

"As you were," she said, her voice booming and fierce in the stillness.

The Yewolyns bent their heads, returning to their conversations and meals. Several of her mages raised their fists to their hearts in a somber show of respect. They did not know of their dead companions yet, and it pained her to think of delivering the news.

As Tyg strode through the main hall, she saw Gallant Myrdah stand. His heavy footsteps followed after her, but she did not bother slowing her pace until she passed into the portico outside. There, she waited beside one of the columns and gazed up at the sky. The sunset had deepened into a copper glow.

The doors opened, and Myrdah joined her, leaning on the other side of the column. "The Valor requested our audience as soon as you returned."

"Of course," she said.

"I take it you know the girl is missing."

"Not missing anymore. I found her," she said as they began to walk side by side toward Callum's quarters. "We will be needing a new kitchen master."

"His brother also caused some trouble while you were away."

"Cyn?"

"Yes, but I will let your husband recount that story. I was hoping I could speak candidly with you before we meet with the Valor."

They halted and faced each other. Tyg gave a sharp nod.

"A sylv sent a golem here, to the lodge. I cannot ignore such a bold move. They are regaining their power. You were right. But I do not believe Queen Innes intends on taking action, and Valor Marigen will stand by her." The giant dren rested his palm against the top of his sword's hilt. "Where do you stand, Magus?"

"I stand for Mysanhal. I did not endure the mage's trials to watch our strength crumble at the hands of a weak ruler. The sylv will be dealt with, Myrdah."

"Then we are allies in this." He held up a hand, and she clasped it in agreement. "I will not doubt you a second time."

"Thank you, Gallant." Pride swelled in her chest. Myrdah did not admit his wrong easily, and she was pleased to have his support. Callum would have no choice but to see reason.

They went to the Valor's quarters. Callum wore a stony expression and regarded them both with a frown. "Tyg," he began, but she already knew the words on his tongue.

"I found the girl wandering the market district. It is taken care of." She traced a line of road on the map before him. "Let us discuss the sylv."

"There is nothing to discuss. I have spoken to Queen Innes. She desires peace, not war. You are not to provoke the sylv, Magus Marigen," said Callum.

Tyg lifted her chin. "A sylv killed three of our mages yesterday, and there were three more golems. She was young, too young to have learned such magic without a teacher. Innes does not understand the threat."

Myrdah turned to her. Only his gaze revealed his surprise. "You returned alone," he said as if he had just realized it.

"Yes." She tugged a pouch free of her belt and loosened the tie. Then, she dumped the three silver hearts onto the table. She watched their expressions shift between shock and horror. "Such alchemy cannot be allowed to exist in Mysanhal. It is dangerous, dark."

The news appeared to weigh heaviest on her husband. He sat down in his chair and fell silent.

This time, Myrdah spoke. "Valor, our queen is wise, but this is—an unexpected development. We must look into it."

"It was one sylv, and she is dead now. We will continue to be vigilant, but we must not overreact." Callum's voice was flat and empty of conviction.

Tyg seized her chance. "Vigilant? It was my scout who reported—"

The Valor slammed his fist against the table. "*Your* scout is probably dead. A golem was sent in her place. None of this would have happened had you left the sylv alone."

"So, we wait until there's another attack? Another spy?" said Myrdah.

"We will wait until our queen sees it fit to take action."

"When did you become so weak-willed, husband?" Tyg growled.

Callum's gaze became flinty, his voice low. "Do not forget your place, Magus."

A stream of vicious spells flooded Tyg's mind. Her fingers curled at her sides. She wanted to strike him with a curse, to remind him of her strength. Instead, she spat on the floor and stormed from the room.

Anger burned in her chest. She hardly saw the faces that turned toward her as she swept back through the main hall. To quell the rising energy, she shot her hand out and shouted a spell. The doors to the lodge burst open violently, thudding against the walls. A stunned silence followed her down the steps.

She could not easily forgive Callum, and her fury threatened to consume her. Thinking an offering would clear her mind, she set off toward the temple. Perhaps Cree would send guidance as he had when Odharan sought to destroy the sylv.

Aside from the palace, the temple was the largest building in the royal city. Its sweeping architecture and colored glass windows looked marvelous by day. By night, the stained glass shone out to the world, and the halls felt otherworldly.

Incense and candle smoke spiced the air. Mosaics lined archways and swirled beneath her feet in rich blues, greens, reds, purples, and golds. Even Innes's palace could not compare to the temple's jewel-like wonder.

In vivid detail, master painters had created scenes telling the story of Cree, their horned god. From his conception in the darkness of Ether to the war against his sisters and brothers, his saga stretched across the ceiling. His strength when he fought the mountain god, Eldrys, and silenced the volcanic Mount Lenali. His cunning when he trapped Kadypha, the sly goddess of the unknown, and gave the fae of Rioc magic. His conquering of Pylis, the spirit realm, where he created a kingdom for the dead. She knew the stories by heart. Her mother told them to her when she was a girl.

The altar was a magnificent tree made of gold. Its bark and leaves were so finely detailed that it almost appeared to be alive. In the flickering candlelight, its branches and leaves seemed to shift as if touched by a gentle breeze. No one quite knew how it came to be. No living artisan could match such craftsmanship, even with magic.

Beneath the tree stood a marble statue of Cree. He held a stone orb in one hand and from his head sprouted two elegant antlers. At his feet were dozens of small, shallow bowls made of copper. It was there that his worshipers knelt and made their offerings.

Tyg stepped up to the altar and pressed the tip of her knife against her finger. Then, she squeezed a drop into one of the bowls. She asked for a vision, an omen, a guide. But when she closed her eyes, all she saw were the dull, orange shadows of flames.

She prayed for victory instead.

Time crawled, and her thoughts began to wander. At last, she rose and made her way back toward the entrance.

As she began to descend the steps outside, she spotted the dren from Innes's dinner party. He stood in the middle of the steps with a book open in one hand. Just as jovial as the night they met, he snapped the book shut when he saw her.

"Magus Tyg Marigen! A pleasure to see you a second time. You look ..." Beneath her glare, his merriment faded, but only a little. "Troubled."

Her frown deepened. "What are you doing here?"

"I am ... close to Cree," he said with a puckish smile. "May I walk with you, Magus?"

"If you'd like to keep your tongue, then no."

"A pity. I was told you are a master transformationist. I would love to hear your perspective on Casyan and Auldymere."

"Perhaps I could demonstrate."

Book still in one hand, he held his arms out. "Well, if you must, but I'm already an ugly, old goat."

A smile flitted so quickly through Tyg's expression that Maol might have missed it had he blinked. She brushed past him. "Have you read Casyan and Auldymere then?"

"Yes," he said, bounding to her side. "Several times, in fact. They had their differences, but I am an admirer of both."

"Yes, but Auldymere revolutionized the art."

"He was a romantic, though. I don't think you would have liked him much."

"You talk as if you knew him."

"We met a few times."

"That would make you—"

"Quite old, yes."

Tyg stopped. "Who did you say you were?"

"Maol Becanan. A merchant by trade."

She studied him more carefully than before and then began to descend the steps again. He kept pace beside her.

"You must be pissing glamour to look like that," she said.

"It is second nature by now."

"You probably are an ugly, old goat."

Steadfast in his good humor, he gestured like a thespian as he spoke. "Wasn't it Auldymere who said glamour is the reimagining of one's soul? An exploration of both self-expression and the discipline of self-control."

Though impressed by his knowledge, Tyg did not spare him so much as a glance as she said, "You're right. Too much of a romantic."

After that, they fell into easy conversation and wandered the streets of Tirnan. Tyg lost track of time as they discussed the subtleties of Casyan's philosophy on visualization, Auldymere's extensive experiments, and the work of other mages who had left impressions upon them.

Maol spoke eloquently but not without the bubbling energy that had captivated Innes and her dinner guests. He drifted into tales of travel. As a merchant, he made most of his wealth by acquiring and selling rare artifacts and magical objects. He claimed to have a knack for stumbling upon such curiosities.

"You are a surprising character," Tyg said and cast her gaze up at the moon. It was waning but still bright in the crisp, night air.

"What do you mean?" he asked with an amused little chuckle.

"You are well read and well-traveled. I would not have guessed it after our first meeting."

"Ah, I'm relieved that it's a compliment. You do not seem to give those generously."

"I do not." She turned to him, a determined gleam in her eyes. "Have you spent much time traversing the Wastelands?"

"Of course. Did you know there's quite the population of impkins? Their teeth are useful to enchanters, but they're not easy to get. Of course, that just means enchanters are willing to pay more."

"Have you encountered any sylvn clans?"

He gave a thoughtful nod and scratched at his chin. "Yes, I'm afraid so. They give merchants plenty of trouble. Of course, that has been good for business in a way. Raise the stakes, raise the price."

"What sort of trouble?"

"If you're going to interrogate me, Magus, I insist we do this over drinks."

"Answer my question," she said, her voice a low warning.

"Magus Marigen, there's no need to intimidate me into further conversation." He pointed to a tea stand on the nearby corner. "Walk with me, and I will tell you about the sylv I have encountered."

Before Tyg could argue, he strolled toward the teamonger. She caught up to him in a few swift strides. "You are infuriating," she hissed.

"I am thirsty. Would you like some tea?" He opened his coin purse and fished out a copper piece.

The teamonger was already pouring two cups of the creamy tea with a ladle. He eyed the Yewolyn warily as he held out a steaming cup. She glowered but took it all the same.

Once Maol paid, they found a place to sit along one of the benches beside the stall. The warm, spiced scent of the tea filled Tyg's nose. She set the small cup beside her.

"How many sylv are left?" she asked.

"How should I know? I've only ever seen a few at a time." With his first sip, he sucked in his breath and grumbled that it was too hot. "I wouldn't worry about them too much, Magus. They're nothing but scavengers, looking for food and supplies."

"So I've heard."

"But you don't believe it?"

She could not tell him about the sylvn alchemist or how she had found the golems. She chose her words carefully. "There are other rumors."

"Ah, so you've heard about the seid."

"A seid?" Her eyes narrowed. "There's no such thing."

Maol shrugged. "Stranger, darker things have come out of the Ether before. At least a seid was once fae."

"Such spellcraft is only theory. No mage has been foolish enough to try it."

As Maol began to speak, a scream pierced the night air. They both leapt to their feet. Tyg watched as fae surged toward the plaza where the crossing lay. Forgetting about the merchant and the tea, she made her way to the crowd and began to push through them.

"You will stand back!" she bellowed.

An eerie hush settled over the throng of nervous fae. Their eyes dropped, and as they parted, she understood their panic.

It was her scout, a young, swift dren called Ayla. If not for the Yewolyn markings tattooed along her arms, Tyg would not have recognized her. Her elk cloak had been stripped away. Dark bruises and cuts covered her skin. Chunks of hair had been ripped from her head. But that was not what summoned the frightened scream.

The Yewolyn scout's eyes had been carved from her head, her ears cut off, and her tongue slashed from her mouth. She was crawling across the stone circle, her hands searching ahead of her.

"Get a healer!" Tyg shouted as she stepped onto the circle. She dropped to her knees beside Ayla and gently touched her shoulder. "You're in Tirnan. You're safe. Can you hear me?"

But the injured Yewolyn seemed unaware of Tyg's presence. She made no sound. Not when Tyg tried to speak to her. Not when the healer arrived. Not when they helped her to her feet and guided her through the lamplit streets. Her body felt cold and lighter than it should have.

The city became a blur of concerned faces and low whispers. Though none knew how the scout had come to be so disfigured, Tyg felt a crushing sense of guilt for what had become of Ayla. The young mage had volunteered eagerly to investigate the sylv. She had been talented and would have risen through the ranks faster than many of her peers. If Tyg had known Ayla would be facing alchemists, she would have sent a more practiced mage.

Once they reached the healing ward, a few thachwings took over. Though none of them said it, Tyg knew Ayla would not last the night. Not because she would die but because she had *already* died. She was nothing more than the reanimated shell of a fae that would fade before the light of dawn. Tyg was certain the corpse had been a message, one meant for her.

As she left the healing ward, the sylvn girl's words returned to her. *Don't worry, Magus Marigen. They will find you.*

"Magus?" Maol stood outside, his hands folded behind his back and concern written across his features.

"I—" Words evaded her, and she shook her head. "I didn't realize you followed."

"I thought it best to stay out of the way." His gaze flickered to the healing ward's doors, and he let out a long, sad sigh. "I know the work of an alchemist when I see it."

"As do I," she said, her voice distant and soft.

"I am sorry to hear it, Magus Marigen. You must be devastated."

"Devastated?" Tyg scoffed. "I am furious, Maol. Mysanhal's greatest enemy is regaining power, and our queen will do nothing about it."

It was more than she had meant to say, and to her great irritation, Maol's lips spread into a gentle smile. "It seems Mysanhal is in good hands."

"Good hands? You think Innes—"

He cut her off. "I was referring to *you*, Tyg Marigen. You do not strike me as the sort to sit idly by when there is a threat. This is why you were asking me about the sylv, is it not?"

In answer, she gave a short nod.

A mischievous look glittered in his eyes as he spoke. "I have little to tell myself, but I have many friends. I will ask around, Magus." Then, he gave a slight bow and left her standing in front of the healing ward before she could say anything else.

Tyg almost called after him, but she thought better of it when she saw a few bystanders gossiping nearby. At least Tirnan had seen some measure of truth that night. *Let them talk*, she thought. Innes would not be able to ignore her people forever.

SIXTEEN

ORA sat on the hard earth with the night sky bright above her. Sleep had not come easily. Every time she shifted in the small bed, the throbbing pain in her hand reignited. Now that she sat in her familiar landscape, she did not care if she ever woke again. The starlit desert of her dreamworld soothed her aching heart. Time did not weigh upon her. It was always night. It was always dark.

A breeze tickled the hairs on her neck. She shivered, becoming aware of her surroundings. She dug her nails into the soil and tried to ignore the feeling that crept up her spine. There was something else there, something pressing into her consciousness. Breath shaking, she got to her feet and turned.

"Who's there?" she called out when she saw nothing but the strange, blue nightglow caressing the land.

A soft rustle came from behind her. She turned again. A piece of paper was caught in the brush. She bent to pick it up and gasped. It was a page from *The Transformative Arts*. As she straightened, she became aware of more feather-light pages drifting toward her across the dusty earth.

One by one, she gathered the pages. The paper was warm to the touch, as if it had been left out in the sun. She stared at the drawing of a pig's anatomy. The lettering around it was nonsensical. In an unconscious movement, she felt for the crystal pendant around her neck.

"You could summon it to you." The voice startled her. It was brisk, almost dismissive. When she looked up, she found the wayfarer standing before her. "You look surprised, and yet you summoned the pig pages with hardly a thought."

Ora drew the pages behind her back, distrustful of the wayfarer, who had swallowed them to begin with. "How are you here?"

"That is difficult to explain." Esi tilted her head as if thinking, but her expression remained impassive. "I imagine we are tethered now. We made a deal, and I must uphold my end."

She wanted to feel hopeful, but she was tired and cautious of giving a dream too much credence. Still, she said, "So you'll give me passage."

"I have no choice." The wayfarer sounded annoyed by the idea but went on all the same. "Call on me when you reach a crossing."

With that, she vanished.

When Ora woke, she did not know if the wayfarer had been a dream or a reality. As she became aware of the hot pain in her hand, she forgot about it altogether.

After Tyg had left, she had slumped down to the floor and squeezed her wrist as if she could stop her mangled hand from shaking. Furious and afraid, she filled the house with another anguished cry. She sobbed until her head stung. Until a numb disbelief settled over her.

The rest of the day had been a blur. She had cleaned the wound and dressed it with a strip of cloth she found tucked in the back of the larder.

Picking up her own severed pinky from the table was surreal. She did not know what to do with it, but she felt strangely attached. She held it in the palm of her good hand and stared at it for a long while. It was a gruesome, cold little thing.

Her mind grasped for a way to make a joke of the cruel injury. What good was a pinky anyway? She had four more perfectly good fingers, and she would give up any of them to return home. She paced through the parlor a few times before turning to the fireplace.

She had felt empty when she set the severed appendage aflame. What else was there to do? It could not be reattached. It would rot. *Smell.*

Now, the pain drowned out all other thoughts. Unable to sleep anymore, she lay in bed and waited until Tyg called for her. In the parlor, she could not bring herself to look at the Magus, so she stared at the hearth instead. She could still see the bones smoldering in the ashes.

"Make yourself useful," said Tyg. Then, she left. The door clicked shut.

Whatever the Magus had meant by useful, Ora did not care. Her mind felt clouded, her body weak. She had not eaten since the previous morning, and now hunger tore at her hollow stomach.

She went to the kitchen and devoured half a loaf of stale bread. She had to wedge it under her arm and rip chunks off with her good hand. Crumbs littered the floor. She found what looked to be an apple, but its skin was brown like a pear. After the dry bread, she welcomed the sweet juice. She licked her fingers clean and drank water directly from the pitcher.

As she wiped her lips with her sleeve, a tap on the doorframe made her flinch. She spun around to find Callum watching her.

"You must think yourself clever for running off like that," he said.

He received a cold glare in answer.

"Tyg took a finger I see." There was no sympathy in his voice. He held out his hand expectantly, and when she did not move, he said, "Let me have a look."

"No," she said bitterly. "I'd rather you didn't."

"I don't have to ask." The Valor stood over her in just a few strides. He took her wrist and began to unwrap the cloth she had tied around her hand. The wound beneath was inflamed and beginning to weep puss.

"You should not let this fester," he said and stepped past her to open the larder. He held out a corked glass bottle. "Wash it in vinegar. You'll be glad for it."

Distrustful but eager to be alone, Ora took the bottle and waited for Callum to leave the house. She set aside the vinegar. The gruesome injury was the least of her worries. She had to find a way out of the house. If that meant attempting a spell to get past Tyg's enchantments, so be it.

She spent the morning searching through book after book for a useful spell. The complex and often unfamiliar words overwhelmed her. As she gave *The Fundamentals of Conjuring Flame* a second pass, she briefly considered setting fire to the front door, but its introduction consisted of a colorful, ten-page explanation on how fire magic should not be attempted without a teacher. Frustrated, she tossed the book across the parlor. It bounced off the chaise and landed open-faced in front of the fireplace.

"Is that some sort of joke?" she asked the book, then got to her feet.

She held her good hand up, palm open to the sky. When she knocked Cyn's chair out from under him, she had not used a spell, and she certainly had not uttered a spell the night she dreamed of the falcon. If it was that simple to summon magic, why did almost all of Tyg's books contain warnings about botched spells?

It mattered little. She still did not know how she managed to channel magic to begin with.

Half lost in thought, she returned the book on fire magic to its place among the rest of Tyg's small library. The night at Fyntolomah's had been an accident, and yet, she had felt the power flowing through her veins.

The magic arose with her anger, but if that was so, why then? Why with Cyn? Why not when Tyg attacked her? Why not in the Hy Borea when she first encountered the fae?

Determined to quell the growing sense of doubt in her chest, she lifted her hand again and recalled the spell Tyg forced her to cast.

The word burst from her, assured and pointed. "Ayluma!"

Warm energy streaked through her arm, her palm, her fingertips. Then, an orb of light blossomed inches from her skin. Ora's breath caught.

It worked.

Stunned, she lowered her hand, and the pale, blue light drifted above her head.

"To the depths with warnings," she muttered, eyeing the books once again.

Ora ran her hand along the spines, plucked one from the shelf, and flipped through the pages in search of another simple spell. Finally, one caught her eye.

Azyna's Featherweight

Less well known than Torsyn's levitation spell but exceedingly more elegant and simpler, Azyna's featherweight is an excellent example of alteration's fundamental truth: reality is subjective and therefore changeable.

The mention of alteration made her recall Berengar's words. If understanding the basics of such magic was the first step in learning how to cast transformation spells, perhaps she still had a chance of changing Hademar back.

She continued to skim the page. Beneath the introduction to featherweight was a drawing of a hand gesture that reminded her of the graceful way her mother held a needle. She laid the book on the table and imitated the illustration. The text continued at length, detailing Azyna's early life as a hermit and subsequent success as a scholar.

While the traditional method of levitation requires adept visualization, featherweight can be achieved by recognizing an object's infinite potential. Much like a sculptor reimagines a block of granite, a mage too can reimagine the bounds of reality. Of course, it is recommended that one starts with a light object as it is easier for the mind to grasp. As with many alteration spells, the mind will rail against the extraordinary and seemingly impossible outcomes inherent to bending reality.

It was less ominous than many of the cautionary tales she had read, so she scanned the rest of the page for the spell. Once she found it, she read it aloud several times. "*Hyferia*, *hyferia*, *hyferia*." The word alone made her heart quicken.

Ora decided to test the spell on a letter first. She swept aside the mess on the table and placed the folded paper in front of her. With some effort, she managed to balance the book in the crook of her arm while she prepared her good hand for the casting.

Several attempts later, she dropped the book on the table and let out a frustrated sigh. The letter remained where she placed it, unmoved and mocking.

"So much for subjective reality," she muttered.

In truth, she craved fast progress. The idea of staying in Tirnan any longer frightened her, and it was difficult to slow the waves of doubt. Every day Hademar lived as a pig was another day he could be hunted, whether by man or beast.

These thoughts staved off any sense of discouragement. She spent the rest of the afternoon trying to pronounce the levitation spell differently, adjusting her hand position, experimenting with different objects. Once, she directed the spell at a cork and thought she saw it wobble.

When the sun began to set, she knew the Marigens would return soon. She rushed to tidy the space, hoping it would look like she had attempted to make herself useful. The last thing she wanted was Tyg's undiscerning anger.

Soon, Ora heard the Marigens approaching the door and recognized the fighting edge in Tyg's voice. Thinking it best to stay out of the way, she rushed to the spare room.

"It's a waste of time," the Magus cried as they burst into the parlor.

Ora held her breath and pressed her ear against the door to listen.

Callum's retort sounded weary, as if he had been arguing with her for too long. "It's a show of goodwill and respect for the Cedar Clan."

Tyg fell silent. Even from the spare room, Ora could sense the tension in the house.

"What about the girl?" she asked.

"Take her to Wynn," said Callum. "There's always plenty of work to be done in the palace."

At the Valor's words, Ora smiled to herself. It was not just that the Marigens would be absent from her life. The mention of Wynn had stirred a memory. On her first day in Tirnan, she had stood at the thachwing's window and looked down on the palace garden. At the time, the stone circle had looked ornamental, but now she understood. It was a crossing, and all she had to do was find a way to reach it, to call for Esi. And this time, Tyg would not be there to stop her.

SEVENTEEN

WIND swept down from the mountainsides in gentle gusts as Tyg led Ora through Tirnan's streets. The Magus said nothing of her conversation with Callum, and Ora began to worry they were heading toward the lodge. It was not until she saw a familiar blue door that she realized they had been making their way to Elder Kavyn's shop.

Just as they reached the front step, a fae woman caught sight of Tyg and drifted across the street with a thin smile. She was snow white in complexion, and an aura of magic charged the air around her. "Magus Marigen," she said in greeting, then looked down at Ora. "I've been hoping to meet this human girl of yours."

"I would think you have more important matters to occupy your time, Aygriel," said Tyg. Her hand curled over the girl's shoulder and pushed her toward the door. "Wait inside."

More than happy to get away from Tyg, Ora stepped into the dim and dusty shop alone. Elder Kavyn chuckled as she shut the door. He sat at his desk, tinkering with some delicate, copper instrument. "Ah, Magus Marigen isn't very fond of the high priestess," he said and pushed his glasses up his nose. "But what does it matter if you hear their conversation?"

"How should I know? I've never met her," Ora said, voice flat.

"Well, since we have some time to ourselves, tell me what happened, Ora." He eyed her hand, which she quickly hid. When she did not answer, he leaned back in his chair and crossed his arms. "I rather suspected your name wasn't properly bound."

Elder Kavyn's words gave her a fright, and she tensed. "You did?" she asked, stunned that he noticed at all. No other fae seemed the least bit suspicious.

"Relax, child. I won't be telling anyone. It hardly matters to me. You may want to be more careful, though. You gave yourself away when you didn't answer."

Ora let her hand fall back to her side, but she still did not know if she could trust the Elder. Hoping to shift his attention away from her severed pinky, she nodded at the instrument that sat before him. "What is that?"

He grinned and pushed it toward her. It had a number of flat, pentagonal faces with glass oculi in their centers. "Go on. Pick it up."

She did so with her good hand, cradling it as if it would break merely from her touch. Like the books, it emitted warmth and energy that crawled up her arms. She began to clumsily turn it over. There were notches and markings carved into the copper that meant nothing to her, even with the help of the amulet. "What is it?" she asked.

"A speculademain by the looks of it," he said. "I think."

"Does it do anything?"

"I'm sure it does a wonderous something, but I'm still figuring that bit out. It's a sylvn tool of—"

"Sylvn?" she said, thinking of the copper orb that had sprouted legs.

"Yes. The sylv are akin to dren, but there aren't many left. They were talented alchemists of a sort. Most of that knowledge has been lost, though." He tapped his desk thoughtfully. "That device is quite valuable these days."

Before Ora could ask any more questions, the door opened. She gave a start and dropped the copper instrument. It thudded against the floor, and Elder Kavyn winced.

"You idiot girl," snapped Tyg as Ora scrambled to pick it up.

With a gentle smile, Elder Kavyn took the device and studied each side for damage. "It's quite alright. I asked her to fetch it for me from the shelf." He set it back down on the desk. "No harm done."

"How fortunate," she said, glaring down at the girl.

He removed his glasses and stood from his desk. "And how is the high priestess this fine morning?" he asked as he stepped toward the backroom.

"Vainglorious, as usual. Queen Innes has seen it fit to honor her with a private villa near the temple." Tyg picked up the sylvn artifact from the desk and began to study it herself.

"Hardly pious!" Elder Kavyn called from the backroom.

She set the device back on the desk and turned toward the shelves of books and enchanted objects. Ora stepped out of the way and lingered near the desk instead.

"Here you are." The elf smiled as he reemerged with a neatly folded elk cloak. "This reminds me, a son of an old friend was looking to join the Yewolyns. His name is Berengar. I admit, I had hoped he would pursue another path. Young as he is, he's a talented mage."

The mention of Berengar made Ora perk up. She shot the Elder an inquisitive look, but he did not seem to notice.

"Yes, I spoke to him yesterday. I'm sure we'll find him useful," said Tyg, still examining the odds and ends on the shelves. The Magus picked up a polished, indigo-colored crystal and rubbed her thumb along its smooth surface. "What were you working on before I arrived?"

Ora watched as Elder Kavyn's smile faded, and he seemed to become paler than usual. His eyes lingered on the sylvn device. "Why do you ask?"

"Simply making conversation," she said.

"Ah, well, I was only tinkering."

"With a sylvn artifact?" she asked, whirling back around to meet his stunned gaze. "It has sylvn writing on it. I'm sure you noticed, Elder. You're well studied."

He cleared his throat and squared his shoulders, trying to appear taller. "It is nothing more than a dusty curiosity. There is no crime in having it."

She raised a brow. "Perhaps not. But where did you get it?"

"Not from a sylv if that's what you're asking. I don't do business with their sort."

Tyg forced a smile. "Of course. I apologize for my assumptions. You have served Mysanhal well all these centuries."

"Good day, Magus Marigen," he said tersely and handed her the cloak before sitting behind his desk. He pulled open a drawer and began to rummage through it.

"Good day," Tyg answered.

As soon as they stepped into the street, she drew Ora aside and bent down to be at eye level with her. Expecting the worst, Ora shuddered, but the dren only asked, "Did Elder Kavyn say anything about the device on his desk?"

She shook her head, eyes wide.

"Are you certain?"

Remembering his lie, she said, "He only told me to bring it to him. I was just doing as told."

"Of course. Why would he tell you anything?" She let out a frustrated sigh. "Come, then."

To Ora's dismay, the Magus took her to the lodge next and marched her up the stone steps. She began to ponder how she could reach the crossing behind the living quarters. Renna would be easy enough to slip away from a second time.

But it was not Renna who stood in the kitchen.

"Berengar," said Tyg as they came to the doorway. "This is Ora. Do not let her out of your sight."

"Yes, Magus Marigen." Berengar wore a clever smile, and Ora could not help but wonder if he had taken the kitchen master's position on purpose.

Heart pounding in her chest, she glanced up at the Magus. "Where is Renna? Did you hurt him?"

"No, your dear little Renna is a coward, and rather than suffer the consequences of his actions, he simply did not show up. *This* is our new kitchen master." Tyg shoved her inside the kitchen, and as Ora stumbled across the stone floor, Berengar's hand shot out to steady her. The Magus turned to leave but then paused. "I understand that you are a talented mage, Berengar."

"That is too generous, but yes, I have studied under several Elders." As he spoke, Ora pulled her arm away from his grip, and he eyed her hand. It was nothing more than a flicker, but she saw the disgust in his eyes.

"I imagine you did not come here to be a kitchen master, then."

Voice steady, he said, "No, but I did not want to argue with the Magus on my first day."

"Elder Kavyn spoke for you. Consider your position as kitchen master temporary."

Before he could thank her, Tyg left. In a few swift steps, she vanished from the courtyard, the elk cloak trailing behind her.

Once they were alone, Berengar turned to Ora and said, "Let me see your hand. I can't regrow a finger, but I can heal what's left."

Ora said nothing. She was afraid she would melt into tears if she did. Instead, she let Berengar take her hand into his own. He chanted the healing spell with a low, gentle voice. At first, she felt only an intense warmth, but then, the pain dissolved. The swelling went down. The skin scarred over.

It took less time to heal than the gashes along Cyn's back. When he finished, he cleaned away the leftover grime with a damp cloth and clicked his tongue. "This was beginning to fester," he said. "What happened?"

Ora held her hand against her chest, relieved to be free of the pain that had kept her awake through most of the night. "I ran into Tyg before I could reach the crossing."

"And she saw it fit to take a finger. I shouldn't be surprised. Tyg Marigen is known for her ruthlessness." He leaned against the worktable, produced his pipe, and then lit the bowl with an effortless spell. Smoke curled from his lips as he spoke. "Do not lose heart, little twig. There is a saying where I come from. *Nosos kiv moria kiv erasi.* Nothing about fate is certain."

The unfamiliar language he spoke sparked the beginning of a realization. She studied him, piecing together fragments of memories and conversations. "Where *do* you come from, Berengar?" she asked.

"Tell me, Ora, do you find it easy to speak of home?"

She answered with a meaningful silence.

"Then you understand." He pointed to the boiling pot with the stem of his pipe. "Give that a stir, please."

She took up the big wooden spoon and swirled it through the thick stew. "You're a sylv, aren't you?" she asked and glanced at him to gauge his reaction.

He blew out a cloud of smoke and then drew close enough to whisper into her ear. "I am more than that. I am the Magus's greatest fear."

The idea that Tyg could fear anything summoned a small, wicked smile. "And what would that be?"

Berengar met Ora's gaze with a dark, prideful stare and said, "An alchemist."

"An alchemist? So, you alter metals?" Her smile faltered, and she blinked. "Why would Tyg be afraid of that?"

"No. Alchemy is more than that. It's complex magic." He paused to puff at his pipe, then asked, "What do you know of Tyg Marigen's past?"

The question was unexpected. She shrugged, feigning indifference, though he had sparked her curiosity. "I know she's the Magus, and most everyone I've met is wary around her."

"Yes, she does have a reputation, but that's not what I meant." He kept his voice low and his gaze fixed on the courtyard in case anyone passed through. "The Magus's father was once the Valor as well as the previous king's most trusted advisor. He was behind much of the animosity toward the sylv, and when they captured him in battle, they sent Tirnan a message."

"What kind of message?" she pressed.

"His reanimated corpse," he said, voice hard and cold. "I have heard it said that little Tyg could not stop screaming when she saw him."

She shivered and inched away from Berengar. "That's terrible."

"*War* is terrible," he said. "The fae of Mysanhal committed many atrocities as well, but they refuse to see their own cruelty. They burned our libraries and universities to the ground. They tortured and killed our masters. They even destroyed our god."

Ora's eyes widened, and she could not stop herself from interrupting. "Is that possible? Destroying a god?"

"Oh yes," he mused, a new plume of smoke unfurling from his lips. "You must know what it's like to have everything taken from you."

Though she sensed there was more to the story, his words tugged at her heart. She gently touched his arm, and he gazed down at her with a mild look of surprise. "Not in the same way. But I know I would do anything for my home and family."

He smiled sadly. "As would I," he said, closing his hand over hers. "Now, we should not speak of this anymore. We'll find ourselves in trouble."

She winced. "Yes, I have a talent for that."

EIGHTEEN

TWO uneventful, unbearably long days passed. The Marigens were distracted with their own affairs. In the evenings, Tyg would lock Ora in the townhouse and disappear for hours. So, Ora attempted more spells from the same book in which she discovered featherweight. It was a thick, redolent old tome entitled *The Mage's Companion to Subjective Reality*. A number of spells were labeled as "simple" or "suitable for learning fundamental aspects of alteration", but her attempts to alter reality failed again and again.

When the Marigens returned home for the night, she would hide in the spare room and listen to their hushed conversations. They intended to leave soon, and it was the only consolation she had for her inability to cast simple alteration spells.

By day, she worked alongside Berengar and told him of the Marigens' plans to resettle the Cedar Clan. She had gleaned few details from her eavesdropping, but he listened with intense interest, pipe in hand. He claimed to know little about the clan. They went into exile during Odharan's wars and had not been seen in Mysanhal since.

He refused to let her out of his sight, just as Tyg had requested. To be sure, she had tested him. On their first day together, she had picked up the broom and stepped toward the open kitchen doors. "The main hall needs sweeping," she said when he raised a brow at her. Without waiting for an answer, she strode into the courtyard.

He was at her heels in an instant. "I will join you, and we'll get it done faster."

"I don't need your help."

Berengar pried the broom from her grip and guided her back into the kitchen with a hand on her shoulder. Then, in a low voice, he had said, "Your time will come if you are patient. Do not ask me to risk the sylv for your freedom."

The sylv. Any chance she got, Ora asked about the mysterious clan. She wanted to know every last detail about the alchemists Tyg feared, but Berengar deflected her ceaseless questions with orders. Fetch more salt. Wash the dishes. Make more dough—if he burned the bread one more time, she swore she would set fire to his beard.

Berengar was less tedious than Renna. Not only did he burn the flatbread, he put too much salt in the stew, and served sour, unripe fruit. Finally, after they overheard several Yewolyns complaining about his cooking, she rounded on him and asked, "Was that all on purpose?"

"No, but it is amusing, isn't it?" he said with a wink.

They had just returned to the kitchen. He sat down on a barrel to smoke his pipe and lit the herb with an effortless spell. As he did, she gave him such a look of longing that he offered the pipe to her.

"No, it's not that." Ora sat beside him and became pensive. She peered into the courtyard to be sure no one stood at the fountain before asking, "Do you know Azyna's featherweight?"

"Where did you hear of that?"

"I read it."

He tapped the amulet around her neck with the stem of his pipe. "Elder Kavyn outdid himself."

"Well?" she said.

For once, he conceded. "Fine, I will teach you featherweight. I assume that's what you're really asking."

With an uncontrollable grin, she nodded. "It's supposed to be simple. I don't know what I've been doing wrong. I tried for hours last night and the day before but—"

"Little twig, be still. Alteration magic takes clarity of mind. You cannot cast such spells if your thoughts are cluttered, as I imagine yours are." He pressed his thumb into the bowl of his pipe, snubbing out the resinous ember. "Grab something light."

Ora chose a discarded plum pit and set it on the table. As she did, he shut the kitchen doors and cast an orb of light.

"Now, what do you think of when you're standing there doing nothing?" he asked and came to stand behind her. "Magus Marigen, perhaps? Your brother? Fears and failures?"

"Yes, all of that," she admitted and felt foolish for it.

"This is natural. Your mind will always seek distractions when it comes to magic, especially alteration. You are defying what you perceive as reality, after all." He placed his hands on her shoulders and adjusted her posture so that she stood straighter. "Still your eyes and focus on nothing else. Envision what you want to happen, the reality you wish to actualize. Then, on a full, clear breath, cast the spell."

Ora settled her gaze on the plum pit and tried to ignore the thoughts flooding into her idle mind. She concentrated instead on the pit lifting up from the table. She imagined it as weightless and as hollow as a feather shaft. Still, when she cast the spell, she could not help but doubt her efforts, especially after so many failures.

The pit remained motionless.

Frustrated, she crossed her arms. "It's useless."

"You cannot cast a spell with a fettered mind. Doubt chains you to reality, Ora. Try again."

Berengar's words brought to mind the falcon and how it had fought against her even as she tried to free it. Then, with piercing clarity, she understood. "You mean I'm holding myself back?" she asked, tilting her head up to catch his gaze.

He grinned. "That's probably a simpler way to put it, yes."

"Why didn't you say so?"

"I read too much. Try again," he repeated.

With a renewed sense of determination, she lifted her hand a second time. "Hyferia!" she shouted without pause or hesitation.

The pit shot up and hovered before her. Unable to contain her excitement, a victorious cry burst from her lips. She almost turned to hug Berengar, but then, the pit quivered and tumbled back down to the table.

"Unusual," said Berengar.

A flush crept across her cheeks. "Sorry, I lost focus."

"No. You did well. That's what's unusual."

"Are you sure?" She twisted around to face him. "I barely got it off the table."

A mixture of wonder and concern filled his eyes, and she did not know what to make of it. He sighed. "You are a natural. You would be wise to find a teacher."

In that moment, Ora did not think of her brother or home. The infinite potential of magic filled her with a strange, hungry yearning. She wanted nothing more in all the Ether than to study spellcraft and alter the world around her. "You can teach me. Can't you?" she asked.

Berengar scratched at his chin. "To study in secret is limiting. I could teach you simple spells and fundamentals, but … No, this is dangerous territory, little twig. If Tyg, or even Innes, learns of your ability, you may face death."

"Why? Why should they care?" Exasperated, she struggled to keep her voice low. He held a finger to his lips before she could go on.

Her shoulders fell, and he answered. "To them you are unworthy of magic, just as I am."

"Because you're sylv." She leaned against the table and gripped the edge hard enough to turn her knuckles white. "I cannot stand their cruelty any longer, Berengar. Teach me a spell to set this city ablaze, and I will leave it in ashes by morning."

"If it was that simple, this city would have been dust ages ago. There is more than Yewolyn strength guarding this place."

Berengar snuffed out the light and moved to open the doors, but she reached out to catch his wrist. Though she withdrew right away, her touch made him pause. "You weren't going to leave it at that, were you?" she asked.

He studied her in the shadows. "You should not concern yourself with this. Focus on returning home, on helping your brother."

She faltered at the mention of Hademar and watched as Berengar opened the doors. The sun stung her eyes. She raised her arm against the stark light as she spoke. "I cannot help my brother if I do not learn magic."

"You can't help him if you're dead either."

He sounded too much like Tyg. She glowered and opened her mouth to argue when they heard the sound of footsteps in the passage. They both turned, suspended in a moment of fear as the Magus appeared in the courtyard. Had she heard them? She looked angry, but she always looked angry.

"Ora!" Tyg barked.

A frightened shiver ran up Ora's spine, but she forced herself to step toward the doors. Tyg had been more impatient than usual the past few days. Ora could not decide if it was because of her attempted escape or because of the Cedar Clan.

The Magus halted a few feet from Ora, her lips thin and shoulders square. Her elk cloak flapped against her legs in the mountain breeze. "Come with me," Tyg said. "I am taking you to the palace."

NINETEEN

IN the grand entry hall, the Magus hissed a final warning as Wynn approached. "Do not forget the consequences of disobeying. I can do worse than take a finger."

"How could I forget?" Ora's voice was tinged with more defiance and resentment than the dren could stand. She watched the Magus's fingers curl around the handle of her blade, but the knowledge that she would soon leave the fae realm made Ora bold. She rolled her eyes.

"Do *not* test me, Ora," Tyg said just as the thachwing reached them.

"Well met, Magus Marigen," Wynn said, clasping her hands before her. "Queen Innes wishes you a safe journey."

The Yewolyn raised a brow. "Does she?"

"Yes, of course. Good day, Magus." Wynn seemed just as eager to part with the Yewolyn as Ora. She drew the girl away with a gentle hand.

Tyg did not respond to the thachwing's farewell, and Ora dared to shoot a final, withering glare over her shoulder. But the dren was already on her way out. "Good riddance," she muttered under her breath.

Pretending not to hear, Wynn led her to the servants' wing. There, she eyed the simple linen smock Ora wore. "I suppose it's more to Tyg's taste, isn't it?"

"It's fine. Really," Ora insisted. She did not want to be laced up into a ridiculous, layered dress again. "It's comfortable and doesn't get in the way."

Unconvinced, Wynn said, "Well, let's at least put you into more proper attire while you're here."

By then, Pons had crept to Wynn's side, head bent down as always. "We're all done with laundry," he said.

"Perfect! You can show Ora where to find some more suitable clothing."

At this, Pons blushed. "It's this way," he said, then led her down to the big laundry room on the floor beneath the servants' quarters. Once they were out of anyone's earshot, he nervously lifted his head. "What happened to your hand?" he asked.

"Nothing," she said and clasped her hands behind her back.

"You had ten fingers before. I—I'm sure of it."

"I'll tell you on one condition."

He winced. "I can't promise anything. You should know that by now."

She leaned forward and whispered in his ear, making him shiver. "I don't want to wear a dress. Get me something like what you're wearing, and I'll tell you what happened."

"I don't know …"

"If Wynn says anything, I'll take the blame. What's another finger?" she asked with a small laugh.

"How can you joke about that?" he said but did not agree to her proposition. He stood with his hands shaking at his sides.

Seeing the strain on his face, it dawned on Ora that it had probably been a long time since anyone gave him a choice. "Come on. I can't imagine Wynn being that angry. She didn't even use our names," she said. "There's nothing stopping you."

His brow rose in surprise. "I hadn't thought of that."

"No? Are you always so dull?"

"Are you always so … so …" But he seemed unable to think of an insult.

Ora smiled triumphantly as he stumbled over his words. "Pons, *please*. I won't ask for anything else. I promise."

"Fine, but it's your problem if Wynn says anything. Don't drag me into it," he said and hurried off for a minute. When he came back, he held a neatly folded white shirt and a pair of trousers the same deep shade of blue that he wore. "You better tell me every last detail," he said.

She grinned. "I won't spare anything."

But it would not be until much later in the day that Ora told him about her missing finger. He worked with a sober vigor. To her surprise, he was meticulous in his work, as if he took pride in the exacting details of polishing golden cutlery and dusting empty rooms. She soon remembered why he had irritated her the first time they met.

There were other bound humans, of course, but they were just as distant as Pons, always keeping their eyes down and speaking very little. They wore the same blue palace uniforms, but they came from all over the human realm. She spotted blonde-haired Galgoans, freckle faced Merinians, and other Nors like her. There were those who she could not place, too. Most appeared young. She bitterly wondered if the fae only stole children away.

Her manners, or a lack thereof, alarmed Pons. He watched in horror as she peered into every open room, stole a pastry from an unguarded spread of food, and chased the palace cat along an empty corridor when it refused to let her stroke its black fur. Nothing he said could dissuade her.

While they were dusting an enormous but cramped study, she opened desk drawers and boxes, rolled a brass paperweight across the palm of her good hand, and flipped through several books. She could feel Pons's eyes following her. When he at last found the courage to ask what she was looking for, she smirked.

"Silver," she said. "Maybe a spell book."

"You're not funny."

"I'm not joking."

A wall of windows faced the mountains. Jagged, gray peaks stretched into the distance like layers of sharp teeth. She pressed her forehead against the glass, trying to see what lay below. "There's a crossing here at the palace, isn't there?" she asked.

"Crossings are useless unless you are a mage," he said.

"That wasn't a no." She had made a point of investigating the view from every window she came across. Unfortunately, the palace was monumental in size, and she could not orient herself. She had relied on Pons all day to guide her through the maze of halls and staircases.

He cast her a furtive look, and she thought she saw a hint of suspicion in his expression. But it was fleeting. He ducked his head and ignored her until they finished the room.

That evening, they ate their supper—a plate of bread and cheese—in a sunny atrium. Pons fidgeted with a loose hem on his sleeve and several times looked as if he might speak. When Ora could take it no longer, she turned to him and said, "Go on. Out with it."

"You promised," he mumbled.

Ora shifted her hand off of her knee and tucked it beside her leg. But he was right. She *had* made a deal with him. She looked about the atrium for anyone who might overhear but only saw the black cat, curled up on a bench not far from them. She lowered her voice and told the whole story, beginning with the day Renna explained the crossings. By the time she got to the part where Tyg sliced off her finger, Pons's eyes could grow no wider.

"I intend to try again," she said in conclusion.

For a long time, Pons said nothing. He pushed a few crumbs around on the plate and frowned. "Y—you're not really bound, are you?"

Ora gave a start and clapped her hand over his mouth. "Don't say that so loud!"

When her hand dropped away, he spoke more softly. "It's true, though. Isn't it?"

"Queen Innes told me to keep my name secret," she said. "Don't say a word to anyone."

"How do I know if you're telling the truth?"

"I have no reason to lie to you. Besides, what are you going to do? Ask her yourself?" Ora's words rushed out harsher than she intended, stunning Pons into silence. Feeling guilty, she muttered an apology.

"I shouldn't have said anything to begin with." His shoulders fell. "You're lucky, Ora. You still have choices."

"So do you," she said. "You chose to get me these clothes, remember?"

"It's been a long time since I've done anything like that. Makes me nervous." He grimaced. "Wynn hardly bothers with my name anymore. It took years to earn her trust. It's as close to being free as I could hope for."

The heaviness in his voice made her heart ache. "Pons, how long *have* you been here?"

He didn't look much older than her, maybe only a year or two. His answer nearly made her choke. "About forty years, I think. I've stopped counting, really."

"What? Forty years? You can't be much older than me. That's not possible."

"Fae magic changes you, whether you realize it or not. Aging takes longer in the fae realm."

The possibility of being trapped within Tyg's home for hundreds of years made Ora draw in a sharp gasp. "Haven't you tried to escape?"

"Now *that* truly isn't possible," he said. "Not for me. They have my name, Ora. My *true* name. I'll be here until I die."

"A name can't be bound forever, can it?"

For once, he held her gaze, and she saw the depth and longing of all those years. "I gave my name willingly to save someone I loved. I would do it again."

Ora could think of nothing to say. She could not imagine Pons, the skittish Merinian boy he was, giving up his name for anyone.

"There you are!" Wynn came bustling into the atrium, her lavender skirts billowing about her tiny frame. "Ora, Queen Innes would like to speak with you. Goodness knows why. I do wish there was time for you to change, though."

"The queen?" Ora repeated, her face pale.

"Yes, get up this instant. She's asked for you straight away."

Ora glanced at Pons, but he was staring at the ground once again. She set the plate of food that had been on her lap aside and followed Wynn out of the atrium. Unnoticed by anyone, the black cat jumped lightly from the bench and scurried after them.

TWENTY

QUEEN Innes sat in her conservatory among her ever-growing collection of exotic plants and butterflies. A human girl was busy tucking pearl hairpins into her long, braided hair, but as soon as Wynn led Ora inside, she dismissed the servant. "You may leave as well," she said to the thachwing.

"Yes, Your Majesty," Wynn said before drifting back down one of the winding conservatory paths.

"Have a seat." Innes gave a small nod toward the chair across from her. She had a fine spread of butter cookies and tea prepared, which sat on the table between them. As Ora took her seat, the queen poured her a cup of milky, sweet-smelling tea.

"Thank you." Distrustful of the queen, she left the teacup untouched.

"Let me see your hand," Innes said.

Knowing it would do little good to argue, Ora held out her hand so the queen could study the scarred over nub.

"Tyg?" she asked with a sad look. When Ora nodded, she let the girl slide her hand away. "I am sorry, Eudora. I did not think she would be so cruel to you. She must have caught on, though. Why else would she take a finger?"

The sound of her true name made Ora's skin crawl. She could sense the power in the queen's voice.

"Perhaps I was wrong." Innes sipped at her tea and watched as a butterfly landed on a sugar cube. "I imagine it would be much easier for you if your name was bound."

Ora held onto the sides of the chair and tried to calm her racing heart at these words. "Queen Innes," she began.

The fae queen went on as if Ora had not spoken. "I have never allowed a human to walk through Mysanhal unbound, but it is Cree himself who has willed it. He is most mysterious at times. The gods are that way, aren't they?" Her pale eyes became less distant and settled on the girl.

"Yes?" Ora said.

Innes rose to her feet in such an elegant movement that she seemed lighter than the air itself. "Come with me, *Eudora.* It's time we find out what you are."

Properly bound or not, a power beyond Ora's own reason compelled her to follow Innes. They slipped out a glass door in the other corner of the conservatory. It opened to a brightly lit stairwell. The queen led her up the stairs, through another door, and then along a labyrinth of hallways without another soul in sight.

They eventually came to a large, open room with a flower-covered altar and hundreds of palm-sized, golden bowls of water. The stone columns came together in arches on the tall ceiling, and huge windows on either side meant light could come in from the east or west.

"On your knees and do not move, *Eudora.*"

Ora's stomach knotted as she lowered herself to the ground before the altar. She gritted her teeth, furious that she could not stop herself from obeying. Her whole body felt rigid, and she could not will even the smallest twitch of a muscle. Though she could hear the brush of skirts behind her, she could not turn her head to see what the queen was doing. Anger and fear coursed through her.

Then, Innes stepped in front of her. She had a thin blade in one hand and one of the golden bowls in her other. "Don't worry. I won't be taking any fingers," she said. "I need only a drop of your blood."

She used the very tip of the blade to prick one of Ora's fingers and squeezed a drop of blood into the bowl of water. It spread out in dark, crimson tendrils. Behind her, the water in the other bowls began to turn a deep red as well.

"When I heard news of your arrival, I consulted Cree right away. I was told something that has been on my mind ever since," said the queen as she set the bowl down on the altar. "Can you guess what that might be?"

"No," said Ora.

"You are, as I understand, a new creature. Not human but not fae either." Innes stood over her, cleaning the blade with a soft, white cloth. "It took some time to find the proper ritual, but now we will know just what you are. And, whether or not you are a threat to the fae."

Ora struggled to understand. She had grown up in Fel, daughter of Hagen and Nel Widogast. Her own brother had been there when she was born, and her uncle swore she looked just like her parents. The thought of her family and her home pained her, and she felt tears gathering in her eyes.

Innes turned away from her to peer into the bowl. She drew in a long breath and began to chant a complex, ancient spell. The water in the bowl rippled.

As the thachwing queen chanted, Ora tried to will herself to stand up. She focused first on her feet and tried to wiggle her toes. Nothing. Pain shot through her all the sudden. She gave a small gasp, and her head spun. She tried again to focus on moving, but the white-hot pain returned, doubling in proportion. It was then that she understood why Pons could do nothing and what it truly meant to be name bound. There was no disobeying. Her own body had turned against her.

With each word that spilled from the queen's mouth, Ora's pulse beat faster. Her cheeks were wet with tears by then, and she had gritted her teeth so hard that her jaw hurt.

Then, something strange happened. She heard a warm voice fill her mind, but it was not the queen's. It was far too deep and mocking.

Would you like some help, Eudora?

She shifted her eyes, trying to see what was in her periphery but only caught the glimmer of golden bowls. Was there someone else there? Wouldn't Innes have noticed?

Well? the voice pressed.

Yes, she thought in a panic. *But hurry.*

Promise you'll help me. Whatever it takes. I've been saving this last bit of magic for longer than you can imagine.

Yes, yes. I promise! She did not believe her thoughts could be any louder. She feared she had in fact said it aloud.

Very well, Eudora. You are now bound to me and to no one else. Your name is mine and cannot be used by any fae. It will hold no power. As long as you breathe, I can call on you however I choose.

Wait! It was not at all what Ora intended when she agreed to the stranger's help, but before she could ask any questions, she felt the force that held her in place dissipate. Shaking, she very slowly got to her feet and stepped away from the queen without making a sound.

Innes gripped the sides of the altar as she uttered the last word of the chant. The water in the bowl grew still. She gingerly picked it up, tilted it against her lips and drank every drop, even licking the rim.

She will be in a trance for quite some time, searching your memories and the memories of your ancestors. I doubt she'll find much of interest. You seem rather mundane to me.

Ora watched as the bowl dropped from the queen's hand and clattered to the floor. She sank down to her knees beside the altar, clutching at her stomach and moaning in pain.

Oh, well, that isn't so mundane after all. Run, Eudora. You will find me in the hallway.

Ora fled past the countless bowls of crimson water as the agonized cries of the queen echoed in the stone chamber. It did not bode well if her blood killed the queen. Tyg would gut her for sure. She flung the doors open and stumbled into the hall. But as she looked up and down the passageway, there was no one in sight. Just the black cat from before.

"I knew you would be useful, but I admit, that was not the outcome I expected." The same voice that aided her in the chamber now rose up from the cat with a feline trill, neither masculine nor feminine. Her mouth gaped open in disbelief.

She was bound to a *cat*?

"No," she said. "No, no. You are *not*—"

"Oh, but I am." It flicked its tail. "Ora suits you better, truly. Eudora sounds too stuffy for a girl that chases innocent cats about the palace."

"How do you know my name?" she snapped.

The cat smiled, showing its pointed teeth. "I was in the conservatory, of course. Queen Innes is more careless than she realizes. An unbound name should not be thrown about so freely." Then, with an impatient sigh, it said, "Let's go, *Eudora*."

She followed, though her arms were firmly crossed. "You don't *have* to use my name, you know. I promised I'd help you."

The cat glanced over its shoulder as it led her farther down the hallway. "I can't be sure you'll want to do the thing I'm going to ask of you."

"Why not?"

"Well, it's a bit dangerous is all."

"That's never stopped me," she said.

"Come along, then." The cat took off running down the hall.

TWENTY-ONE

THEY did not make it far before they heard the rush of footsteps coming up the stairs. The cat stopped and pressed its paw against the nearest door. Ora looked down at it expectantly. "What are you waiting for? Missing finger or not, you're the one with hands," said the cat.

Feeling foolish, she twisted the doorknob and hurried inside with the cat at her heels. She shut the door gently before turning to see where they ended up. There was a large fireplace against the wall and three tall, south-facing windows. A long wooden table with plush dining chairs sat in the middle with a grand, crystal chandelier hanging over it. Paintings of regal-looking fae filled the walls.

"Ah, perfect. One of the dining rooms," said the cat. "There should be a secret door somewhere. The servants were once required to use it for discretion."

With little time to think or question the cat, Ora began feeling along the trim and pressing on the walls. She even tried tilting the larger paintings to see if there was a door behind them. When she had searched every corner of the room, she stood back with her hands on her hips and tried to think of what she might be missing.

"New plan," called the cat. It had its paws against one of the windows. "Are you scared of heights, by chance?"

She approached the window without answering and pressed her face against the glass. There was at least a ten-foot drop to the terrace below. She would have to jump.

"Do you know where the terrace leads?" she asked but was already opening the window. It swung out and summer air warmed her cheeks.

"It's better than staying here," said the cat. It balanced on the windowsill. "If you hesitate, I *will* use your name."

"I'm not scared of heights," she said.

With a laugh, the cat leapt from the window. It landed on all fours, as cats do, and then looked up at her, waiting. She felt especially grateful to be wearing slacks instead of one of those silly dresses as she stepped up onto the windowsill. Then, she jumped.

The hard landing made her stumble forward, and she caught herself with the edge of a lounge. "Not so bad," she said, though she had to catch her breath from the rush.

Inside was another room with countless paintings. Velvet lounges and chairs filled the space. A thin layer of dust sat atop the tables as if the room had not been used in a while. Ora hurried past it all and opened the door to peer into the hallway. She saw a guard walk into another room and a lady in sage green skirts ascending the stairs on the opposite side. Neither noticed her, but it still made her heart quicken.

The cat glided past her, and she heard its voice echo within her thoughts. *It's clear. Just keep your head down, and do not speak to anyone.*

Ora took a deep breath and stepped out into the hall. The black cat once again led the way, but this time it did not use her name to make her follow. Still, it kept glancing over its shoulder as if she might change her mind and run in the other direction at any moment.

When they went up a staircase rather than down, she began to question the cat's intentions. Why would it lead her right back to the queen? It had been the one to help her escape. Only to bind her to it … But when they emerged on the landing, she realized they had come to yet another corridor she had never seen before.

"Where are we going?" she whispered after glancing around to be sure no one noticed them.

If we are to escape this palace, I will be needing your help. As promised.

And what sort of help do you need? It felt strange to be carrying on a conversation silently, especially with a cat, but it was certainly more discreet.

I need my power back. I told you that was the last little bit of magic I had, said the cat.

"What business do you have here?"

The sudden voice made her wince. She hadn't heard any footsteps. It took immense effort not to look up. She saw the hem of a lavender-colored skirt when she peeked from the corner of her eye. Fumbling for an answer, she said, “I—I’m just—”

Tell her you’re to light the fire in the queen’s study.

The words rushed from Ora’s lips as soon as the cat delivered them to her. Her shoulders relaxed as the woman huffed and went on her way. *That was close,* thought Ora.

Come on then. The cat led her to the end of the hall and sat before a red door. *The queen’s study*, it said. *I cannot pass through the door. It’s enchanted. But I believe you can.*

You’re not certain? She glared down at the cat.

Well, why should she want to keep you out? I’ve seen plenty of servants in and out of there.

Ora tapped the crystal doorknob quickly, and when it did not burn her hand, she gave it a cautious twist. The door swung open without any incident, and she stepped inside. To avoid drawing attention, she shut the door behind her. The sun had nearly set, and it was difficult to make anything out other than piles of books, a large desk near the window, and a reading chair in one corner. *Now what?* she asked.

There should be an orb of some kind. All cloudy inside.

She walked about the study, running her hand along the spines of books. There were countless odds and ends tucked onto the shelves: ornate boxes, bronze instruments, jars of herbs, and figurines. Then, she rounded the desk and began opening the drawers. When she gave the bottom handle a tug, it did not budge.

Do you think she’d lock it away? she asked the cat.

Perhaps. Why do you ask?

There's a locked drawer in her desk.

Any sign of a key?

Not that I've seen. All the same, she began shuffling through the papers and quills strewn atop the desk. She doubted Innes would be leaving the key in such an obvious place. *Do you know a spell?*

I know many, but now isn't the time for such conversation.

I mean, do you know a spell to unlock the drawer?

The cat did not answer right away, but just as she began to grow impatient, it said, *Place your hand against the drawer and say to it, politely, pasij.*

She pressed her hand on the drawer as instructed and tried to focus, but she was in too much of a hurry. When she cast the spell and pulled the handle, it held tight. *It didn't work.*

With more confidence, Eudora, the cat said impatiently.

I told you, you don't have to use my name. She took a deep breath, pushing aside her annoyance, and tried again—not that she had a choice. "Pasij," she said, careful not to sound too harsh. This time, she heard a tiny, almost inaudible click.

It worked, she said.

You are *full of surprises. Is it there?*

She pulled the drawer open. A muted light burst through the crack. When her eyes fell on the orb, she could not smother a proud smile. *It's here,* she said. She lifted it into her hands, and its warmth spread through her palms. A whirl of black, shadow-like energy swirled inside of it, shifting and bumping against the glass. *What* is *this?*

An ash crystal. Now hurry up before anyone finds us here.

Ora closed the drawer and wasted no time in returning to the cat.

You've done it! It smiled up at her. *Now, smash it.*

What?

I said smash it, Eudora!

At the sound of her name, Ora's hand let the orb roll from her fingers and drop to the marble floor below. The crystal cracked but did not shatter.

The cat no longer bothered with their secret conversation. "Again, Eu—"

"I keep my promises, cat," she said, cutting it off before it could utter her name again. She picked the orb back up and, raising it above her head, threw it hard against the tile.

This time, the crystal exploded into a thousand tiny shards. Light and energy rushed out so violently that Ora covered her face. The hairs on her arms and neck stood on end, and she could hear the cat laughing joyfully. When the bright light faded, she slowly lowered her hands. The cat had vanished.

"Cat?" she said, dumbfounded.

Something soft tickled her arm, and she covered her mouth to muffle a cry of surprise. A formless, black shadow whirled around her, and then, it settled on the marble floor, taking shape until it resembled an enormous wolf.

"What do you think?" asked the wolf. It was nearly as tall as her, its gaze level with her own and bright green. "A much more useful form than a cat, yes?"

Instinct made Ora back away from the wolf, though a wolf frightened her less than Tyg. "Who are you? *What* are you?"

At this, the wolf grinned. "Well, now you're curious, aren't you? You may call me Eiko. I am one of the very last pukhas of the Cedar Clan."

"*The* Cedar Clan?"

"You've heard of us?"

"In a way." She frowned, thinking back to the Marigens' hushed conversations. Tyg had clearly hated the idea of dealing with the fae clan, but they had not mentioned pukhas. "What is a pukha?"

"We're the most talented shapeshifters. The fae have their glamour, but we can take whatever form we please." To prove its point, Eiko began to hop about, changing so swiftly she could hardly decide what it was at any given moment. A fox, a badger, a horse, a falcon, a raccoon, a goat, a bear—all with black hair and the same emerald eyes—danced about the corridor until it settled once again as a wolf before her.

"I will never be a cat again," it vowed.

That's when the terrified cry rang out, echoing down the hallway from the opposite end. "A pukha! A pukha! In the palace! Guards!" It was the lady in the lavender-colored dress.

Before Ora could speak a word, the wolf took off down the hall, barreling toward the frantic woman. She screamed at the top of her lungs and nearly tripped on her own skirts to get away. Just as Eiko reached her, she burst through one of the doors and slammed it shut in the pukha's face.

"Eu—" Eiko paused and smiled at the girl. "Ora, let's get going."

She nodded in approval when it called her Ora and ran toward the pukha, grinning ear-to-ear. It seemed as if she had made a powerful ally, one that other fae feared.

Eiko charged down the stairs so quickly that the guard who had been rushing to the lady's aid did not have time to draw his sword. The pukha only had to growl and gnash its teeth, and the guard flattened himself against the wall with his eyes squeezed shut. The two flew past him in an instant.

They returned to the room full of chairs and lounges. As the pukha ran onto the terrace, it shifted into a griffin with its black wings spread wide. Ora had never seen a griffin before, though her uncle had described them to her. It flicked its lion tail impatiently as she slowed to a walk and looked at it with wonder.

It snapped its beak. *Surely you did not expect us to simply walk out.*

Nervous with excitement more than fear, she climbed onto the griffin's back and clutched tightly to its black fur. "No," she said. "This is much better."

When the terrace dropped away, Ora let out a shout. The rush of wind filled her lungs and made her chest feel light. Eiko swooped downward at first before rising past the white stone of the palace. By then, she was hugging its neck and laughing. She was at last free from Tyg, free from the fae queen.

But as the palace faded behind them, so did her initial joy. Now, she had to figure out the pukha's intentions.

Where are we going? she asked, reaching out with her own thoughts this time.

Aren't you the natural telepath, replied Eiko, a note of amusement in its voice. *Then again, we are uniquely connected now. Aren't we, Eudora?*

She scowled. *You bound my name,* she said bitterly.

It was necessary.

The pukha did not answer her question about where but turned toward the darkening eastern horizon. Only a sliver of light remained in the day, and above them, stars began to glitter in the clear sky.

I must return to the Hy Borea, she insisted, pushing aside her other questions.

You are in luck, then. I too must return to the Hy Borea.

These words made her relax a little, and her expression softened. Whatever business the pukha had in the Hy Borea, she did not care. She would at last be able to find Hademar.

TWENTY-TWO

TREETOPS and steep cliffs passed below. At first, Ora leaned over the side of the pukha to peer down at the world. The terraced foothills, the waterfalls, and the sharp precipices were an endless source of awe. She did not dare blink for fear of missing some spectacular detail. As the night deepened, the landscape became inky black. Only then did the sky with its countless stars draw her eyes upward.

In Himil, she could name the constellations. Lupin would take her to one of the basalt cliff tops to point them out and tell their stories. The maiden, Isil, and her lover, Auphren, danced in opposite hemispheres, unable to cross paths. The twin wolves, Aliph and Ausin, nipped at the heels of the warrior, Gisalt. The spider queen, Miseris, and her triangle web of three red stars, which sat just above the southern horizon in the summer months. There were more, but now, she saw nothing familiar.

Eiko, she said. *The stars are different here.*

That's because you are looking from a different place altogether, but Rioc and Himil look out into the same infinity.

With those words, the pukha began to descend. She saw the glint of water beneath them. The glassy, dark surface extended toward the looming silhouettes of mountains in the distance. A cool, fishy scent filled her nose.

Eiko landed on the shore, graceful and quiet. She slid from its back, and it shifted into a wolf. They walked side by side to the tree line and found a clearing with soft grass and the gentle, pulsing lights of fireflies. Ora had never seen fireflies before, but the wonder faded. She was too tired and shaken.

"Will we be safe here?" she asked.

"There is nowhere safer than by a pukha's side." In the dark, Eiko's expression was difficult to make out, but it was easy to imagine a sharp-toothed grin.

They sat beside each other. Ora pulled her knees up under her chin. Despite being far from the palace, she still felt uneasy. The unexpected turn of events and the pukha did not seem quite real. Even if it had agreed to return her to the Hy Borea, she would not rest well until Hademar was safe.

Thinking of her brother, she asked, "Can you turn a pig back into a human?"

A warm, deep chuckle shook the pukha's sides. "Why? Are you in love with a pig? Have you tried kissing him?"

"Don't mock me. He's my brother," Ora said. A sharp, irritated pitch crept into her words. "Tyg turned him into a brush pig. I've been trying to find a way back to the Hy Borea so I can help him."

Eiko sat up and nudged her arm with its head. "The real trick will be finding him I'm afraid. He may very well have forgotten himself. That sort of magic twists the mind, Ora. It is not so simple. Even if I change him back, he may still be lost in other ways."

The pukha spoke with unyielding patience, but its words shot a pang through her chest. "But I have to help him! He can't live the rest of his life as a pig."

"Ora, you have helped me more than you realize, so I will help you find your brother."

She sat up straighter, unable to believe her ears. "You will?"

"Yes, now we should rest. We will have to go to the Basin, and there's a day of flying ahead of us."

"What's in the Basin?"

"A crossing, of course. More importantly, it will be unguarded."

"So, you know the words of passage?"

It paused but then said, "I have crossed the Ether many times."

"That doesn't sound promising," she said, recalling Renna's warnings. She had no intention of being shredded to pieces in the Ether. "No matter. I made a deal with a wayfarer."

"Ah," said Eiko. "I'm not sure how you managed that, but do not waste your passage. It may be useful one day. I will take us through the crossing."

"Isn't it dangerous if you don't know the words?"

"There is more than one type of magic, Ora. One does not have to be limited to words and spells."

Magic without spells. It was a topic she had not been able to find in any of Tyg's books. She leaned into the pukha's soft fur and asked, "What types of magic are there?"

"There are three," it began. "When you unlocked the drawer in the queen's study, you used corporeal magic. It draws from the energy that flows through your blood, and it's what the fae of Mysanhal rely on. It is summoned with words and spells."

"I'm not fae, though."

"In theory, there is nothing stopping humans from harnessing their inherent power. It just seems to be more difficult for you. Well, for most of you anyway."

This comforted Ora. She did not want to entertain the idea that she was anything other than a Nor. "What are the other magics?"

"Ah, yes. The second is elemental or alchemical, depending on who you ask. It can be harnessed through spellcraft and ritual as well. The sylv once had vast libraries dedicated to the art, but that is all lost now."

"And the third?" she asked.

"Ethereal magic. There is nothing more powerful. It is not drawn from your body or the elements around you but from the Ether. This magic requires no spellcraft and cannot be written. It resists explanation. Not that this has stopped some from trying."

Her heart thumped in her chest. "Can—can it be cast while you sleep?"

"That is an odd question."

"Is it?"

"Yes. Why do you ask it?"

Without looking, she felt the pukha's eyes fasten on her, and she grasped for the right words. "I dreamed of magic once," she said at last. "That's all."

"Dreams are not always truthful."

The words rang in her ears, and she thought of Hademar. He had said the same, but the cliff elk in her dream had been an omen. One that she did not understand until it was too late. And then, there was the orb of light she woke to after the falcon clawed through her chest. The soft, bluish light had been all too real.

Whatever the dreams meant, she did not want to explain the strange landscape she visited each night. It was a private world of her own, one that she did not wish to share. So, she shifted the conversation away from dreams and asked, "Can you really change into anything?"

"You don't think I can?"

"I mean, if you can be anything, what are you *really*? What do you look like if you aren't something else?"

"That's like asking for someone's true name."

"In that case, it seems fair that you would show me."

A glint of starlight caught in its wolf eyes, and though it did not shift, she saw a beast before her. A dangerous snarl licked at its next words. "You don't know what you're asking. Not really. Do not speak of it again, *Eudora*."

Ora wanted to press the subject, but she could not form the words. Her tongue felt like lead in her mouth each time she tried. Cheeks growing hot, she finally managed to blurt, "That's not fair."

Voice still feral, it said, "You would be wise to remember that you are bound to me. Not the other way around."

Her heart sank, and she grew silent. Even if the pukha had agreed to help her find Hademar, even if it had helped her escape the palace and Tyg, she was still name bound. She would have to answer to Eiko. No matter what.

Eiko's words made Ora even more restless, and sleep evaded her. Would the pukha let her go once they found Hademar? Would she be able to return to her family? And if not, how would she get away from the pukha? No matter how many scenarios she imagined, she could not think of a single way to escape the name binding. The pukha would always be able to call on her.

She sat with these thoughts until she could take it no longer. She crept away from the pukha and wandered down to the edge of the lake. There, she hugged her sides and began to cry.

"Ora." The animosity had faded from Eiko's voice, and she heard it pad softly toward her.

She turned her head away and wiped her cheek against her shoulder. "Go away."

"What I said …" The pukha sat down beside her and searched for the right words. "I didn't mean to sound so harsh. But you must understand—"

"Leave me be."

"Ora, you must listen to me. Your life will always be intertwined with the fae now. They will not let you return to your old life."

"No." She turned to the pukha, her grief overflowing. Her words came between gasps for breath. "*You* won't let me return. *You* bound my name. No other fae did that."

"Would you prefer to be Queen Innes's little pet? Or worse, *if* that ritual killed her, and it very well could have, you would be tortured and executed without any trial. Far from home, far from your family or anyone you love. Then, your brother would be a pig forever, probably to be hunted down as you fear."

The tears stopped, and she stared blankly into the wolf's eyes. She had not considered any of that.

Eiko went on. "If you wish to return home, I will let you. But you must do so with the knowledge that they will come for you, Ora, and I will not be there to protect you. Because the queen was right in one regard. You are *not* an ordinary human."

"What do you mean?"

It looked up at the night sky. For a long time, it did not answer. "I'm not sure yet, but your blood should not have poisoned the queen. Not even a fae's blood would have done that," it said.

A chill coursed through her. Were the queen's tormented screams truly because of one little drop of *her* blood?

TWENTY-THREE

TYG hated pukhas. They were unruly, unpredictable, untrustworthy. Why the queen agreed to let the Cedar Clan return to Mysanhal was beyond her. Their allegiance meant nothing. They were probably just sick of the cloudy skies and fog looming over the Hy Borea. They had no interest in the affairs of other fae, and they would never devote themselves to Cree. Like the sylv, they had their own god.

A dozen Yewolyns accompanied the Cedar Clan to ensure they settled where they were instructed. The seven shapeshifting fae followed with little trouble, but they remained silent as they journeyed through the Hy Borea. Tyg had no doubt that they were trading secrets and plans telepathically. Tyg hated telepaths too, even if the queen was rumored to be one. Not many fae mastered the skill, and only pukhas took to it naturally.

Out of the corner of her eye, she saw one of the pukhas shift into a black cliff elk. It pranced ahead of the Yewolyns with a mocking gaze. Tyg pushed back the hood of her elk cloak, anger flickering in her chest. "Enough," she snapped. "Do not think your impudence will go unpunished."

All seven pukhas burst into laughter.

"She's frightening, isn't she?"

"I don't think she could catch one of us."

"Not if we become shadow."

"Not if we become small."

"What about large?"

"A bear, perhaps?"

"Have you ever wrestled a bear, Magus?"

The pukhas' ever-changing forms and collective way of speaking gave Tyg a headache. She slid her glare to Callum, who had just lowered his hood as well. When she caught the spark of amusement in his eyes, she let out a furious huff. "Valor, surely you do not think their behavior acceptable?"

"I thought you had an appreciation for transformation," he said with a wink.

The other Yewolyns shifted nervously around them, not sure what to make of their Valor and Magus. Another fit of laughter trickled from the pukhas' lips, and they all became cliff elk.

Tyg's face reddened, but before she could speak, she caught sight of a shabby, gray bird perched on a branch above them. She had to look twice. "Callum, a sluagh," she said, nodding toward the grim messenger.

The company became tense all at once; even the pukhas stilled. Sluaghs only delivered bad news, and when not delivering messages, they only appeared to consume suffering and death. Though the Yewolyns employed at least a dozen, Tyg had never been able to shake the discomfort she felt around them.

The avian fae fluttered down to the ground and transformed into a woman with feathers poking up from her hair. She clenched her fists at her side, irritated to have the earth beneath her feet. "A message from Aygriel," she said.

The mention of the high priestess caused Tyg's expression to darken further. "What business does Aygriel have sending a sluagh to find us in the human realm?"

"I did not question the high priestess's motivations. I am only a messenger. You know that well, Magus," said the sluagh with a thin-lipped smile.

"Out with it then," said Callum.

Before the sluagh could speak, Tyg cut in. "Perhaps it would be best to receive this news privately."

Callum considered this, then nodded. He gave orders for the other Yewolyns to keep an eye on the pukhas. When Tyg tried to follow them away from the group, the sluagh glowered but did not protest. They walked until they were well out of earshot before the sluagh spoke.

"The queen has perished," she said and paused to let the two dren process these words.

"Perished?" Callum repeated.

Tyg's blood ran cold. It was not what she expected. Innes had been preparing to cross over to the spirit realm for years. It would have been a very different fate than death.

"Yes, she has died. A ritual gone wrong, as I understand."

"And why have you been sent to us now?" asked Tyg. The news could have waited until they returned to the fae realm. There had to be something more for Aygriel to justify sending a sluagh to find them in the Hy Borea.

The sluagh gave a sly, knowing smile. "Because, my dear Magus, it is *your* human girl who was last with her. And it is *your* human girl who has disappeared with—oh, but this hasn't been confirmed, this is just rumor now." She giggled at the shocked expressions both dren wore.

Tyg nearly shouted her next words. "With who?"

"It's quite unlikely, but a guest and one of the guards swear the girl was with a *pukha*." She punctuated the creature's name in delight as Callum's face went pale and Tyg's turned red with anger.

"It's impossible," said Callum, shaking his head. "The girl was—she was name bound. She couldn't have."

Tyg's rage felt as if it would burst from her chest. Between clenched teeth, she hissed, "She shouldn't have."

"A pukha?" her husband asked next, baffled by the whole story. "How did a pukha get inside the palace?"

The sluagh shrugged, pleased to have rattled them both. Without another word, she laughed and leapt into the air as a gray bird once again. While Callum contemplated what he had just heard,

Tyg stormed back toward the Cedar Clan. Surprised by her anger, he ran after her and caught hold of her arm.

"Where are you going? Shouldn't we discuss this?"

She jerked away from him. "I'm going to kill every last one of those pukhas," she roared.

Tyg saw a flash of black fur in the brush. She knew right away it was one of them. Exasperated, she drew her sword and chased after the cursed creature. There were only seven of them. How had no one noticed it slipping away? How much had it heard?

The pukha barreled out of the brush as a hare. Tyg's furious cry of "stop the pukha" followed, and all the Yewolyns looked up at once, throwing back their cloaks. The nearest tried to catch hold of the runaway pukha, but it slid through his hands like water.

"Eiko has returned!" the pukha cried to the rest of the wide-eyed clan as it ran past.

They looked between each other for only an instant. Then, in a swirl of black shadows, they dispersed and flew after the hare. Each took the same form, mimicking the first. The Yewolyns did not know what to make of it all, especially when their furious, red-faced Magus stormed past.

Just as Tyg lost track of one, she would see another and charge after it. This went on for several minutes until she at last gave up altogether and slashed at the brush with her sword.

"If you ever set foot in the fae realm again, I will skin you all alive!" she shouted, a preposterous threat against a pukha. It was almost impossible to catch one without snaring it in an enchanted trap. And so, her mad chase had been just that. *Mad.*

Knowing she had made a fool of herself, she did not return right away. She sheathed her sword and kicked at clumps of moss. Whenever she got her hands on that stupid, insolent, disrespectful brat of a human, she would do far worse than she promised. A gutted pig simply was not enough.

"Tyg!" It was Callum. He pushed aside a hemlock branch, having finally caught up to her. "The girl is not bound, is she?"

She froze, chest rising and falling with heavy breaths. A long silence passed between them as she searched for the right words.

"Did you know?" he asked.

"I knew," she said slowly. "But I thought I could keep her under control. To preserve your reputation, Callum. Bringing an unbound human into Mysanhal is—"

"You should have told me," he said, voice growing colder. "This could have been avoided."

But she would not so readily take the blame. "It's that stupid thachwing who Innes lets watch over the humans. She's useless. You know that!"

"No." Callum took a step toward her, gold eyes aflame. "It was foolish of you to think leaving an unbound human with Wynn was a good idea. I would never have allowed such a thing."

"Callum—"

He cut her off, unwilling to hear any excuses. "You lied to your queen, and you have lied to me. Because of you, she is dead. You have betrayed us."

"You would have been made a fool! You would have lost rank!" she shouted. "Is that what you wanted?"

"It could have been handled privately." He took another step toward her and grabbed her arm. She tried to pull away, but he only held on tighter. "I'm taking you back to the palace. We will let the court decide what to do with you."

Tyg met her husband's gaze with a look of shock. "You're joking."

"It is not the first time you have defied the will of our queen. When you went after the sylv, I stood up for you, but this … this I cannot overlook. It's treason, Tyg!" He rarely raised his voice, and she did not know how to respond. He even managed to pull her along for a few steps.

If Callum had known his wife better, he might have guessed that she would fight tooth and nail to avoid being held accountable before their peers as a traitor. She was too proud. Neither prison nor execution would be her fate. No. In Tyg's eyes, it was Callum who had betrayed her.

"If you do not stop this instant, Callum, I will no longer call you my husband." Her voice fell darkly. Like all Tyg's threats, this one was not empty.

"As if I could call you my wife after this," he said without slowing his pace.

"Have it your way." She drew her knife with her free hand.

The movement did not go unnoticed. Callum turned just in time to block the blow. He held her wrist at a distance. The blade shook in her grip. Incredulous that she should even consider drawing his blood, he searched her gaze for regret.

"I have always known you to be cruel, but I did not think you so entirely heartless," he said.

"I'm the heartless one?" she scoffed and struggled against his grip. "You want to have me tried as a traitor! I only sought to do what's best for you. For us."

She was hysterical. It was the first time Callum saw tears in her eyes, but he did not know what provoked them. Was it sorrow or the heat of her own anger? "Drop your knife, Tyg," he said, voice hollow.

"Very well." With a little smirk, she let go of the knife. Then, she pulled him into her knee. Breathless and taken off guard, he staggered back. As he did, she swooped down to retrieve her blade.

"Tyg!" he growled as he regained his balance. "Think of what you're doing."

"Oh. I am."

She lunged at him.

He blocked the knife and struck her face, bruising her cheek.

She took another jab at him. He blocked and hit her hard in the stomach.

Winded, she doubled over.

Callum twisted her arm behind her, peeled the knife from her grip, and pressed it against her throat. "Tyg, do the honorable thing and—"

Her fist slammed into his groin. The knife nicked her throat as he crumbled.

She drove her knee into his face, breaking his nose. The pain blinded him for an instant. Then, with a swift spell, she sent him sprawling into the mossy earth.

Tyg could have run from him. She could have left him there until he regained his senses and returned to the others. There are so many things she could have said. But her mind had become twisted with anger, with pride. He had betrayed her. He had chosen his side.

There was no hesitation in what she did next. She picked up the blade and drove it into his neck.

"I will decide my own fate," she growled and let him drop to the forest floor. Then, she lifted the hood of her elk cloak and fled.

TWENTY-FOUR

THE day after they escaped the palace, Eiko took Ora high into the mountains. They flew most of the day, only stopping in a tiny village long enough to find some food. Eiko chose the form of a sleek, black dog and played the part, its tail wagging and tongue lolling.

A thachwing woman took pity on them and shared a fresh loaf of bread and a wedge of sharp-tasting cheese. They sat on a stone bench outside, surrounded by a thriving vegetable garden. Their host did not ask how a human girl ended up in the middle of nowhere, and she did not seem to care. Instead, she spoke at length about her family and garden.

Ora pretended to listen and nodded along with the fae woman's long-winded stories of domesticity. Not caring if she appeared rude, she stood up as soon as she wiped the last crumbs from her mouth. "We are in a hurry," she said. "Thank you for the food."

As if seeing the girl for the first time, the thachwing swept an inquisitive—or was it a suspicious—gaze over Ora. Her eyes lingered on the missing pinky. "A hurry? What for?"

The first tendrils of apprehension snaked their way into Ora's gut. She stepped back from the fae. "We have a long way to go is all," she said.

"Who did you say you were?"

"No one." Before she could be asked any more questions, she hurried toward the garden gate. The pukha rushed after her.

They walked at least a mile before slowing their pace. The trees and the landscape had long since hidden the small village from view. Still, Ora could not shake the flutter of anxiety in her chest. She strained her ears, trying to listen for the telltale snap of twigs or shifting of rocks beneath boots.

As if it sensed her worry, the pukha sniffed the air and then said, "No one followed us."

She willed her shoulders to relax but could not convince herself they were safe, not truly. "I don't like the way she looked at me," she said and sank down onto a rock. "How far are we from Tirnan?"

"Far enough that you needn't worry. Your missing pinky might be problematic, though," it mused. "A four-fingered hand is difficult to forget."

Irritated, Ora curled her hands into fists. "It won't matter. We'll be in Himil by the end of the day."

Eiko gave a small nod but said nothing more. It didn't need to. She could not forget its warning. Despite this, she tried to convince herself the fae would not bother with her once she returned, and if they did, they would be met with silver.

They drank water from an icy mountain spring before taking to the sky once again. Ora spent the rest of their journey peering over the pukha's side at the rocky cliffs and pine forests, watching the landscape change the farther north they went. Eventually, the mountains sloped down into an enormous caldera with rolling emerald grasses. Beyond that, were barren flatlands that stretched as far as she could see.

Is that the Basin? Ora asked, eager to at last return home.

Yes, said Eiko, *we've made it.*

Like an island, an odd hill sloped up from the middle of the Basin with a stand of pines growing on it. It made Ora think of a tortoise shell. The pukha landed at the bottom of the hill, and she slid off its back. Aside from the brush of wind in the trees, there were no other sounds.

The crossing is at the top of the hill. The pukha shifted into its wolf form as it spoke.

The hill looked taller than it appeared from above. They walked through the quiet trees until they thinned and gave way to a slab of dark granite. The crossing appeared as if it had not been disturbed in ages. Moss grew over the glyph-like carvings, and pine cones and twigs were strewn across it.

She followed the wolf to the center of the circle. A powerful, old magic rose from the stone. She could feel it in her bones as she walked across it, like the lowest of vibrations when a distant horse approached, or when faraway thunder shook her family's home. It both thrilled and terrified her.

"Breathe in and close your eyes," said the pukha.

"Must I close my eyes?"

"No, but it is advised."

"Fine," she said and did as told.

Eiko said nothing. She opened one eye, puzzled by its silence, but then, the ground dropped away so violently, she nearly lost her footing. The shock of movement made her eyes fly open. The world shifted and spun for only a moment, but it was enough to leave her doubled over and retching when it stood still again. A high-pitched ring flooded her ears.

"My head won't stop spinning," she groaned.

It sat beside her and said, "Be patient. Breathe."

Ora pressed her head against the cool stone, unable to move for several long minutes. At least they had crossed the Ether in one piece.

As the ringing in her ears faded, she heard the crash of waves in the distance. She breathed in deeply, the familiar scent of the Hy Borea nearly bringing tears to her eyes. Careful not to move too fast, she sat up and looked into the branches of ancient spruce, hemlock, and fir. Moss hung from the branches like wiry green beards. Below, the ferns and brush grew thick.

She wobbled to her feet and flung her arms around the pukha. "Thank you," she said, burying her face against its neck.

"You're most welcome, Ora."

But as she pulled away, her smile faded. Nearly a dozen cliff elk stood on the other side of the stone circle, motionless and almost invisible in the brush. "Eiko," she whispered. "There are Yewolyns."

With a snarl, the giant wolf turned. The Yewolyns stepped from the brush and shed their cloaks. Some drew swords, and others raised their hands, ready to cast spells. The pukha clearly unsettled them, but they had strength in numbers. Cyn was among them. He hung back from the rest, holding up a dren with a slumped over head and bloodied cloak.

"Let us pass, and I will not kill all of you," said the pukha, its voice curling and feral.

Only Cyn looked past Eiko; his eyes lit up in recognition. "It's her," he said. "The Marigens' human."

"Are you certain?" asked another.

"I am."

Then, it struck Ora. The fallen Yewolyn was Callum. She stepped back with a small gasp and looked between them all. If that was Callum, where was Tyg?

"Give us the girl," Cyn said. "You have no right bringing her here."

The pukha laughed darkly, making even Ora shiver. "How very wrong you are," it said.

In a blur of shifting black fur, teeth, and claws, Eiko attacked the Yewolyns. The first fell with a broken neck, the next doubled over with a gash in her stomach, and by the third, the Yewolyns had scattered. They could not make out the pukha in its ever-changing forms.

One of the swordsmen ran toward Ora in the chaos. Still nauseated from the crossing, she bolted clumsily into the brush and wove her way through the old growth as fast as she could. A slick tree root made her lose her footing, and she fell forward. The earth dug into her palms as she caught herself. Panting, she flipped over just as the dren caught up.

"Eiko!" she shouted.

Before the dren could grab hold of her, something thudded against his head. He fell, the back of his skull bloodied.

And there stood Tyg.

She looked half-mad. She was covered in blood, and hair stuck to her face and neck. Her cheek was purple and swollen. But it was her eyes that frightened Ora most of all. Rage burned in her gaze, consuming all else.

Ora leapt to her feet and staggered back. "Eiko!" she screamed again.

Its voice filled her mind. *I'm coming. Where are you?*

She did not have time to answer. Tyg bore down upon her and slammed her hard against the trunk of a tree. "I should kill you for what you've done," she said and wrapped her hand around Ora's throat. "But that's not good enough for you. No. I will take you back to Mysanhal so that you'll live for hundreds of years, and I will personally see to it that you suffer every single day."

Ora's desperate hands wrapped around Tyg's wrist as she struggled to breathe. The dren's eyes fell on her mutilated hand.

"Perhaps I should start by taking your whole hand?" she said with a predator's smile, but when her eyes rose to Ora's face, she took pause.

The girl's eyes had always been dark, almost black orbs, but now they were changing. Silver light swirled in them, and the delicate veins in her face emitted a soft glow.

"What are you doing?" Tyg's voice rose in a high-pitched panic.

All sense of place and time dissolved. Ora wondered if she might be dying, but then, a white-hot flame spread through her hands and up her arms, as if it coursed through her very blood. She met Tyg's gaze and watched with cold indifference as pain and shock twisted through the dren's features.

At last, Tyg relinquished her grip with a furious roar and staggered back. Ora stepped away from the tree. Her silver eyes glittered. She did not know what compelled her, what power flowed through her veins, but when she lifted her hand, a force burst from her fingertips and struck Tyg like a boulder. She heard the snap of bones and branches as the brush swallowed the Yewolyn. Then, came a black rush of shadow, and she felt herself slump into the pukha's soft fur.

*****

The boughs of evergreens and dappled sunlight swam above Ora. Her time in the fae realm felt like a dream, the stuff of her uncle's stories rather than reality. She smiled to herself, happy to be awake at last and breathed in deeply. But what was she doing sleeping on a bed of moss?

"Ah, you're awake." It was Eiko, its voice warm and relieved.

The mist of sleep dropped away, and she closed her eyes again. "I'd rather not be," she said with a groan. It came back to her then, and she gingerly touched her throat. Tyg had almost killed her. Again. She remembered slipping from consciousness only to come to with a lightning bolt of vigor.

Ora sat up and looked at the pukha. Her brow wrinkled with confusion. "What happened?"

It had a wolfish smile. "It seems as though you have a bit more magic in you than I thought."

"But—"

The pukha went on as if she had not spoken. "And by a bit of magic, I mean you seem to be quite powerful, Ora. You were glowing when I found you. Don't you remember?"

"Not—exactly?" she said. The details were foggy, but she did remember the dren being flung away from her. But that couldn't have had anything to do with her, could it?

"I should think anyone would remember glowing like that."

"Glowing?"

"Yes," it said. "There is strong magic in your veins, Ora. And it would be wise to accept it now."

"Eiko …" But Ora did not know what to say. She had not summoned it or meant to use it at all.

"Magic, without control, can be quite dangerous," Eiko said. "You are lucky it did not harm you."

She shook her head. "I'll worry about that later. I have to find Hademar."

"I thought you might say that, which is why I very much want you to meet the Cedar Clan."

"The Cedar Clan?" She felt ridiculous repeating the pukha's words, but her mind was too clouded to make sense of anything. She wished it would be quiet.

"If anyone has seen an odd brush pig running about, it would be one of them."

She rubbed her palms against her eyes, trying to focus. "I—I need a minute."

It laughed. "Unfortunately, they're already here. Look up."

Ora tilted her head back to peer into the hemlock. Peeking down from its thick branches were seven silky, black pine martens. The weasel-like creatures looked between each other, having their secret conversation, and then climbed down, their little claws scraping at the bark. Once on the ground, they each shifted into a wolf, though they changed less fluidly than Eiko. Their limbs took a little longer to change, and their forms settled less elegantly.

One of the shadowy wolves stepped toward her and sniffed her wild, curly hair. Its wet nose swept past her ear, and she jerked away. "Sorry," she said when it gave her an incredulous look. "Tickled a bit is all."

"You are Eiko's human?" it asked, dark eyes narrowing. None of them had the bright splash of green in their gaze. "It has bound you to it?"

Name binding is a cruel, unthinkable thing to a pukha, Eiko explained, its words sliding into her thoughts. *It does not sit well with them.*

They're right.

It kept you from an unfortunate end.

Whether or not Eiko's words held truth, she dropped the subject and swept her gaze between the wolves. "Well, yes. In a way. But … it seems we have become good friends."

"Indeed," said Eiko and looked pleased to hear her say so.

The wolves looked between each other approvingly.

They introduced themselves, but she could not distinguish one from the other. As she tried to recall their names, Eiko asked if they had seen an odd brush pig that might not know it was a brush pig, not entirely.

"There has been one."

"He lives in a secret place."

"We saw him contemplating his reflection in a spring."

"It's not really a secret place."

"But it's not so easy to find."

"We can show you where."

"It does not move from that spot."

At last Eiko interjected, cutting the swirl of speech to an end. "Please, take us there," it said. "Ora, are you ready?"

She nodded.

The seven pukhas began to lead the way, their movements like black water beneath the brush, taking no form but the shadows. Ora walked alongside Eiko, who remained as a wolf, and grew more and more anxious as she went. What if Hademar had already forgotten himself? How long had it taken her to escape? Was it too late?

They walked for the better part of the afternoon before they came to a hill cluttered with enormous boulders. Ora ran her hand along the dark, damp stone faces and looked to the pukhas, who stood around her as pine martens once again.

"The brush pig is in there."

"We will not go there."

"I would."

"Don't lie. You won't go without us."

"Eiko, take the girl. We will not go."

"It stares into a spring night and day."

"We will wait here."

The Cedar Clan pukhas climbed a nearby tree and peered down from the branches. Eiko took a step toward an opening in the stones. Though the Cedar Clan's words made her heart race, she followed Eiko into the wind-carved rocks. They wound through open passageways, at times narrow and at times opening up to small stands of alders.

The farther they went into the labyrinth of rocks, the more she became aware of how the air changed and the ground beneath her seemed to emanate a secret power. The hairs on her neck prickled.

"Why wouldn't they come?" she asked.

"Old magic is often best left alone. A pig staring at its own reflection is not a good omen to them."

They went deeper into the stones until they at last came across a clear, babbling spring. There stood a brush pig staring into the water.

"Look," said Ora.

They crept up behind the pig, not wanting to frighten it, but it did not budge even when they were close enough to touch its spotted hide. They peered over the pig's shoulder. There, reflected in the clear water, was the face of a man.

Ora gasped. "Hademar."

But the sound of his name did not rouse him. He continued to stare into the water, unmoving and silent. She reached out one shaking hand and rested it against his side.

"What is it?" Eiko asked as her expression grew somber.

"He's cold," she said.

The pukha studied the spring, and when Ora looked up from her brother, she glimpsed another face in the water as well—a sharp, fae-like face with dark skin and emerald eyes. Long, black hair spilled over its shoulders, and she could not tell whether it was a man or a woman. Right away, she knew she had seen Eiko's true form. Remembering what it said, she did not let her gaze linger, but she could not stop herself from turning a bright shade of red.

Pushing aside all other thoughts, she tried to pull her brother's head away from the spring. But Eiko stopped her as it backed away from the edge of the water. "Don't move him. There is something strange about this spring."

"I can't just leave him here!"

"You said he is cold?"

"Yes."

"Ora, his spirit has left his body."

"What?"

"It is a nymph's spring. If you gaze too long, your spirit becomes ensnared in her waters. If you move him now, his spirit will be severed from his body forever."

She looked between the pig and the spring. The reflection of her brother made her heart ache. "How do I help him, Eiko?"

The pukha hesitated to answer. "You must find the nymph and kill her. But, Ora, it is not so simple. This spring is only one manifestation of the nymph. It's fed by underground streams. You will have to find the fountain from which all her waters flow."

"How?"

"We will need a seeing stone."

TWENTY-FIVE

RAIN. She could hear rain. For a brief, careless moment, Tyg thought she lay in her own bed. Then, the pain rippled through her. Every fiber of her body felt as if it had been set on fire. Head throbbing, she flung off the covers and tried to sit up. Her body failed her. She crumbled back into the sheets, recalling the sting of magic that had crawled up her arms, spread through her chest, and sent her flying into the ferns. The girl's eyes had flashed silver.

But it couldn't have been Ora. Had the pukha attacked her? She could hardly remember. There had been a streak of black fur. No, that happened after the girl—she groaned and sat up again, this time more slowly. The room she lay in was dark, so she lifted her hand and uttered the spell for light.

An orb flickered to life above her palm. Its bluish glow filled the small room for only a breath before fading in a wisp no brighter than the first light of dawn. Something was wrong. Tyg stretched her fingers, and a pulsing, twitching pain coursed through her hand. Crying out, she caught hold of her afflicted hand and tried to steady the shaking.

The door swung open and lamplight flooded the room with its cool glow. Tyg looked up to see a pallid thachwing in a plain, gray healer's smock holding up a lamp in one hand. He had glossy, black wings and smelled of dried herbs.

She had been taken to the healing wards. This brought her some comfort. They did not know the truth about Callum, or she would have woken in a prison cell.

"You're awake, Magus Marigen," he said. "We were beginning to worry. Nothing we did could rouse you."

"What do you mean *nothing*?" Tyg asked as she slid her shaking hands beneath the covers.

"There's no question that you suffered a curse, but none of the usual reversals worked. We even called on Elder Eslyn," the healer said. "But she could not wake you either."

"Elder Eslyn?" she echoed. The master of curses and hexes only ventured down from her mountain home with the promise of novelty. "Well, whatever it was, I'm awake now."

"Yes, I can see that," he said, setting the lamp on the table beside her bed. "Do you feel any lingering effects?"

"Just a bit sore," she lied.

"We have elixirs that may help."

"Keep your elixirs. All Yewolyns are taught to welcome pain."

"Taught to, yes," he said as if he had slipped such remedies to Yewolyns many times before. With a small smirk, he dipped out of the room and left the lamp behind.

Irritated by the healer's snide response, she swung her legs over the side of the bed and pressed her feet against the cold stone. She refused to stay in the ward any longer than she had to. She found her elk cloak folded atop a chest at the end of the bed, but her shoes were nowhere to be found.

"Fine," she grumbled, limping toward the door. "Bare feet it is."

Tyg's body protested against each movement, but she ignored the searing pain. None of the healers stopped her as she left the ward and stepped into the rain. There was a chill in the air. She wrapped the elk cloak tighter around her shoulders and descended the steps.

By the time she reached her home, the rain had soaked through the cloak and gown. She fought back the cold biting at her skin and drifted across the parlor to stack logs in the fireplace. With a deep breath, she held her palm over the wood and cast the spell for flames.

A few sparks hopped across the logs. The scent of smoke filled her nose. Tyg gritted her teeth and cast the spell again. Pain sliced through her hand. Furious, she coiled back from the hearth.

"Only lingering effects," she told herself. "It will pass."

She made tinder from a crumpled piece of paper and cast the same spell, this time ignoring the pain. A spark caught, and she nursed it with her breath until the flames began to grow.

Before the fire, she shed her wet clothes. It was only as she let the silk gown fall from her hand that she noticed the scarring. Thin tendrils snaked up her arms and spread across her chest. It was unlike anything she had seen before.

"What in Cree's name?" She sank down onto the carpet before the hearth. For the first time, she wondered if Innes had been right. Perhaps Callum had brought a new creature among the fae.

*****

"Tyg, wake up." Cyn's urgent voice roused her. He touched her shoulder just as her eyes opened. "You're freezing."

Confused, she pushed his hand away and sat up. She had fallen asleep on the floor, still naked. A chill crawled up her spine despite the warm sunlight that streamed in from the south-facing window beside the bookshelves. Had she slept through the morning?

Cyn lifted up her elk cloak, which she had left to dry by the fire, and draped it over her shoulders. "What are you doing on the floor?"

She pulled the cloak tightly around her. "I fell asleep," she said as he sat down beside her. She smelled ale on his breath. "Are you drunk?"

"I had a drink with Alish is all," he said.

"How did you get in?"

"The door was open."

She looked past him with wide eyes. Had she truly forgotten to close the door behind her? She shook her head. The previous night felt distant. "You must think me foolish."

"No," he said. "You suffered a terrible loss."

At first, she did not know what to make of his words. Did he truly not suspect her? She grasped for a lie, but he spoke before she had to fill the silence.

"Tyg, those scars—what attacked you?"

She met his gaze, and the girl's name came readily to her lips, though she still hardly believed it to be true. "Ora."

Cyn ran a hand through his hair and nodded. "She was at the crossing with a pukha. It injured most of our Yewolyns, killed two. And you, you just barely survived."

This news struck her like a stone. One pukha had taken down nearly a dozen Yewolyns. It sounded impossible. "What happened to the girl?" she asked.

"She's gone, along with the pukha."

They stood but did not speak for some time. A breeze swept into the room and rustled the corner of a map spread across the table. With it came the cool scent of mountain forests and snowy peaks. Tyg gazed out the door and felt out of place within the walls of her own home. The world without her husband, the great Valor Marigen, was a new one.

"I will leave you be," Cyn said, turning toward the door.

"Have Callum's rites been performed?" she asked as he reached the threshold.

He nodded but did not face her as he answered. "We didn't know if you would wake."

"I will go to the temple then."

After Cyn left, she raised her palm and attempted the spell for light once again. She only managed a brief flash. With a cry of dismay, she snatched up a book and tossed it across the room. It hit the wall with a loud thud.

If she went to the temple, it would not be to perform rites for her husband. After all, he had died by her hand. Her prayers would mean nothing. No. She would go to offer her blood and ask Cree for guidance. All curses had a cure. She only needed a little help to find it.

Tyg waited until nightfall to go to the temple. She did not want eyes following her as she limped along the cobbled streets with the help of a staff. It took nearly an hour to reach the temple steps. Few fae visited the temple so late, and she walked between the columns alone.

High Priestess Aygriel was ceremoniously tending to the hundreds of candles that filled the main hall. She looked up as Tyg approached her, the wooden staff clicking against the marble floors. "I'm surprised to see you here," she said. "You look to be in poor condition."

Without slowing her uneasy gait, Tyg said, "I've come to perform rites for Callum." She drove her staff even harder against the marble as she passed the high priestess.

When Tyg came to the altar, she set the staff aside and got to her knees.

A drop of blood would not suffice. This time, she wanted to gain the god's attention. She gritted her teeth and slit her wrist with the ceremonial knife, a thin golden blade. She let the blood flow into the offering bowl. "Cree," she said, looking up at his marble statue. "My blood and—" She swallowed hard. "The magic that flows through it is yours. Please, I beg of you, guide me in this troublesome time."

The god, at first, did not respond. Not even the faintest wind rose up to lick the candle flames. But then, she felt a sensation like cold water wash over her. All at once, the candles went out. The smell of smoke filled her nose. She breathed deeply, and her eyes closed. Cree had heard her.

When her eyes opened, she found herself before the oracle. Her skin was the color of sage leaves and eyes the color of bright, green moss. Her white hair was braided and hung down to her waist. The gown she wore was made of such a delicate fabric that her figure showed through as a faint shadow. She ran a finger along the rim of the offering bowl and regarded Tyg without an ounce of emotion. She rarely made an appearance, and she spoke even less. Rumor had it that she spent months in prayer without sleeping or eating.

Tyg bowed her head. "Basirah, it's an honor."

"Well met, Tyg Marigen." The oracle had a voice that held all the clarity of a perfectly tuned bell, but she spoke as if from a distance, her voice coming from a ghostly place. "You have asked for guidance."

"I have—I …" But she could not bring herself to say it, not even before the oracle. It filled her with shame to be without magic.

"Be still. Your blessings have only begun to manifest."

"Blessings?" Tyg could not hide the resentment in her voice.

The oracle stepped around the altar, took Tyg's chin into her hand and pressed her other hand against the dren's eyes. "Look."

The vision filled Tyg's mind at once. She saw a wreath of jimsonweed that wrapped around an ornate golden crown. She knew right away that she would take the throne. This knowledge spread through her veins like wildfire. Cree surely recognized that she would make a fierce queen, one who would ensure his will was carried out no matter the cost.

But then, the crown faded, leaving behind another image that wrapped itself like a dark shadow around her heart. It was a knife held by a hand with only four fingers.

Basirah withdrew. Though her face remained unreadable, Tyg sensed the slightest hint of apprehension in the oracle's voice. "Few plants carry such dark warnings as jimsonweed, with its foul-smelling trumpets and thorns. But that is not what troubles you, is it?"

Eyes alight with anger, Tyg rose to her feet. "That is none of your concern."

"Perhaps not, but it would be wise of you to heed the warning." Basirah gently took hold of Tyg's arm and drew her fingers over the bleeding cut on her wrist, suturing the skin with a powerful spell.

The dren's resentful gaze did not falter as she pulled her wrist away and snatched up her staff. "It's only a vision. It means nothing," she said.

Basirah donned the faintest of smiles. "The hand belongs to that human girl of yours, does it not?"

"Yes. How did you know?"

"Cree sends me many visions." Basirah drifted toward her. "Magic is returning to Himil, the human realm, for the first time since their fall. Innes has weakened Mysanhal with her foolishness, and now, Cree has chosen you for your strength. His warning is meant to guide you, not threaten you."

Tyg leaned heavily on her walking stick as she took in Basirah's words. "And what does Ora have to do with it?"

"She is the harbinger of a new era and a threat to Mysanhal."

The oracle's words did not move Tyg. She frowned. "I did not come here for a fanciful vision, Basirah. I have been cursed and—"

The oracle cut her off. "It is not a curse that afflicts you. It is something else. A new sort of magic."

Tyg's heart began to beat wildly in her chest. "The girl, she—she did this."

"And she must be stopped." Though Basirah's voice remained soft, her words were resolute. "You will possess greater power than you did before. Cree will reveal your path when the time is right."

TWENTY-SIX

EIKO described a seeing stone as nothing more than a rock with a hole in the center. What sounded like a simple search turned into days of crouching over the earth and pushing aside rocks. Each night, Ora returned to the stone forest to be sure Hademar still stood by the spring. She feared he might be killed by a mountain lion. But perhaps even the mountain lions shied from the strange nymph waters. Whenever she drew near, she felt an inexplicable urge to run away.

The Cedar Clan helped in their search, but they often became distracted, wrestling each other in the brush and taking naps in the sun. Though they were pukhas, they seemed nothing like Eiko, whose air of composure and wit had grown on Ora over the past week.

They ate rabbits, mushrooms, and berries. Eiko pointed out signs of small, elemental beings, who were so entangled with the forest that they were closer to beasts than fae. She even saw a few. There were gnomes who cultivated mushrooms, tiny thachwing-like fae who wore pinecone caps, and rock sprites who, if disturbed, would bite at her fingers.

"Why haven't I seen them before?" she asked, thinking of her childhood filled with wanderings through the Hy Borea.

"They are usually very secretive," said the pukha. "Most curious."

Ora had an endless number of questions. At times, Eiko would grow tired of answering and pretend to take a nap while she continued to search for a seeing stone.

She felt sure she had overturned every rock and looked beneath every tree root and crouched over the shore of every creek in the forest. At last, she reached down one afternoon to pick up a smooth, gray stone. When she held it up, she saw a perfectly round hole carved into the middle of it.

"I found one!" she shouted in triumph.

Eiko's shadow form glided toward her and settled as a wolf. It sniffed at the smooth gray stone cradled in her palm and said, "Good. Now, we must return to the spring."

They had wandered far that day, and by the time they returned to the stone forest, daylight was fading. Eiko kept its distance from the spring, and Ora wondered if it knew she had glanced its true form. She stood next to the pig and studied Hademar's face. Her brother did not seem to notice her. His eyes looked distant, emotionless. It pained her to see him in such a state.

"Hold the seeing stone in the water and ask it to show you the water's source," said the pukha.

Ora knelt beside the spring, and, careful not to let her eyes fall on her own reflection, she held the seeing stone beneath the surface. "Show me the water's source," she whispered.

"With more confidence, Ora."

She scowled over her shoulder at Eiko but then raised her voice. "Show me the water's source!" But nothing happened. At least, nothing she noticed. She stood up after a few agonizing, long moments and threw up her hands in frustration. "Why isn't it doing anything?"

The pukha laughed. "Look *through* the stone."

Ora peered through the hole in the center and turned until she saw it. Pale, green light spread from the spring, flowing beneath the earth in spectacular underground streams. She lowered the seeing stone.

"Well?" said the pukha.

"It's this way," she said, pointing to the east.

They asked the Cedar Clan to watch over Hademar, and with the seeing stone against her eye, Ora led them through the Hy Borea. Sometimes the trail of light was but a trickle, and other times it expanded beneath their feet, revealing vast underground rivers and lakes. But she did not care how long or how far they walked. She did not want to wait any longer to get her brother back. She would free Hademar that night.

At last, they heard a waterfall. When Ora looked ahead, she saw many streams of light converging beneath the trees from all directions. "I think we're close," she whispered.

"Ora, I cannot go any farther," said Eiko.

She lowered the stone and whirled around to face the pukha. "What do you mean? You're not going with me?"

"If she sees a pukha with you, she will turn to water and be impossible to catch. You must go alone."

"But I don't know what to do, Eiko. How do I—how do I kill a nymph? I've never even seen one before. What if—"

The pukha cut her off gently. "You must find her heart and smash it."

"Her heart?" Ora felt as if her own heart might leap from her chest.

"Yes. She will have hidden it, I'm sure. But Ora, remember this: she will try to trick you. Do not trust a word she says. Do not trust anything you see. The only power she holds is illusion. She cannot harm you any other way. Do you understand?"

The pukha had not mentioned any of this before. "How will I know I've found her heart if I can't trust anything I see?"

"Because wherever it is, she will do anything to keep you from it."

She gripped the seeing stone tighter in her hand. "What if I don't come back?"

Eiko stepped toward her. "Do anything it takes to return to me. Do not believe your eyes or your ears. Find the heart and destroy it. *Eudora,* I command it."

She smiled, and for the first time since she was stolen away to the fae realm, she felt strength as her name was spoken. "Thank you, Eiko," she said.

Ora then turned and raised the stone to her eye once again. She followed the trail of light down a steep hillside that sloped to a pool of water beneath a thunderous waterfall. As she came to the shore, she tucked the stone in her pocket and squinted into the dark.

"What a pretty girl."

She felt the voice like a whisper against her ear.

"You have a seeing stone. You were looking for me."

"Yes," said Ora. She began to walk along the shore, looking for anything that might be a heart or a nymph.

Then, the water began to ripple, and a pale-skinned fae woman rose from the pool. She was very beautiful, with finely carved features and eyes that seemed to glow with the smallest amount of moonlight. Even though she was wet, her long dark hair curled over her shoulders and breasts in an elegant way, swirling into the water around her hips. "Come closer." She held her hand out. "I will take you to your brother."

At this, Ora stopped and met the nymph's gaze. "Let him go, and I will leave you be."

The nymph moved toward her but could go no farther than the edge of the water from which her very essence flowed. "Come with me. Your brother is waiting for you," she said. "Don't you want to see him?"

Though part of Ora wanted to believe her words, she could not bring herself to go with the nymph. But what if she had to go into the water to find the heart?

The nymph reached out and stroked her cheek with a clammy hand. "What is your name?"

Of course, Ora realized, tricking the nymph would be simple. "I'm Ora," she said.

"*Ora*." The nymph's voice dripped with magic. She took hold of Ora's hand and led her into the pool. "Would you like to see your brother?"

"Please," she said, pretending to be enthralled by the fae's words.

The nymph led her deeper into the pool until the frigid water rose up around the girl's waist. The nymph tucked a few strands of Ora's wild hair behind her ear. "Such a pretty human girl," she said. "Come stay with me, *Ora*. Come stay with me and your brother."

Then, the fae drew her close and sank beneath the surface of the water. Ora felt the pull of the nymph's magic, a dark, silent warmth beneath the surface. But she could not be tempted. She wriggled free of the nymph's embrace.

Ora dove to the bottom of the pool and drew the seeing stone from her pocket. She peered through it, hoping it might help her figure out where the nymph's heart was hidden. When she saw nothing of interest, she turned to swim back up to the surface for air, but a hand wrapped around her ankle and pulled her toward the bottom.

"You lied to me!" She heard the nymph's voice rumble in the water.

Ora twisted around to see eyes glinting in the dark water. She knew she would run out of air soon. She could feel the mounting desperation to breathe. As hard as she could manage, she slammed her free foot into the nymph's face. The hand fell from her ankle, and she broke the surface just as her lungs felt like they might burst for air.

She turned to the waterfall next and raised the seeing stone to her eyes once again. "Show me the nymph's—"

Before she could finish her sentence, the nymph caught hold of her hair and pulled her back beneath the water. She struggled violently against the nymph, and the seeing stone dropped from her hand. As she reached for it, the nymph dragged her to the bottom of the dark pool.

Ora sensed she would run out of air soon. She thrashed at the nymph, tearing at her hands and clawing at her face. Again, she managed to break away, and this time, she swam toward the waterfall.

Gasping and choking, she pulled herself through the pounding curtain of water and felt her way along the slick stones behind the falls. She heard the nymph's voice behind her. "You should not be here!"

"Let my brother go!" she shouted back, nearly slipping on the rocks as she turned to face the nymph, but she was nowhere to be seen. In the dim, silvery glow of moonlight, Ora instead saw a figure sitting on the rocks with its knees held close to its chest. She hesitated at first to approach, but then it looked up and met her eyes. Hademar.

Eiko's words pressed into her mind. *Do not believe your eyes or your ears.*

She stopped herself from running to her brother, though she desperately wanted to. "You're not real," she said.

But then he spoke to her. "How can you say that? I am your brother."

"You're not!" she shouted and turned away, tears in her eyes.

"Please, Ora. Don't leave me. I need your help."

He went on, and she covered her ears. She searched the outcrop beneath the waterfall, bent and feeling her way through the shadows. Then, her foot bumped against a small wooden box. She picked it up carefully and began to lift the lid.

"Don't open that," Hademar snarled.

Ora paid him no mind and looked inside the box to find an assortment of trinkets, from pocket watches to hairpins. Puzzled, she began to dig through the box. There were arrowheads, wedding bands, a rusty cup, and an old tinderbox. No heart to be found. She nearly set it back down but then thought better. Perhaps the box was not what it seemed.

She closed her eyes and reached into the box again. She let her fingers brush over each object.

"What are you doing?" her brother asked.

Ignoring him, she continued until a spark of cool energy ran up through her arm. She opened her eyes and lifted out a heavy, round stone. It fit perfectly in the palm of her hand.

"Put it back!" the nymph roared, shedding her brother's appearance and lunging up over the rocks. Her hand barely brushed Ora's arm.

The girl raised it above her head, ready to smash it against the rocks. "Not unless you give me back my brother!"

"I will, I will, I will! Just put it back! You will find him by the spring! Right where I left him. I promise. Just please, please put it back."

Had Eiko not used Ora's true name, she might have believed the nymph and spared her heart. She would have returned to find her brother's corpse curled up beside the spring and realized too late that the nymph had lied out of spite. But she could not help it. She was bound by Eiko's words. With every ounce of strength she had, she slammed the stone against the rock.

It shattered into thousands of glistening shards, and the nymph screamed, clutching and clawing at her chest. Ora watched as the nymph stumbled back into the pounding falls and washed away as if she had never existed.

*****

Eiko carried an exhausted Ora on its back all the way to the stone forest. The only thing that kept her from nodding off was the excitement of seeing her brother again. As they drew near, she leapt down from the wolf and began to run.

"Hademar!" she shouted as she rounded the last boulder.

Still a pig, he stood beside the spring with seven pukhas surrounding him. He was frightened but unable to get past the growling pine martens. When he saw Ora, he looked past the clan longingly.

"Hademar," she said. "Please. Don't be afraid. They're friends."

The pukhas grinned up at her and let her walk past them without any trouble. "See?" she said, but the brush pig still wore an uncertain expression. She threw her arms around his neck and hugged him tight. He nuzzled her shoulder. "We've come to change you back," she said as she pulled away.

But then he saw the giant black wolf. With a squeal, he tried to push Ora behind him.

"Wait, Hademar, this is Eiko," she said. "Another friend."

The pig eyed the wolf suspiciously but allowed it to walk closer. Once near, Eiko spoke in an unfamiliar tongue, its voice booming.

The reversal was less gruesome than the transformation. Hademar's hands parted the pig's chest. Then, the speckled hide rippled off of his body, leaving him naked and shivering on the mossy earth. Hademar sat up with a puzzled expression and held the hide against his chest. When she touched his shoulder, his gaze shot up. "Ora?"

Unable to form words, she dropped to her knees to embrace him, and he began to sob. She held onto him until he grew quiet and then wiped tears from her own cheeks.

"Can we go home?" he asked, his voice strained.

"Yes." She laughed and kissed his forehead. "Hademar, I am so happy you are safe. I was afraid that …"

The pained look in his eyes made her words trail off. She grabbed his hand and helped him to his feet. When he draped the hide over his shoulders, Ora cast a worried look at Eiko.

"All will be well," it said. "That skin is his now. He will always have a second form, should he want it."

Hademar bowed his head. "Thank you for helping us, Eiko," he said.

"I only played a small part. Ora is to thank."

She felt her cheeks grow hot. "I will tell you everything after you rest."

They found the path home with the Cedar Clan's help. It was a long walk, and by the time they smelled woodsmoke on the air, the sun had begun to rise. At last, the trees thinned, and she saw the outline of cabins farther up ahead. She paused and caught hold of Hademar's hand. He looked at her, eyes tired and watery.

"How long has it been?" he asked.

She felt as if she had spent a lifetime in the fae realm, and she had trouble counting the days. Almost in awe, she said, "Two weeks, I think."

"What do we tell them?"

"We will say that we were lost in the woods. It will be easier that way."

She let her hand slip from his and returned to Eiko's side. It sat warily near the forest's edge. "Will you be staying in Fel?" it asked.

She looked down at her hands. Ever since she awoke in the fae realm, she had only wanted to save her brother and go home. But now, she felt uncertain. She did not know if her enemies lived or what that meant for her. And there was also the small matter of the magic that flowed through her. She thought of Berengar, how he had told her to find a teacher.

But she could not imagine abandoning Hademar. Not after what he went through. She would be the only one who could understand.

Heart heavy, Ora asked, "Will you be close by, Eiko?"

The flash of disappointment in the pukha's green eyes surprised her, but it nodded its head once. "I will be with the Cedar Clan."

She wrapped her arms around the wolf's neck. "Thank you for everything. I do not know what would have become of me if you had not been there in the palace."

Its voice filled her mind with a final, grim warning. *I do not know if the fae will leave you be. Should they find their way here, call for me. I will come and sink my teeth into every one of them.*

"I will," she whispered and withdrew from its side. "Goodbye, Eiko."

"Goodbye, Eudora."

She glowered at the mention of her name, but it was already turning, its form becoming shadow and sinking into the dark ferns.

TWENTY-SEVEN

ON the night of the divining ceremony, the moon sat full and bright over the Sylamor Mountains. Court officials and representatives from each fae clan crowded the Great Hall, their voices a low rumble of rumors and politics. When the oracle last named a new monarch, there had been a dispute between Odharan and his brother over who she had indicated. It ended with his brother's head rolling across the marble floor of the Great Hall.

Though certainly not a child, Tyg had been young for a dren and could remember how pleased her mother had been with the news. Odharan ruled fiercely. Back then, the sylvn clans had grown too powerful and treacherous. The fae had wanted a strong king to quell the threat. It was Odharan's cause that first inspired Tyg to join the Yewolyns. Now, faced with taking the throne, she vowed to strengthen his kingdom once again.

In anticipation of the divining, she chose to wear a dress of deep, red fae silk. It was the same red the Yewolyns used for their war banners. Though simple, it fell elegantly over her strong figure. She wore her black hair down, letting it spill over her shoulders and breasts in long, soft waves. More unusual still, she painted her lips a dark red to match her dress. She was strikingly regal in her beauty. More than a few sets of eyes followed her as she entered the palace.

When she stepped into the Great Hall, Aygriel drifted toward her. "Magus Marigen, you look well," she said.

Tyg did not wish to speak with her, but Aygriel reached out to touch her arm. She drew back with a grimace.

Still, the high priestess persisted. "Might I have a word with you?"

"Whatever you'd like to say, say it now," said Tyg.

Aygriel dared to lean in closer to the Yewolyn so that she could speak quietly. "I know what Basirah imparted to you. Perhaps it would be wise for you and me to put aside our differences. It's all just politics, isn't it?"

Amused by the high priestess's words, Tyg smiled and replied softly, "Perhaps."

"Magus, I simply want what's best for Mysanhal. I have no wish for—"

Tyg cut her off. "Aygriel, your duty is to carry out Cree's will, is it not?"

"Of course."

"If it is Cree's will that I should take the throne, then it is his will that you should be a loyal little priestess and obey your new queen. Is it not?"

"I—" Aygriel seemed ready to argue, but then she bowed her head. "Of course."

"Good. Then, we don't really have any differences to set aside, do we?"

"No, Magus Marigen."

Tyg whispered into her ear, "Try again, Aygriel."

The high priestess's lips parted, and she seemed incapable of making a sound. The dren waited with her hands folded behind her back as Aygriel struggled to humble herself. At last, she murmured, "No, My Queen."

"It's a shame you are so pithless," said Tyg. "I might have enjoyed your counsel otherwise."

Aygriel's bewildered gaze rose to meet the Yewolyn's. "You might have?"

Tyg did not answer but brushed past her to find a seat instead. Despite the vision from Cree, doubt still managed to gnaw at her thoughts. Basirah knew well what Tyg had seen, but did that mean she would speak with clarity when naming the new monarch? Would she have to confront another over the crown? So absorbed in her thoughts, she did not notice her cousin arrive until she felt a firm hand grip her shoulder.

"Pyri," said Tyg, surprised to see her cousin. She took her hand and drew her toward the empty place beside her. "Please, sit. It has been too long."

Pyri sank down onto the bench carefully. She had also dressed well for the occasion. She wore their clan color, Kieran green. "It has," she agreed. "I am training with Usyngol to regain my strength."

Though long since retired, Usyngol was a renowned teacher of the fighting arts. She smiled, pleased to hear it. "I cannot imagine time better spent. You're recovering well, then?"

"Well enough," said Pyri, but she pressed her hand against her chest and grimaced. Then, she lowered her voice. "I was sorry to hear news of Callum's death. He will be remembered as a great Valor."

Tyg closed her eyes and drew in a deep breath, searching for suitable words. At last, she muttered a simple thank you. To her relief, the conversation did not have to continue. The oracle arrived.

Basirah waited in the entry until the hall grew silent. The high priestess stood at her side, crown in hand. They walked noiselessly to the front of the Great Hall, and dozens of hungry eyes followed them. Every fae in the room felt the same hope—that Cree would honor them with the crown.

An altar had been erected before the court with a golden bowl and ritual knife. Basirah pricked her finger and squeezed a drop of her blood into the bowl without any formalities. Tyg felt Pyri shift beside her, leaning forward to see the oracle better. Every fae seemed to be holding their breath.

Despite the initial lack of pageantry, she made a great show of calling upon Cree, swirling her hands about, and drawing in deep breaths over the bowl of water. She spoke in the old language as lamplight shifted on her face. The court sat transfixed and waiting. At last, she opened her eyes and looked out upon them all.

"Our queen will be of Kieran and Marigen blood. Cree has willed it, so it shall be."

The court officials began to turn their heads. Remarkably, only one among them could claim both names. A Kieran by birth and a Marigen by marriage, Tyg could not hold back a thin smile as she rose to her feet. She glanced down at her cousin, who had a mixture of pride and shock written across her features.

A murmur rose around Tyg as she made her way along the center aisle to stand before them. Her walk was still jagged, but she refused to take the throne with a crutch in one hand.

Aygriel bowed deeply before Tyg, and then, the dren slowly lowered herself to her knees so that the crown could be placed on her head. But even as she rose back to her feet the queen of Mysanhal, all she could picture was the dagger and the hand that held it.

Pushing aside dark thoughts of the human girl, she held her chin high and addressed the court. "Cree has revealed a vision to me as well," she began. Her words caused an eruption of hushed conversations. Irritated, she bellowed over them, "Quiet! You will hear your new queen speak."

The fae settled back down but stole nervous glances between each other. This was no Innes, after all. Anyone could guess how Tyg would handle irreverence.

"The human girl who killed our queen is only a harbinger. Magic has returned to Himil, and it is time we regain our strength.

For too long, the fae have hidden in this realm as the lands and power of man have grown unchecked. Our outposts have been abandoned since the time of the ancients, and the fae have been all but forgotten in the realms beyond the crossings.

"My duty is to Cree and to Mysanhal, as it has always been. I led our Yewolyns against Hisinger's mages and crumbled their sylvn colleges to stamp out their blasphemy. Surely none of you have forgotten. It is written in our histories, our songs. My duty is to you, to our future.

"If magic is truly returning to Himil, then I will lead the charge in quelling it. Magic in the hands of men threatens our way of life. Would you have them passing through the Ether to our realm? They would drive silver through our hearts to take our lands! Do not forget the stories of our grandfathers and grandmothers.

"By the power and blessing of Cree, I stand before you not only as your queen but as your Valor. Under my banner, a new era will dawn. Under my leadership, Mysanhal's strength will be known, and we will destroy the queen killer and every last trace of magic in the human realm."

One by one, the court officials went down on their knees and bowed their heads to show their fealty. Never in her life had Tyg felt such power. She lowered herself into the throne with her heart beating wild in her chest and a smile upon her face. Despite everything, Cree still awarded her what she had rightfully earned. But if she was to keep it, she would have to destroy the girl.

Though she would not admit it to anyone, not even herself, she feared Ora. Whatever the girl was, her magic was unlike anything the fae had seen before. Spells, curses, and charms were one thing, but the girl used magic without any ritual or practice. It erupted from her violently, without direction or warning.

That night, Tyg sat before a wall of windows, gazing upon the mountains and letting the moonlight touch her skin as she contemplated what she would do once she captured the girl. Ora would be stripped of power, of course. She would be lashed and perhaps hung in a cage somewhere in the mountains until she was a breath away from death. Then, Tyg would send her to the healers so it could be done all over again.

"Your Majesty," came a servant's voice from behind her. "Master Becanan wishes to speak with you."

Without looking, she raised her hand and said, "Very well."

Maol's soft footfall grew closer, and she gestured to the seat beside her. For the divining, he wore a fine shirt of dark blue fae silk. It was the royal color of Tirnan. Amused, Tyg wondered if he had hoped to be crowned king.

"Please, forgive me for the late hour." He bowed before he sat down, much to her pleasure. Her revelry did not go unnoticed as he lifted his head. "You seem to have taken to your new role rather easily."

"What have you come to discuss, Maol?"

"Your hands." He held out his own and received a baleful look. "The *scars* on your hands."

How he had noticed in the Great Hall, she could not surmise. Though wary, she undid the small clasp on her sleeve and drew it back to reveal the scarring that wound up her arm. "Not just my hands," she said and gave him a slight nod.

Maol took the hand she offered and studied the scars. He traced one of the pale lines on her arm, and she shivered. "My apologies," he said and then withdrew. "Your magic has been severed from you, hasn't it?"

"You've seen this before then," she said. "What is it?"

"I have seen it once before. Have you heard of the ash crystals?"

"Of course. They were used to slay the old gods."

A strange smile quirked into place, and Maol shook his head. "A god cannot be slain. The ash crystals were used to steal their power."

"What does this have to do with anything?"

"The scarring is not from a curse."

For once, Tyg looked rattled. Her face paled, and her lips parted as she searched for the right words. "You mean … my magic, it's gone?" she said, voice flat.

"Yes, but my dear queen, what would you say if I told you that I could help you find an ash crystal? That you could take the power of a god?"

Tyg pulled her sleeve back down over the scars and rose to stand before the window. The oracle had been right. She was meant for greater power.

"Maol," she said. "You are a godsend."

TWENTY-EIGHT

THEY had just finished sparring. Ora crouched at the edge of a tidal pool and prodded speckled anemones with a smooth piece of driftwood. The air smelled crisp, almost sweet. The tide would be coming in soon, and the ocean would swallow the small puddle of marine life. On a nearby rock, Lupin smoked his pipe and watched the waves. He had been quiet since she returned but so had she.

A few days after reappearing, she had visited Lupin in his cabin to talk about the fae without her ma overhearing. When he first told her how he found the sword and no other trace of the Widogast siblings, a deep sadness filled his gaze. He admitted that he feared she would never be found, and the weight in his voice brought tears to her eyes.

After that, Ora spent an agonizing month trying to return to normalcy, but a longing had rooted itself in her chest. She craved magic. At night, she would brush her fingers across the amulet Elder Kavyn enchanted just to feel the power emanating from the crystal. There was also Hademar's brush pig cloak. He would not part with it, and when he stood near, an intoxicating force charged the air around him. She asked if she could wear the cloak, but he sheepishly told her no.

Several times, she tried to sneak off on her own to practice featherweight, but neither her ma nor her brother would let her out of sight, unless Lupin was at her side. They were made nervous by her silver eyes, the pearly nub where her pinky had been, and the distracted, cool demeanor that she had adopted since returning.

For once, she was grateful for her mother's anxious nature. On several occasions, Nel had opened her mouth as if to ask Ora a question but could never manage more than a bit of unintelligible mumbling. The rest of the time, her ma seemed content to have her children back, even if they had returned somewhat different than before.

Only Lupin knew the true story, but Ora had left out one detail. He did not know about her magic.

The truth weighed on her. Perhaps, he would understand, and then she would be able to practice a spell or two. It would be no different than their secret sparring.

The sea wind tore at Ora's braided hair, and she found herself wondering what sort of magic could be woven from the chilly gale, from the waves, from the battered rocks beneath her feet. Eiko had said power could be drawn from the elements.

The longing felt like a coil twisted around her chest. She could take it no longer. She tucked a few curly strays behind her ear, picked up her sword, and rose to her feet. "Uncle Lupin," she said, pulling his attention away from the glittering horizon. "While I was in Tirnan, I discovered something."

She felt almost light-headed at the idea of telling him. Her heart quickened.

When she did not go on, he said, "I imagine you discovered a good deal."

An anxious, breathless laugh passed through her lips. "Yes, but this is different. This is something about me."

His brow rose, but he looked past her. Confused, she glanced over her shoulder and saw a stranger approaching them.

"Do you know him, uncle?"

"No." He got up from the rock and tucked his pipe into his coat pocket.

They waited. The stranger drew closer. He was a tall, dark-haired man and carried a small satchel over one shoulder. He could have been a Nor, but there was something off about him. When he reached them, she understood why.

Ora drew the silver sword from its sheath. "Who are you? And do not lie. I can see your glamour," she said, more than ready to take a swing if he proved to be an enemy.

But the man smiled. "Hello, little twig."

In shock, she lowered thc blade. "Berengar? How did you find me?" She could not hide the high-pitched twinge of fear in her words. If he could find her, how simple would it be for any other fae?

"Your innkeep, Mathilde, was kind of enough to point me in the right direction."

"You used her name?"

"It was necessary." He glanced at her uncle. "Are you kin?"

"Yes, we are kin," Lupin growled. "If you are fae, and I'm guessing you are, you had better have a good reason for coming here."

"Yes, I think I do." He held Ora's gaze and slipped into the fae tongue so only she would understand. "Tyg Marigen is now queen and Valor. She has vowed to destroy you and all magic in Himil."

The world felt suspended for a breath, and Ora felt a buzzing sensation spread through her. Recognizing the first prickling of magic, she swept her hard gaze out to the ocean and drew in several, slow breaths to calm herself. Eiko had been right when it warned her about returning home, but she did not want to contend with the idea that she would no longer be safe in Fel. Leaving would be an impossible subject to broach with her family.

Berengar went on, the fae language a familiar lilt. "I have been allowed to join the Yewolyn mages. I must return—"

"Whatever you have to say, say it in Norrish," Lupin interrupted, voice rising over the pounding waves.

"It's alright, uncle," Ora said, returning her gaze to Berengar. "I can understand him. Go on."

Despite Ora's reassurance, Berengar gave a swift, Norrish apology before continuing in fae. "I have friends here in Himil, sylv in exile. They have hidden themselves well. I will tell you how to find them, but the rest is up to you."

She nodded once.

"They are to the south, in Galgoa. Seek out a tribe of nomads. The locals call them wind walkers, but they are sylv." He reached into his pack. "You will need this to see them. They use strong wards to stay hidden."

Right away, Ora recognized the object he held. She sheathed her sword. "A speculademain?"

"Ah, you must have seen it in Elder Kavyn's shop. There aren't many left." He held it out and winked. "I doubt you'll have any trouble using it."

"Were you planning on telling me how it works?" she asked as he placed it in her outstretched hands. The rush of magic at her fingertips made an unbidden smile spread across her face.

"Let's see. It's really just a matter of finding the right spot." He felt along a seam in the copper, then gave it a twist.

Air hissed out of the hollow device. The pentagonal faces began to unfold, and she shifted her hands to give it more space. When finished, it lay flat. From the glass oculi rose a ghost-like landscape of dark trees and mountains.

"The Hy Borea," she said in awe. "Uncle Lupin, look."

He shifted closer, still cautious of Berengar. "It's remarkable," he said. "What is it for?"

Berengar answered in Norrish. "It will always show the world as it truly is." In fae, he added, "It will reveal the wards that hide the sylv. It does more, but you will have to figure that out on your own. I must leave."

He tapped the center twice, his finger sinking into the trees. The glass and copper faces began to fold, and Ora watched on in fascination.

"Thank you, Berengar," she said as the last panel clicked into place.

"I hope to see you again, little twig."

His words made warmth blossom in her cheeks. In their short time together, she had grown fond of him. She wished he would stay so that she could at last ask him to teach her alchemy. Pushing aside these thoughts, she gave a deep nod. "And I you."

"Be safe." These were Berengar's final words before he parted, leaving the two Widogasts where he found them.

Lupin cleared his throat. "Would you like to explain to your old uncle how you came to see glamour and learned the fae tongue so quickly?"

"It's what I was about to tell you." Ora's eyes followed Berengar as he made his way back up the beach. The speculademain felt powerful in her hands, and the energy washing up her arms made her light-headed. Already, her mind turned with the possibilities of what such a device could do. Before her thoughts could drift any further, she tore her gaze away from Berengar and met Lupin's incredulous stare. "You see, Uncle," she said. "It's a complex enchantment."

ACKNOWLEDGEMENTS

As an indie author, I have many kind souls to thank for listening, reading, and giving advice. When you work so closely with a manuscript, it can lose its magic, and I do not think I would have finished without patient encouragement from a community of friends and fellow writers.

First, a lifetime of thanks to my family. You have always believed in my writing dreams, and I am extremely fortunate to have you. Dad, Emmy, and Silas, without you this book would not be nearly as good. You have infinite patience. I love you all so much.

To my mother and grandmother, though you're not here to read about Ora and Tyg, you were the earliest influences on my writing and reading life. Thank you for cultivating my love for books and art at an early age.

To my editor, Libby Copa, thank you for asking just the right questions and for the kind words of encouragement. You truly have an eye for editing, and I will be forever grateful for the time you spent on my manuscript.

To all my beta readers who picked up the earliest renditions of *Ora and the Old God*, thank you for reading and pushing me as a writer. Shawna, Tina, and Jon, you are all such talented writers, and your perspectives helped me more than you know.

Many thanks to my wonderful cover designer, Sarah Oliver. They say don't judge a book by its cover, but we know that's not true. There are many readers who would have never opened this book without your help.

Finally, I would like to thank Sarah Cole for helping me add the finishing touches. You helped me get this book across the finish line.

ABOUT THE AUTHOR

Sarah Day grew up in the Ozarks and has also lived on the Washington coast, a place she still returns to for inspiration. She married a philosopher, who she is madly in love with. They live with their two feline friends, Miko and Merlin, in Northwest Arkansas. In 2014, she graduated from the University of Arkansas with a bachelor's degree in creative writing. This is her first novel.

Follow on Twitter, Facebook, and Instagram: @sarahdayauthor

Sign up for updates: sarahdayauthor.com

CPSIA information can be obtained
at www.ICGtesting.com
Printed in the USA
LVHW041113161020
668888LV00004B/125

9 781735 533407